The

ELEMENT

of

LOVE

Books by Mary Connealy

The
ELEMENT
of
LOVE

MARY
CONNEALY

BETHANYHOUSE
a division of Baker Publishing Group
Minneapolis, Minnesota

© 2022 by Mary Connealy

Published by Bethany House Publishers
11400 Hampshire Avenue South
Minneapolis, Minnesota 55438
www.bethanyhouse.com

Bethany House Publishers is a division of
Baker Publishing Group, Grand Rapids, Michigan

Printed in the United States of America

Library of Congress Cataloging-in-Publication Data
Names: Connealy, Mary, author.
Title: The element of love / Mary Connealy.
Description: Minneapolis, MN : Bethany House Publishers, a division of Baker
    Publishing Group, [2022] | Series: The lumber baron's daughters ; 1
Identifiers: LCCN 2021029280 | ISBN 9780764239588 (paperback) | ISBN
    9780764239816 (casebound) | ISBN 9781493435999 (ebook)
Subjects: LCGFT: Romance fiction. | Western fiction. | Novels.
Classification: LCC PS3603.O544 E44 2022 | DDC 813/.6—dc23
LC record available at https://lccn.loc.gov/2021029280

Scripture quotations are from the King James Version of the Bible.

Cover design by LOOK Design Studio
Cover photography by Aimee Christenson

Author is represented by the Natasha Kern Literary Agency.

Baker Publishing Group publications use paper produced from sustainable forestry practices and post-consumer waste whenever possible.

22 23 24 25 26 27 28   7 6 5 4 3 2 1

This book is dedicated
to my four very smart daughters.
It was easy to believe in women engineers
in the 1800s because I know my girls
are capable of anything.
I'm proud of you,
Josie, Wendy, Shelly, and Katy.

ONE

MAY 1872

NORTHERN CALIFORNIA

THEY WERE RUNNING AWAY from the threat of misery, pain, and degradation.

And running straight toward danger. Deadly danger.

Margaret Stiles Beaumont chose danger.

What's more, she chose it for her daughters and prayed without ceasing that she'd chosen right.

Even worse, the girls had to face that danger alone. Going back by herself was the only way to be sure the girls made their escape.

In silence, Margaret and her three daughters slipped into the night.

She waited until they were far enough from the house no wandering servant, absently looking out the window in the night, could see. Then she lagged behind her rushing daughters, her beloved, precious girls.

Clouds scurried across the sky. The dew-damp grass around the house ended in a dense forest. As soon as the forest swallowed them up, she stumbled and fell. Well, truth was, she stopped running, sat down, and cried out in pain. Softly. She most certainly didn't want Edgar to hear, though he drank enough that he usually slept heavily.

Laura whirled around and rushed back, Jillian a step behind. Michelle brought up the rear.

Laura, her sweet, compassionate child. The blue-eyed blonde who was a fine-boned, feminine version of her father, Liam Stiles. Laura, who knew how to blow things up.

Jillian, with her oddly mathematical mind and nearly photographic memory and the skills to use them wisely. She'd been educated to build trestles across vast gorges and railroad tracks into the heart of a mountain. A fiery green-eyed redhead, a throwback to her papa's Irish grandmother.

Michelle, the calm one who took charge of the sweet Laura and the fiery Jillian, and they mostly let her. Michelle, the mechanical engineer who saw all the details and made everything and everyone work together. And in her spare time, she worked with machines, mechanisms to help the girls' future projects excel. She already had two patents with plans for a dozen more, if she could just get the ideas in her head to become reality. Michelle was the oldest, the brunette with the shining blue eyes who looked like her mama the most.

"Mama what happened?" Laura dropped to her knees on Margaret's right.

"Let us help you up." Jillian rushed around to her left and took Margaret's hand, ready to lift.

"No." A sob broke from Margaret's throat. The tears

were easy to find. Her daughters were about to risk their lives because of Margaret's mistake.

Michelle stopped, hands on her hips, at her mother's feet. They were all dressed in breeches. They needed to move silently and safely through the dense forest.

"I've hurt my ankle." Margaret fought down the tears. To overdo it would make the girls suspicious. "It might be broken."

Her ankle was fine. But she wore a heavy stocking with a bit of padding under it to make the ankle appear swollen. Her girls were very smart, so Margaret tried to be smarter. She had to stay behind, and the girls might stay with her if she didn't handle this just right.

"We'll carry you." Laura slid her arm under Margaret's shoulders.

"No, I can't."

Michelle knelt at her feet and reached for her ankle.

Margaret used every bit of the emotional pain of her second marriage to let out a quiet, true cry of pain.

"It's swollen. It might be broken, Mama. We have to take you up to your room."

"Michelle, no. You have to go." Margaret didn't want them examining the padding on her ankle too closely.

"We'll wait until you're healed. And pick a new night to run." Michelle was planning, reasoning, just like always.

Margaret leaned forward and grasped Michelle's hand to stop her from pulling down her stocking. "You have to go. You know tomorrow night the men will come."

She'd asked them to go without her exactly once—right at the start of this. The protest had been so great she'd never suggested it again. But they'd never get away if Margaret didn't stay. She had a plan that was going to give her girls time.

"It's out of the question, Mama," Michelle insisted. "We aren't leaving you with him."

Margaret squeezed Michelle's wrist until she left the ankle alone and paid attention out of pain.

"Go. You know we can't wait." Her voice broke, and she struggled to speak. "Go, please, I am begging you. I know we planned to escape together, but I'll never make it. If you go on alone, you have a chance. If. You. Go. Now! Tonight. You know I'm right. You know what happens if you're here tomorrow."

Michelle endured the pain and met Margaret's eyes dead-on. Margaret had to win this daughter over. If Michelle agreed to this, the others would follow.

The wind whipped up and made the branches dance and wave. They were in a dense woods in northern California. Liam Stiles had created a dynasty here. A massive treasure trove measured in cordwood. When the country ran west to find gold, he'd realized, after he'd dug a nice stack of nuggets himself, that wood was selling for as much money as gold, or near enough. And while gold was hard to come by, the whole of northern California was covered in trees.

He'd parlayed his gold into a stake to hire men, build a sawmill, and invest in vast acres of trees. And he'd become a titan. The house behind them in this remote woods was possibly the most beautiful home in all of California.

But her beloved Liam was dead, and the girls had to escape.

"No, Mama. No! We won't leave you." Jilly's voice had a note of panic. "He's going to be furious, and he'll take it out on you. He might—might k-kill you."

Jilly's voice broke, and she wasn't one for tears. But then Margaret knew Edgar had done something to Jilly, though she wouldn't admit it when Margaret had asked.

"Mama." Michelle caught hold of Margaret's hand. "Please, we'll make it. Let us carry you."

"Jilly, he will *not* kill me, and furthermore"—the strength of her voice drew all of them deep into her words—"your father's will makes it so he loses everything if he kills me."

"It does?" Jilly watched with such intensity that Margaret realized this must be at the root of everything. What had Edgar told her? Had he said to Jilly the same threatening things he'd said to Margaret?

"Yes." Margaret looked from one of her girls to the next. "Because of that, I've decided I'm not taking another second of his abuse. I've let him scare me, dominate me, but no more. If he comes at me with his fists, he'd better be ready to take a fireplace poker to the head. Today begins the day I fight back. I can do that if you girls are gone. He won't be able to hold harming you over my head."

She saw that they'd never realized before that he did this. A second look at Jilly gave her pause. Maybe one of her daughters suspected. But what point had there been in telling them before now?

"Tomorrow night those men come," Margaret said. "I wouldn't put it past Edgar to let them take you along when they go, even without wedding vows. You have to be far away before they arrive. Please, I am begging you. Go now. Fast. Find husbands to secure your inheritance. Find men strong enough to protect you from your stepfather. But good men. Don't make the same mistake I did. Find good men, then get back here and save me."

She paused, letting her words sink in. All her girls liked to analyze, think before they acted. She gave them time for that now. She looked hard into Jillian's eyes and watched her quietly reason it out, adding and lining it up. When it had been long enough, Margaret went on. "I raised you girls to be smart. Jillian, you especially have an analytical mind. You know you have to leave me. It's the only way."

A crack of thunder rumbled across the night sky. Margaret turned to look to the east and saw jagged lightning. It was still miles away, but it was coming. It made this a harder night to escape, but the sound of their passing would be hidden, any tracks would be covered.

"She's right," Jillian said the words as if they tore her in half. Her green eyes were drenched with tears. Very little made her middle daughter cry.

"Mama, no!" Laura sobbed as she launched herself into Margaret's arms. No great surprise in Laura's tears, she was prone to them.

"There's no time for this." Margaret tore Laura's arms loose from her neck. "Please. Go. Go. Go."

She touched the cheek of each of her hovering daughters. "Go with God. I need you to escape, find husbands, then get back here."

She looked to Michelle, the oldest, the leader. The orderly one. Michelle's skin was ashen as she swiped a tear from her eye. Then she gave her chin one hard jerk.

"She's right. Laura, Jilly, she's right. We can't be here to-morrow, and Mama will be safe." Michelle leaned close. "I've got a pistol tucked in the bottom drawer of the wardrobe in the bedroom we sleep in. Use it if you need to."

Margaret gasped in shock. She had sensed that her daughters might have kept things from her just as she'd kept things from them. Trying, each of them, to bear burdens alone to keep them off the shoulders of one another.

"You should have taken it with you," Margaret said.

"I didn't think it would survive the water." Michelle, the one who knew mechanical things, including guns, was probably right.

"We need to help you back to the house first." Michelle reached down.

"No, there's no time. I'll crawl or hobble or whatever it takes. You're not going back into that house."

That earned her a long moment of silence.

"Go with God, Mama." Jillian leaned down and kissed Margaret on her forehead, brushing back the dark curls.

Laura hugged her again, but she didn't cling. "I love you, Mama. I'll go snag a husband and be right back."

That wrung a smile from Margaret when she'd've said no smile was possible. Laura was the one who'd probably marry first. She was lighthearted and cheerful and a bit of a flirt, and as pretty as a picture. It all covered what was probably the finest, sharpest, most educated mind in the family.

"Now, sisters. Now. We go before we're found out." Michelle took charge again. She'd either find a husband she'd be able to take charge of, or if she did well, she'd pick a husband so smart and strong, she'd be glad to let him take charge of her.

The first kind of husband would be easier to find than the second because few people on this earth were as smart as any one of her girls.

"Go with God, my girls. I love you."

One by one, they nodded, then turned and ran into the woods.

Margaret listened. She had to make very sure the girls were long gone. The thunder cracked again, and lightning flashed. She sat on damp grass that was mostly gone only a few paces farther into the woods.

When she was sure, and with long prayers that she'd made the right decision, she hopped to her feet and, on two perfectly fine ankles, ran toward the house. As she reached the edge of the woods, despite the darkness and the threat of a storm, she paused to look at her house. Her and Liam's house.

They'd had highly trained architects and skilled workmen in to build it. But Liam and Margaret knew lumber, and both had ideas of how they wanted their home to be.

Some might have called it a castle. But those who knew the Stileses were aware they wanted to create something beautiful, and they'd succeeded.

Two full stories and a third story of fanciful turrets, peaks, and gables. A porch wrapped all the way around with sweeping steps up on three sides, and a roof over the open porch was supported by elaborately turned support posts. When the Victorian mansion was done, Liam had declared it the most beautiful house in the world.

Shaking away the sadness the house held for her because she'd failed Liam and her daughters so terribly, Margaret ran on.

She had a lot to do before dawn. A lot to do to prepare herself, including getting the padding off her ankle and taking off these footman clothes before Edgar met her announcement about the girls with rage and a heavy fist.

TWO

L AURA STUMBLED, SLID, AND CRAWLED through the woods in silence. She was third in line as always. They did things in order of age. Michelle led, Jilly came second, and Laura brought up the rear.

Not a word was spoken between them. Tree roots tripped them. Branches grabbed at their clothes. They all knew what they'd left Mama to face, and what they could imagine probably wasn't bad enough. The thought of it had struck them all dumb as they rushed into the heavy forest.

Abandoning Mama, they moved on with the plan, grimly aware that there was no choice. Tomorrow was the end of their hopes and dreams if they stayed here.

As soon as they were out of sight of the house, they lit the lantern.

The house. Their beautiful home. Laura forced herself not to look back.

Papa had built it, and it was the most beautiful building any of them had ever seen. And they lived half the year on Nob Hill in San Francisco, so they knew beautiful homes.

Its majestic beauty was warmed because of the love within its walls.

Even after Papa died, the thorough education he'd provided for them, with professors on sabbaticals from top universities, had continued. Mama had shared his dream of teaching the girls to take over Stiles Lumber. And she'd gone on caring for them and loving them. She'd gone on running the lumber business, and the girls had helped her. For four years they'd managed, sadder without Papa but smart and well trained. Laura felt the weight of how much they had to learn and how badly Mama needed their help. If there were days she'd have rather read a book or walked among the trees, she kept that to herself and studied.

And then Edgar.

Mama made the terrible mistake of marrying Edgar Beaumont. And home had become a place to dread.

Bad enough for the four of them with each other to cling to. Now they'd left their Mama to face Edgar's untender mercies alone.

They each carried a satchel rigged so they could hang it across their chests. Each dressed in scandalous trousers and carrying a dress fit for a maid, clothing cast off by their servants when Mama had gone through the elaborate ruse of declaring the staff needed new uniforms. And they each had a leather purse full of money—a lot of money—hanging around their necks, tucked inside their shirts. Mama had severely told them to keep what they carried small, but Laura had tucked a book into her satchel and a waterproof packet of chemicals. She could do a lot with some of their powders. She dreaded some of what those powders could do.

They'd taken one lantern between them. Michelle carried

it, held high, to light their way. But the way was so dark that the lantern light only helped a little. They were reduced to inching along, feeling their way.

"Watch out. We'll have to climb down this stretch." Michelle, out front, taking care of them.

Laura slowed, and the trip was already painfully slow. She turned and went backward down a stretch that was more handholds and toeholds than a trail.

She felt the bundle of bills and coins tucked into her purse. It bounced and dragged on the ground. Laura was careful not to snag it.

She tried to imagine getting Mama down this stretch without the use of her ankle and knew they'd've never made it.

This was all Mama's plan. They were to behave as servants. Edgar would search for them among the young women of their class. Many arrogant, powerful men didn't even see a servant's face. Mobcaps and drab clothing were a fine disguise.

They weren't to show the money or live well. But discreetly used, the money might save their lives, so they each had a goodly sum.

The clouds overhead darkened what little of the night sky they could see. The moon was gone. The stars hidden behind the clouds. Now, save for that one gleam of lantern light, the forest was as good as pitch-black. Tripping, skidding, bumping up against tree trunks when they missed a curve on the rugged path to the trailhead of the logging camp, they fought their way along.

The wind rose and rattled the trees. It howled like wolves, and Laura knew well what that sounded like in these deep woods and wild lands.

Laura raced and plodded, zigged and zagged. She churned and raged inside her head. *Go back. Do something awful to Edgar.* Laura was gifted with easy smiles and a fine charm. But anyone who knew her—and very few knew her well— knew inside she was as dangerous as the chemicals she loved. Mix her up just right, mishandle her, shake her, or make her hot and agitated, and she just might blow.

You'd never know the explosion was coming until it was too late.

Blow up the house.

That was about all she could come up with.

She even had the right chemicals stowed in her satchel. Enough to blow the magnificent Stiles mansion into matchsticks with Edgar inside.

She'd have to get Mama out, and all the hired help. This murder was getting more and more premeditated every moment.

And she wasn't a murderer, so that made the whole thing just a frustrating exercise in internal rage.

She prayed for forgiveness because she most certainly needed it.

Lightning cracked overhead. The trees bent and branches reached out like clawing hands. The thunder sounded like Edgar coming to get them, stop them. Sell them as wives to his vile cronies. Truly vile. Mama knew the men, and she said it was unthinkable, unbearable. It would cost their lives to marry those men.

The wind howled again, and Laura's fears howled just as loud. She knew what was in store for them if they didn't run. Run fast, run far, run until they had that most precious of possessions: a husband who would give them the legal right to claim their inheritance and kick Edgar out of the business he now possessed through his marriage to Margaret Stiles, the fabulously wealthy widow of lumber baron Liam Stiles.

"We're here." Michelle had done it. She'd led them fast and straight to their escape route. "Help me get this water spout turned on."

They'd all planned and planned and planned. They knew exactly how to set the water to flowing down the flume.

If Papa were still alive, they'd never get away with this because his camp was so well run any water flow that was on in the morning when it'd been off at night would raise up a hue and cry. With Edgar in charge, no one would mention it.

Of course, if Papa were still alive, they wouldn't be making their desperate escape attempt, now would they?

But Papa knew his lumber dynasty. Papa knew his crew. He was out in the woods every day, paying attention, working hard himself.

Not Edgar. That gave Laura hope he'd never figure this out.

Thunder rumbled closer. Laura smelled the rain coming. A bolt of lightning drove them to hurry. They weren't the highest things on this mountain, but they were standing under the highest things.

The flume was a wooden trough that ran all the way down the mountain, heavily framed to form what looked like a massive gutter. Instead of rainwater, they routed springwater into it. Then pushed logs in, which the water carried down the mountain. It ended at the river. Papa had built this flume, and now it might save his girls.

The wind whipped their clothes, pressing them against their bodies. Wearing trousers, outrageous though it was, might save them because this ride ended with being dumped into the river. The oilcloth was to preserve their clothes, their lantern, themselves.

"If it rains heavily, they might not work tomorrow." Laura hoisted one of the half barrels, open on top and covered on each end. They sent things besides logs down the flume, including orders to the general store, mail, all sorts of things. And tonight, they were sending three women. Three when it should have been four.

Laura's heart wept to think of Edgar's rage at Mama. Could she really protect herself? Laura wanted to believe it because Mama was right. They couldn't have carried her the long hike to the flume. So they'd abandoned her. Choking back sobs, she lifted the barrel, Jilly on the other end.

"You go first, Laura." Michelle ordered, handing her their single lantern. She was smart, no doubt about it. But no smarter than any of them, just blessed with a take-charge manner. Oh, go ahead and say it, she was a bossy big sister.

That was how they'd always run things, with Michelle in charge. Laura didn't like it, but now wasn't the time to change the habits of a lifetime.

"Get all three half barrels close. I don't want us to be separated any more than necessary."

Laura's stomach twisted as she realized a detail they hadn't planned on. Getting that last barrel in the flume would be hard for one woman alone. Michelle would have to do it. There was no going back.

"The water's flowing slowly. Let's get all three of us launched before it comes full force." Jilly, the engineer who made ideas and drawings come to life, studied the flume as they lined up the barrels.

"Laura, you go, then Jilly and me. We'll all get going right together so we're close for the ride down."

They quit talking to work.

The moment came. Jilly and Michelle prepared to swing the barrel into the flume, and Laura would jump in. She dug deep for a prayer and came up with mostly *Lord, take care of Mama*.

The barrel splashed into the flume. Laura jumped even as it hit. And she was off. Flying. Flying to freedom. A splash behind her. She looked back. The wind blew her blond hair over her eyes. She pushed it aside, and the barrel swayed. Laura saw Jilly coming, but there wasn't time to see more. Another splash. That's what she'd heard, wasn't it? Could the barrel roll in the flume? Not wanting to make a move that would possibly tip her, she clung to the sides, stayed desperately still, and held on for dear life. She pushed all her desire to scream into her prayers.

For Mama. For all of them. The three sisters were breaking free.

Edgar knew none of this. He only knew how to count Papa's money, spend it, and make everyone's life a misery.

Mama had done poorly marrying him. But they'd all met Edgar. He was a charmer, warm and funny and easy with the kind words and flattery that sounded sincere.

And they'd all been so lonely for kind words from a man. The girls had welcomed him into their lives, and he and Mama had married just over a year ago.

It hadn't taken them long to figure out he was a monster.

A curve ahead had her clinging to the edges of the barrel. Laura moved fast, and the flume was steep for a long stretch with a wild sweep of a curve following the edge of the mountain.

A trestle appeared below the flume, holding it high in the air when a deep gully opened.

Laura felt like she was flying through midair. No ground beneath her for a hundred feet down. Then she swooped around a mountainside and got splashed as the barrel careened from one side of the flume to another.

And that's when the rain began falling. It was only sprinkling, but they'd planned to stay as dry as possible, and she'd forgotten her oilcloth.

Her movements cautious to keep from tipping, Laura got out the oilcloth packed in her satchel. She wrapped it around herself. She kept her arms out, but her satchel, the lantern, the money, all were protected. She couldn't wrap the oilcloth around her shoulders, even if they ended up soaked, because this ride would most likely end with her taking a swim. She'd need her arms free.

The curve went away from the mountain, then veered back, and for a sickening second, she saw she'd be slammed right into the face of a cliff. And then she saw the hole. The tunnel.

Laura blasted into the dark.

The roar of the water and the echo of the tight tunnel made her dizzy. All she knew was noise and motion, no vision. Blindness while the world exploded around her.

She couldn't breathe. A scream built in her chest. She fought a violent urge to throw herself out of her barrel, to make contact with something that wasn't moving, wasn't roaring. It was irrational, and she knew it.

But still, every second she endured was a battle.

Fighting it, she remembered the need for quiet. She had to be quiet. But surely they were far enough from anyone that a single scream, which pushed to tear free from her throat, wouldn't be noticed. She swallowed it down. Clutched the sides of the barrel, fought the dizzying fear she'd tip over or be crushed by the dark and speed and roar.

Then out.

Gasping for breath, she went into a sudden descent that was almost a straight drop. The sky had opened up while she'd been in the tunnel. Rain poured down and hit like needles. She lifted the oilcloth up to cover her face so she could breathe and had to keep her head ducked low because her hands were busy clinging to the barrel.

The flume gradually leveled a bit to a less terrifying fall. The flume carried logs for nine miles. She knew that. She had to ride nine miles from the mountaintop to the river below. Nine miles and there was no way to figure time because there was no way to figure speed. She'd heard once it took the logs an hour to get from top to bottom. Another time she'd heard half that.

It all depended on the force of the water. Had they opened it full blast? She wasn't sure. It was science: force times distance times descent patterns. She should be able to do the math in her head while she careened downward, but she was missing key numbers.

Mathematical calculations were more Jilly's thing. In fact, Laura wouldn't be surprised if Jilly was keeping herself calm by counting in prime numbers or doing calculus problems. Laura did science. Her favorite was chemistry. And right now, she'd love like mad to use her smuggled chemicals to blow the flume into a million pieces.

She couldn't blow it up. She couldn't do the mathematical calculations. So she played guessing games about what would happen when the men discovered the flume running. She ripped around a curve in the flume, clinging to the barrel sides.

The men, think of the men.

They'd be coming to work at sunrise. Or the next day if the thunderstorm held on. No one logged mountaintop woodlands if there was lightning. Whenever they came back to work, the men would see the flume open.

Would they wonder if it hadn't been turned off at the end of the last shift? She knew one thing: they wouldn't report it to Edgar. His punishment was always as rapid as the blade of a guillotine. His wrath would fall on the neck of whoever reported it. And they'd be fired.

No, Edgar would never hear about it. And all of the hardworking lumberjacks were loyal to the Stiles family and held Edgar Beaumont in contempt. So between fear of Edgar's wrath and disgust with the man, even if he tore the mountain apart looking for runaway daughters, which he just might do, he'd never hear about a flume found running overnight or any suspicions about the mad decision to use that flume to escape.

By the time he quit looking close to home, they would be miles away, and putting more space between them with every minute they were free.

The storm became a deluge. The slicker Laura had wrapped herself in and used to cover her face helped. Her head and shoulders, with her hands out to cling to the barrel and swim when this ended, were soaked. But the rest of her was doing all right. The lantern probably wouldn't survive the landing, but they'd needed it to get to the flume, and they didn't dare leave it behind.

Lightning crashed close enough that a tree exploded right in front of Laura. Burning, it began to tilt toward the flume.

She'd heard of the flume being damaged by falling trees or rocks, but they'd cut the trees back. She didn't think it would hit her. Watching it slowly topple, branches flaming, Laura zipped past it. Did it hit the flume? Did Jilly and Michelle both make it?

She waited until the next curve, then, careful to keep her body centered, she lifted her face from the oilcloth and twisted her neck, hoping between the curve and the twist she could see behind her without tipping the barrel over. Through the sheeting rain, she saw Jilly behind her, coming along at the same speed as Laura. But the curve wasn't wide enough for her to see farther. If Michelle was there, she was out of sight.

She saw the tree crash harmlessly to the ground, missing the flume. It was still burning, but she hoped and prayed the rain would douse the flames. A forest fire was a deadly and tragic thing.

Before Michelle could appear, the curve straightened and plunged down.

Laura faced forward, ducked back into the oilcloth as best she could, and prayed for her sisters. Prayed for her mama. Prayed for the right kind of husband, one who'd help her come back and wrest the Stiles Lumber dynasty from the foul hands of Edgar Beaumont.

And then, because her prayers were long and fervent, it snuck up on her.

The end of the line.

THREE

L AURA WENT SOARING into the air. A scream would have ripped loose, but she was inhaling at the time, and no real sound came out.

It seemed like hours.

And it was over in seconds.

She slammed into the water. Her barrel rolled, dumping her underwater. She struggled against the tumbling. She'd just inhaled that scream, so she clamped her mouth shut to keep the water out.

Her eyes burned from going under with them wide open. She was upside-down, then sideways, then she didn't know up from down. Releasing the oilcloth out of pure self-preservation, she flailed about, barely aware of what she was doing. Then she started using her brain. *Relax.*

Let the water lift.

She became still in the water, and after a few seconds, though she hadn't begun to surface, a splash overhead told her which way was up.

Using strokes her parents had insisted they learn, she

clawed her way to the night sky. And found it almost as wet as the water.

The rain still poured down. The night was as black as the belly of that tunnel. Laura dragged in a breath. Her thoughts snapped to Jilly. That had to have been her hitting the water.

Looking frantically, she saw two floating barrels but no sister. Where was Jilly? Where had the splash been?

A swooping object hurtled toward her, striking the water inches from her head. Michelle's barrel, complete with big sister, skidded along the water and submerged.

Laura used the strength of a well-developed swim stroke to get to Michelle, latching on to her before she sank.

"I can't find Jilly."

Michelle's somewhat dazed eyes focused. Without a word, she went one direction, Laura went the other. Beneath the surface, she saw a white blur.

"Over here." Laura dove. There was no motion. If that was Jilly, then she was unconscious, unless—*please, God*—she was floating, letting the water lift her as Laura had.

Laura's hand brushed across the sodden fabric, and she clamped on. It was Jilly. It had to be. But there was no movement, no sign of life.

Laura dragged upward against the dead weight. Suddenly, there was someone else. Michelle grabbed hold, throwing her strength into the rescue. They got their middle sister above water. Her red hair, black in the cloudy sky, covered her face.

"Let's get her to shore."

"No, Michelle, going ashore here wasn't the plan. We can't leave any sign that we were down here."

Michelle met Laura's eyes. Her big sister listened well. She took all the pieces of any problem and organized them, then made a decision and plotted a course of action.

While Michelle did her fine plotting, Laura lifted Jilly higher in the water, then dragged her toward the nearest barrel. When they got there, Laura saw that Michelle came along.

"The water is freezing." Michelle rarely just talked about minor things. Especially not in intensely important moments.

Laura, holding Jilly close, said, "I feel a heartbeat. She's unconscious, maybe from a blow to the head. Hard to say. Let's slap her on the back. That might get her to choke up some of the water if she drew some into her lungs. If she's knocked cold, then she'll come around."

"Hug her against your chest. I'll slap her."

Laura wondered why Michelle sounded like she was looking forward to that. But then Jilly was always a pill, hard to handle, hard to argue with. Maybe Laura oughta take a turn slapping Jilly. For Jilly's own good, of course.

Laura hugged Jilly tightly against her chest, and Michelle as good as pounded on her back. They really didn't know what else to do.

Finally, Jilly vomited a chestful of river water onto Laura's face and dragged in a deep breath.

"Being in the water is as good a time to get vomited on as any, I suppose." Laura rolled Jilly onto her side, thinking to clear out the rest of the water in her as she gasped and vomited and gasped some more.

"Yuck, Jilly. Wake up and help us." Michelle took charge of the unconscious woman.

"I don't think we can get back in the barrels. There's a log. Let's see if we can start it floating downriver." Michelle pointed at the edge of the wide spot, dug deliberately by their father as a landing place for logs coming down the mountain.

Laura was impressed that Michelle recognized the log for what it was in the rain.

Another coughing fit from Jilly stopped them from making any progress. When it was over, she was still knocked out. Laura ran a hand over Jilly's head. "I think there's a bump on her forehead right here." She took Michelle's hand and guided it to the goose egg.

"She's not going to be any help for a while. But she'll come around and be all right." Michelle's relief belied the rather bristly relationship she had with Jilly.

For all Michelle's skills at organizing, Jilly was also very smart and very orderly. The two of them clashed frequently. Both of them thought they should be in charge.

No one ever expected such a thing from Laura, even though she was quite sure she was smarter than both of them.

Having a log snag on the river's edge wasn't unusual, but fighting them off the snag was a big job, and since every day there were more logs coming, knocking into the snagged logs, the men didn't put too much effort into getting every single log to go on its way. Any they missed today, they'd deal with tomorrow.

"We can get the log loose, or another one if this one won't come," Michelle said. "It's common for logs, snagged at the end of the work day, to have taken off down the river by morning."

"Yes, and with this rain and the 'oh my, who left the flume running' discovery tomorrow, they won't even notice if a log here tonight is gone tomorrow." Laura paused, then added, "They might notice the barrels we rode down on though."

"Let's hope they decide the storm blew some off the shore. We can't take time to do anything with them. We have to get out of this cold water. It saps body heat until it can be dangerous."

They arranged Jilly on her back. Michelle brushed her sister's hair away from her face, and the two of them swam awkwardly toward the log.

"It's as wet out of the water as in." Laura drew herself along, feeling the current of the river catching her and helping them make progress.

"The rainwater isn't as cold as the river water though. Unpleasant and certainly wet, but even up this high, in May the average temperature of rainwater is around fifty-five degrees. The river water is still getting run off from the snowcaps. I hope it's not cold enough to reduce our core body temperature to a dangerous level. Did your satchel survive?"

Laura touched her chest. "Yes, it's still here. No lantern though." Exploring, she said, "Jilly's is still strapped onto her, too."

"Good. And feel this, she's wrapped in the oilcloth."

"I lost mine. Should I dive for it? Will it give us away?" Laura couldn't think of anything she wanted to do less.

"It's impossible to find a black cloth in black water on a black night, so forget it."

The open flume, the barrels, the oilcloth. Laura could do nothing about those things but pray God closed the eyes of those who came upon them.

"We'll get to the log," Michelle went on, "see if we can get it loose and start it floating. Then we'll hoist Jilly on and climb on ourselves if possible. If it rolls too much or is too slippery, we'll spend our energy getting Jilly on it, then we'll cling to it as it goes downstream. By then, if the oilcloth has floated up, maybe we'll be able to pick it out on top of the water. If not, we'll manage without it."

The rain was still pouring down. Lightning crashed, but not directly overhead. It was flaring in the mountains. Any closer and it might be too risky to stay in the water.

"You hang on to Jilly, Michelle." Laura was a better swimmer, and even as bossy as Michelle was, she knew it.

Laura went to check out what had snagged the log to the side of the river. It was not neatly trimmed like logs always were before they were sent down the flume. If there were branches sticking out here and there, they'd snag in the flume too easily and stop the log coming behind it, and the one behind that and so on. It had never happened to Stiles Lumber. It was just discussed because it would create a disaster.

Laura swam back to Michelle. "This tree must have fallen in the river. It's got branches and bark, and it's impossible to move. I'm going to look around."

"I'm awake, L-Laura. Thank you for finding me and pulling me up. Michelle said you saved me."

Laura took a moment to rest a hand on Jilly's face. In the wet and the darkness, touch was a lot more important than giving her sister a smile.

"I was two feet ahead of Michelle. She'd've dragged you out the same as me. And you'd have done it for us. We're in this together, big sister. And it's a good thing we are. We'll make it by working together."

"Thanks. I'll try and save you sometime, though I'd as soon not find ourselves in too many more life-and-death situations."

At that moment, a tree floated toward them. Also not a trimmed log. But this one was loose.

"God has provided a ride for us," Laura said. "It's coming even with us right now. Let's not let the ride pass us by."

Hanging on to Jilly, Laura and Michelle swam forward with Jilly giving some help now. They caught a very soggy train downriver.

"It's easier to climb and stay on than a trimmed log would've been. You know how they roll," Michelle said. "With the wide branches and that big clump of roots, this tree has already decided which side is up."

"Grab hold, Jilly. Drag yourself up. Michelle and I will boost you."

It all worked well, though Laura felt like she was using up more than the last ounce of strength she had. Praying fervently for God to give her strength sufficient to the task, she scrambled on after Jilly, closer to the top branches. She heard more than saw Michelle climbing on.

"Are we set?" Laura asked.

"I'm aboard," Michelle said.

"I'm alive." Jilly sounded vague, like she wasn't all that sure.

"I wonder if we can catch a nap on this thing," Laura said.

"We'll take shifts. I'll stay awake for the first shift," Michelle said. "Sleep, Laura. If you can't sleep, then rest. Jilly, you too. I'll holler if I need help steering away from the bank."

"Get your feet up out of the water. It's too cold. We'll lose too much body heat." Laura found a forked branch she could drag her feet up onto. She couldn't really see Jilly, but she heard her rustling around, Michelle too, so she trusted her sisters to be managing.

Laura found a spot on the log where another branch stuck out and rested her head there. Between her legs in one fork, her head in another, and lying on her back with a few more branches around, Laura felt safe.

Safe enough she fell asleep.

FOUR

MICHELLE HAD EYES LIKE A FLOCK OF EAGLES, ears like a colony of bats, and a grip like a troop of monkeys.

Even using all three of these skills, she saw only pitch-black. She could make out no sign of the bends and beaches of the river ahead. She applied her grip more than her eyes and ears and went on her river ride.

Both her younger sisters were asleep, for what little bit of time they had.

For the first time since Michelle launched herself into that barrel to ride the wild flume, she thought of how they'd abandoned Mama.

They should have found a way. But how? Carry her? Down the faces of steep cliffs with one ankle sprained or possibly broken?

They were smart women, but none of them had an idea, so they'd gone on, as Mama had begged them to, leaving her behind to face Edgar's wrath.

She'd sacrificed herself for them.

A cold, harsh anger filled Michelle's belly as she considered what Mama might face at the hands of that horrid Edgar.

Mama, Mama, Mama. Michelle's thoughts became prayers. She reached out to God to beg His protection for Mama. To beg Him to help them do what had to be done to save her.

The tree floated faster. The rain still poured like a curtain of water. They curved around a corner Michelle couldn't see, moving faster still. Her sisters slept, or maybe Jilly had passed out. Inhaling a shuddering breath, Michelle kept her eagle eyes sharp. Looking for danger. Looking for an oncoming bank. There were some rapids, some stones on this river. Neither of those were truly dangerous. But that was a truth for someone rowing a boat. In daylight.

Mama, Mama, Mama. A heavy branch on their long-dead tree cracked under her hand and snapped all the way off. It was the first she'd realized how tightly she was holding on.

Lifting the branch close, Michelle didn't see a fine paddle or even a tidy pole. But she'd use it for both to push herself off banks, to avoid tangles, and, maybe, with some intervention from an almighty God, to steer. The tree chose that moment to spin dizzily in the water. Michelle had her sisters in front of her before, but now they all faced upstream. With the trunk end now downstream, Michelle could see this was a more natural way for the tree to float. The water pressing on branches aimed upward, toward the top of the tree, had less resistance. And it didn't hurt that Michelle could turn herself to face downstream and not have branches blocking her view. With some trepidation, she dug her branch deep into the water and stroked.

The tree cooperated, at least a bit. She could speed them

up. Direct them a little. She could have some kind of control over the night's madness.

And once they got control, everything would go according to plan.

As Laura had said, they'd round up husbands to secure their inheritance and be right back. They'd do what they had to do to wrest back possession of their lumber dynasty, and they'd take great pleasure in kicking Edgar right off their mountain.

Michelle, unlike her little sisters, was practical. She'd marry the first decent man . . . or the first manageable man, she came across.

No, decent was definitely more important. Because if he wasn't decent, she might end up with someone like Edgar.

And he'd fooled them all.

The tree coasted along at a steady speed that was much less rampant than the flume. She had no idea how far they'd come, but she knew how far they had to go. Searching for landmarks she could make out, she guessed the first town they'd pass waited only a mile or so ahead. She had hoped to be well past that town before dawn. And this soaking, miserable rain was certainly cooperating. In fact, the river was running faster than usual, though still nothing like the flume.

They'd pass that town soon. It had to be after midnight. Their journey had started late, and they'd been an hour or more hiking to the flume, then about that long riding down it. And now maybe a third hour had passed getting aboard this tree and floating along.

Michelle was usually good at judging the passage of time. She decided to trust herself but with some misgivings. Three in the morning, when sleep was deepest and spirits were at the lowest ebb, was a good time to try to sneak past a town, and that would be one more step of their escape.

The flume and this water ride were step one. And hopefully, the only part of their escape that risked life and limb.

The rest of their plan was more about sneaking than escaping. And the three Stiles sisters needed everything to go just right.

"WHAT'S WRONG WITH YOUR FACE?" Edgar had a weakness.

Well, he had ten solid weaknesses, and about fifty other personality deficiencies. Oh, he was a wretched man.

But this one weakness Margaret could parlay into her daughters' escape: he was afraid of sickness.

"I'll only be in the room for a minute, Edgar." She did her best to sound weak and helpless, like a mewling, pathetic, whipped dog. It wasn't easy because she was just waiting for an excuse to do some serious damage. But he liked her best that way.

She also tried to sound sick. And she was. Poison ivy was dreadfully uncomfortable. "I woke up this morning with this rash. I'm afraid it might be the measles."

She was lying, and she knew it for a sin. She prayed for forgiveness even as she spoke. She had never needed God to be with her more.

"We must have caught it from . . . oh, I don't know . . . maybe a deliveryman? The girls have it, too. I'm quarantining all four of us in the girls' room."

The girls used to each have their own room in the massive

house. But since Edgar had arrived, they'd moved in together. Safety in numbers.

"We won't come near you or expose you. The cook and maids will bring us what we need. You must stay away, Edgar, uh . . . unless you've had the measles?" Margaret feigned a more hopeful expression and began walking toward him. "As I understand it, you can only get them twice or was it three times?"

"Get away!" Edgar erupted from the table and backed to the wall. "And stay away."

"Yes, of course, Edgar." Margaret scuttled toward the door.

"We had plans!" Edgar's face was so red with anger he almost looked like he had a rash himself. "We have company coming tonight. What am I supposed to say?"

"The girls are feverish and even more rashy than I am. Jillian is sick to her stomach, too. And she might be vomiting blood."

Margaret was just making up the most disgusting symptoms she could think of.

"Michelle has other, um, complaints. She needs to always be near a chamber pot. And Laura is developing a hacking cough."

Margaret covered her mouth with her fist and coughed into it. Loud and long.

"Get out. Now. I'll be able to send a wire and stop the men from coming. I hope. Maybe I should send a rider. Maybe I should go myself. I'll handle it. You just get away from me and keep those girls shut up behind their door. I don't want to find them wandering the halls."

"The rash only lasts a couple of weeks. Sometimes the

cough a bit longer. Another week or two or three and we can have your visitors then, Edgar."

She simpered as if she didn't know the horrible nature of the men he'd invited here tonight and didn't know Edgar's purpose. Didn't know or didn't care.

Three men. All three old, wealthy lechers. Men who would destroy her girls in body and soul. Men who would pay to be part of an exclusive circle of powerful deal makers in California industry. And no one was higher in that circle than Edgar Beaumont.

Giving him thousands of dollars to secure his stepdaughters' hands in marriage was a strong connection and would lead to wealth and power beyond what the men already had.

More power for Edgar, too.

Margaret coughed as she turned and hurried away from the room. Oh, why hadn't she just gotten serious here and applied that fireplace poker appropriately?

She very much suspected her time for that would come.

She ran up to the empty bedroom and wondered how long she could keep the lie going that the girls were sick in bed. Most of the staff were loyal to her, but she wasn't sure if they all were, so she didn't tell anyone that the girls were gone.

Not much later, she heard the clatter of hooves outside. She looked out the window and saw Edgar riding away as if chased by a pack of wolves.

Oh, if only that would happen. There was never a good pack of wolves around when you needed them.

For now she was safe. She'd maintain the illusion of sickness, but she could breathe easier than she had for a while.

And she had plenty of poison ivy in the room in case her rash began to fade.

FIVE

THE RAIN FINALLY ENDED, but the river was high, and they were moving fast.

Dawn broke into a gray morning. Foggy and dismal. When Laura studied the day, her eyes narrowed on a black object twisted between the branches of the tree.

"There's our third oilcloth. Huh, we brought it with us." Those were the first words Laura had spoken. The oilcloth didn't matter at the moment because they were all as wet as a human being could possibly be. She regretted she hadn't started the day with a prayer and remedied that, fervently thanking God they'd survived and asking Him to guide them on their quest.

And then she prayed for Mama.

Michelle's eyes met hers. Michelle was at the front of their odd raft. Hadn't she been at the back last night? Jilly stirred and shoved herself against the tree. Her hands slipped, and she fell facedown. Her arms went into the water.

"Have a care, Jilly. We're floating on a log on the river."

Laura thought it was highly possible her sister was confused, considering she'd been unconscious last night.

Jilly turned her face to see Laura. Jilly's long red hair was a rat's nest. Laura had cobbled hers into a knot at the back of her neck.

Michelle's thick brown locks were bedraggled. She must not have had so much as a ribbon to confine them.

"We lived through the flume then?" Jilly sounded groggy.

"Yes, and we've floated past the first town."

"Hush, here's the second." Michelle's voice was just above a whisper. "No one seems to be out yet. And the fog is good cover. Let's hope we slip right past it."

Laura knew these towns, and she knew this river. But she'd never had quite this sort of acquaintance with them.

The river flowed with its tumbling liquid racket. The tree seemed steady. They were midstream, so hopefully they wouldn't land against the bank and get stuck.

"Let's stay low," Michelle whispered. "Cover your red hair as best you can, Jilly. Even if they see the tree, they might not notice us."

But there was no one to notice. Not a day for early rising it seemed. A soft breeze followed them downstream. The ripple and gentle rush of a moving river covered small sounds. A few morning birds cried and chattered from the treetops. Jilly's hair was nearly the only colorful thing in this misty world, and she had it well concealed. The moments slid past as they floated by the sleeping town. Laura smelled woodsmoke and wondered if someone was up stoking the stove for the morning's breakfast. She was careful not to move until they were well away, the town out of sight.

"Stay quiet in case someone is out fishing in the early hours."

Michelle, always with good advice. Well, always with advice. Not all of it was good.

They floated on. Sometimes a small creek would empty into the river. Sometimes the banks were steep, and the river would narrow and rush faster. Sometimes it would spread out, and they'd see sandy beaches emerge along the edges.

None of them snagged hold.

Jilly managed to sit up and bind her hair into a knot. She checked that her money pouch had survived the dunking, then reached into the pack on her back. "A bit of food might help me feel stronger."

Michelle opened hers, too. Laura followed.

Between bites of bread, Michelle said, "I estimate five hours floating until the next town. There is a train station there. You all know the plan. Get onto land. Change into housemaid dresses, slip onto the train separately. Maybe we could even stow away. Or one of us could, so there's no witness to three women boarding."

They debated, much as they had before they'd taken this desperate action. It was nearly impossible to plan when they had no idea what they faced.

Would the train be in the station, and they could board immediately? Would it be days before it came, and they'd need to hide out in the small town until it arrived?

All their talk was just to fill the time, and for plenty of it, they floated along in silence. Laura spent that time praying for Mama.

Praying for them.

Praying for a husband of her dreams. A strong man who'd

face Edgar Beaumont and not flinch, not back down. And if Edgar had laid a single hand on Mama, then Laura asked God to send a man who could thrash Edgar to the ground. Make him sorry he'd ever tangled with the wife and daughters of Liam Stiles.

PARSON CALEB TILLMAN TICKLED the chubby baby under her chin. "She is so beautiful, Gretel."

"*Ja*, she's my sveet little one." Gretel Steinmeyer rubbed her nose against baby Willa's.

Caleb smiled at the woman with a head full of red curls and only the slimmest grasp on the English language. But she always had a smile, and she carried her share of the work and then some. Her dark-haired husband, Heinrich Steinmeyer, was also willing to work hard. And they had a precious baby girl. A well-behaved baby with a belly laugh and a tummy that just begged for tickling.

Gretel and Rick were newly arrived from Germany and hadn't found a community that was kind to two people who struggled with English. But they were people with strong faith, and the missionary who'd come to their church had spoken to their hearts.

They'd worked hard with Caleb, and also with the Hogan sisters, to learn more English on the long trip out.

Caleb looked at the two maiden ladies who'd agreed enthusiastically to come along. He thought Nora and Harriet Hogan wanted adventure. They were both in their mid to late thirties, spinsters and gifted teachers. They were sisters and had always lived together, but they couldn't be less alike.

Nora was thin and sharp featured with a crisp way of talking, and she brooked no nonsense. Harriet was plump and quick to laugh. They were both dark haired and brown eyed, and strong women of God. They'd been enthused with the idea of a new life.

Caleb had felt the calling just as the rest had. A parson who'd never found a church because he had a reputation that was hard to live down. His desire to serve a church had gone unfulfilled until he'd joined this mission group. Prison time makes it hard for a man to find any job, but a job as a parson? It was no surprise that people had misgivings.

He was new to the church where the missionary had come to speak, and the Steinmeyers and Hogans hadn't heard of his past. He hoped they never did.

Now they all climbed off the train, glad for a chance to stretch their legs before their journey continued. He stood on solid ground and smiled at the baby. The little one had been their entertainment during their journey.

Caleb ran both hands through his overlong dark blond hair, wishing for a haircut, knowing that wasn't possible with the short layover here. He wasn't all that sure which town this was. In fact, he wasn't sure which state this was. But he thought they'd finally crossed into California.

Please, dear God in heaven, let us be close to the end of this journey.

The train was wearing down on him. And he usually had boundless energy. Well, it was flagging now.

He'd set out in February with his willing team on a ship from Savannah, Georgia, to New Orleans. They'd taken a steamboat up the Mississippi River, then sailed on a smaller vessel up the Missouri. A vessel meant more for livestock than people. But Caleb and Rick had been able to sign on as deckhands, the Hogan sisters as cooks. Gretel kept busy with the baby and was the only one who had to pay a fare, and on a cattle boat, it was a very low fare. Their group didn't have money to spare and planned to use every cent they had to start their mission work.

The high waters of spring kept them on the ship longer, if Caleb was to believe all he'd heard. Later in the year, they'd have had to pull a keelboat up the river, walking on land with long ropes that drew the boat along against the current.

Instead, in early spring, the steamboat had churned its way easily until they reached Omaha. There they boarded the relative comfort of the train. A generous benefactor had made this leg of the journey possible. And they'd rattled along through Nebraska, Wyoming Territory, Nevada, and into California.

They made the states out west much bigger than back east.

Oh, Caleb had *known*. But he hadn't really realized it all. This was an enormous country, and to think how many pioneers came out here in horse-drawn covered wagons.

He was exhausted. Filthy. Hungry. He'd eaten, but it never seemed like quite enough. And the smell of those cattle on his original steam vessel clung to him even yet. Or maybe he just smelled like them all on his own, and those cows deserved none of the blame.

Finally, today, they'd take the last leg of their journey. He knew, to the extent he could really know anything, that he had much hardship ahead. He was wading into a terrible mess, a land torn apart by the lust for gold. Men who worked themselves near to death and then drank or gambled away their earnings.

In the particular area Caleb was heading to, there were hurting families. Men who left their wives and children in harsh conditions without enough food or good shelter. Who suffered from heat and cold, floods and fires. And they did it all with no education to nurture and develop the minds of their children and no church to nourish their souls.

Caleb felt the calling to this mission field. He'd talked for a long time with a man who'd come from this area. He'd heard of the terrible need for a spiritual and civilizing influence.

There'd been a time when Caleb had needed that himself, so when God had opened his heart to coming west, he'd done it.

And these four good souls had felt the calling to come along. Bringing the baby, a fifth good soul, was an act of complete faith on the part of the Steinmeyers. Caleb thanked God for them every day.

The train whistle blasted, and Caleb gestured to Gretel to board first with baby Willa.

"*Danke*, Parson Tillman."

Nora and Harriet, his teachers on fire for the Lord, went next. Rick followed, and Caleb stepped forward just as a woman came into view. She wore a rather tired looking gray dress with a drab, work-stained apron that covered the dress all down the front. She had some kind of lace mobcap on her head that drooped down to cover most of her face. Caleb stopped, gestured toward the train, and said, "You first, miss."

The woman halted, looking up at him, and he stared into the most beautiful blue eyes he'd ever seen. She smiled and his heart turned in his chest. He'd never had such a reaction to a woman before.

"Thank you, sir."

Her blond hair was disheveled. She looked exhausted and delicate and in need of help. She walked past him, up the steps to the train, and chose a seat just inside the door. Caleb's team was just ahead of her. He sat down because he'd learned from experience that the train often jerked hard enough when it started that it could knock a man off his feet.

The pretty, tired woman was just across the train aisle. Nora and Harriet, who sat on the bench just ahead of the poor woman, turned to her.

"We're headed to a mission field near Sacramento. We're to work among the miners. A tough, uncivilized lot, or so we've heard. In the area we're headed for, many of them have families. We're schoolteachers."

"I had wonderful teachers as a child," the young woman said. "It's one of the most honorable professions. To work at it as part of a Christian mission must give you great pleasure. I'll pray for you." The woman's voice was . . . was . . . He couldn't say just what, but there was no strong accent. No slurred syllables or slang. She sounded educated and rather refined.

And women who sounded like that weren't usually servants.

Harriet continued speaking, as she often did. Nora was more prim but warm and a fine listener.

"We go with God leading us like a pillar of fire. We hope to offer kindness and generosity in a place unusually full of cruelty and greed. Gold, why does it turn people mad?"

"'For the love of money is the root of all evil.'"

The pretty blonde knew her Bible.

"That's so strange when you consider it," Harriet said.

"Why love of money? Why is that the root of all evil? There is so much sin in the world. Why that one?"

The delicate blonde said, "That's a really good question. We know it's the root of much evil but why all?"

Caleb watched her as she considered it. He saw a rare intelligence in her eyes as she thought over her own question.

"The rest of the verse helps," Nora said. "'For the love of money is the root of all evil: which while some coveted after, they have erred from the faith, and pierced themselves through with many sorrows.'"

"So the love of it, the coveting of it, lures them from their faith," the blonde said.

"You wouldn't think money would pierce someone with many sorrows." Harriet turned more fully around. "But I suppose the love of money takes the place of the love of God."

"I know a man who has abandoned all decency because of his pursuit of money. His love of it." The delicate blonde tugged at the brim of her mobcap.

Her hand trembled. Caleb looked more closely at her and realized that delicate impression she made went deeper than just her fair blond hair and fine bone structure. She was really upset, possibly hungry. Maybe sick or hurt.

He'd help her. Feed her. Save her. He'd—

Someone came down the aisle of the train, moving fast without running. The woman, this one with dark hair and eyes the color of blue lightning, paused, took one hard look at the delicate blonde, then moved on to a small water dispenser a single pace past them at the back of the train.

The blonde stopped talking and looked down at her hands.

The blue-eyed brunette drank her water from a little paper

cone kept by the dispenser, then returned to the front of the car.

There was a water dispense at the front, too. Why had she walked back here for water?

Why had the delicate blonde fallen silent?

"I'm Harriet, and this is my sister, Nora. We always love to talk of the Scriptures."

There was a stretch of silence. The moment the blonde should have filled in with her own name. That was such a natural human reaction, Caleb found it very telling that the woman, so friendly just a moment ago, didn't respond.

"I had a bit of a sleepless night. I'm afraid I'm fading quickly. It was nice to meet you, but I should try and sleep. I've got a long journey ahead." Still just as friendly but not open. Not happy anymore. And the brunette was to blame.

Caleb knew it at the same time he didn't really know anything. The blonde scooted to the train window and rested her head against the wall. She fell asleep, or maybe she just pretended. He had a feeling it was the latter.

Caleb was a man called to care for God's sheep. And right now, God was telling him this little lamb needed help.

JILLY KNEW WHY she was in the freight car.

This blasted red hair.

Lots of blondes in this world, lots of brunettes. She could count the number of redheads she'd met on one hand. Green-eyed redheads were even more unusual.

Jilly had found a cold campfire and, using a very light hand, brushed the ash over her eyebrows. She'd even brought a little twig she and Mama had worried the end of until it was a tiny brush for that specific purpose. She also used it as best she could to color her red lashes.

She tugged on one of the hanks of hair that had flopped out of her cap. At least they'd brought along the mobcaps. Jilly hadn't particularly wanted to wear one of the oversized, floppy creations. Mama said the caps were to cover a maid's head when she was dusting and such, to keep her hair clean. Jilly suspected it was to mark them as servants, in the unlikely event anyone would dare to treat them as an equal, a hardworking person worthy of respect.

She'd get up on her soapbox right now and give a rousing speech, if she wasn't sitting on the floor behind a row of barrels. By the smell of them, they carried molasses.

Wrangling around inside her head didn't suit her. She liked to speak out. Air her opinions. Her parents had always encouraged it, if she would speak out without insulting listeners. And that training had held her in good stead. She'd learned to craft an argument, state her reasons rather than just rant.

A click at the door on the far end of the heavily laden freight car shoved her love of airing her opinions straight out of her head. She wasn't visible back here. She'd chosen her spot carefully, with barrels in front of her and shelves overhead lined with wooden crates. She'd as good as crawled into a tiny crack in the solid mountain of freight.

Once in, she'd never moved, never stretched her legs. Never gone seeking water or a chamber pot.

Michelle had told them they'd ride this train through the day and get off when it stopped for the night, so there was no way for Jilly to get separated from her sisters, with their normal colored, and therefore less memorable, hair.

Jilly breathed through her mouth, thinking that was quieter, as heavy boots walked the length of the car. Whoever it was walked to the back door and on through. He'd be coming back soon. He'd walked this same route an hour before. He was a train inspector. Maybe a brutal one who'd cast stowaways off the train while it was still moving. She'd heard of these men and their ugly behavior. They often gave stowaways terrible beatings before ejecting them.

Curling her arms around her drawn-up knees, she waited, prayed, wondered about her sisters. Wondered about Mama. Had she broken her ankle? She'd be even more vulnerable to Edgar's cruelties than before.

Long moments passed before the back door opened. The man coming back. She hadn't attempted to see who it was. If she could see him, then it stood to reason that he could see her. And though she considered herself one of the smartest people alive, she didn't fool herself. A man didn't have to be a genius to be very good at his job.

She'd seen too many lumberjacks swinging an ax with impressive skill. Sure, she'd beat him in a spelling bee, and she'd talk circles around him if the topic was mathematics, but that didn't mean she could outfight him.

The man's footsteps stopped right in front of the barrel she'd squeezed in behind.

She heard a bit of creaking, then a voice.

"I have two daughters of my own. It makes my blood run cold to imagine 'em hidin' on a train headed for . . . I might not know where. I have to ask myself what kind of trouble is behind a woman to make her do such a risky thing as ride the rails this way."

She guessed he was sitting on the molasses barrel in front

of her. He had to know exactly where she was. She'd thought herself well hidden but apparently not well enough.

"I'd never harm a girl, nor any woman, come to that. I know us train inspectors have a reputation that is frightening, but I wouldn't be party to that. If you wanted to come out of there, I'd tell you true, I wouldn't lay a hand on you nor throw you off the train. I won't be coming back this way again. You'd be safe from discovery if you wanted to stretch your legs. I've left a sandwich on a plate on the barrel beside yours. And there's a chamber pot in the front corner of the car that I'd be willing to tend if it got some use. I'm not sure of your circumstances, miss, but I'm leaving a few coins for you here, too. The end of the line is little more than two hours ahead. If you get off there, I won't be noticing nor mentioning it."

He stood and walked out of the train car. She heard the door thump shut. Then heard the door to the next car open and shut.

She sat there in silence and reminded herself there were good people in the world and having a terrible experience with one of them—her stepfather—or several of them— the men he'd lined up to marry her and her sisters—didn't extend to them all.

It took a little wiggling, but she got out of her corner, still not sure what part of her had shown. He'd not only known she was there, he'd also known she was a young woman. She ate the sandwich. The coins were few, and it wasn't right to take them from a man who might not have much to spare. But she didn't want him to think his generosity wasn't appreciated.

And she'd tend the chamber pot herself. Grateful beyond words to have it.

W AKE UP, MISS. You're dreaming." Caleb slid into the seat beside the blond woman and shook her shoulder gently but persistently when what had to be a nightmare held her in sleep.

A groan followed her into wakefulness.

Then her vision seemed to clear, and she smiled and looked him right in the eye. Looked at him with no subservience at all. No, not the behavior of a servant. He wondered at the mystery of her.

"Thank you. I *was* dreaming. It was a mercy to have you wake me."

"I'll leave you, then. I didn't mean to intrude. I'm a parson, and I'm at your service if you need any help at all."

"Where are you headed?"

"I've been called to the mission field."

"In California?"

"Yes, I've been journeying for weeks. I intend to start a mission among the hard-pressed families of the less success-ful miners." He burned with the spirit of his calling and loved to talk about it. He'd made a lot of mistakes in his life, but he'd made his peace with God and loved to preach.

Yet he'd never found a way to become a parson to a church back in Savannah. He'd been too well-known. The church had accepted him fully as a member. But it seemed accepting him as a parson was a bit too much.

When he'd heard a stirring speech from a frontier missionary he felt God opening a door that might otherwise be closed. There was a place where his call to preach would be needed.

It was God's leading, but it also enabled Caleb to leave a past behind him that would make this pretty woman tell him to get away from her. Probably at the top of her lungs.

And he *should* get away from her, leave her in peace now that she was awake and her nightmare over. He suspected she wanted that without any knowledge of his past and the one thing he never dared tell anyone.

But his enthusiasm for his mission, and some worry for her kept him beside her.

Speaking quietly because most everyone on the train was sleeping, he said, "Many found great wealth in the goldfields and were wise enough to take that stake and make something of it. But far too many were caught in the grip of gold fever, and it became more than just work. More than a way to make money. They let it take over their lives. It's a shame when it's a single man, but the gold rush is over twenty years old. Some of these men have been there long enough to have wives and children. The ones I'm traveling to live under very undesirable conditions. The two ladies you spoke to earlier and the young couple sitting in front of them are all with me. We had a mission pastor come to our church who had worked out in this unfertile field. He inspired all of us to this mission."

He smiled, and she smiled back, and the moment stretched. Then she blinked in a funny way he didn't quite understand.

"We spoke of love of money being at the root of all evil."

"I heard you talking to Harriet and Nora. You know your Scripture, miss."

"It's Laura." She didn't tack on a last name, and he wasn't comfortable calling her by her first. But that discomfort came second to his curiosity about what she was thinking. She was cooking up a plan of some sort, and he was almost certain she was in some kind of danger. Or distress. Or she'd come upon hard times.

"And can you withstand that temptation, Parson?"

"It's Parson Caleb Tillman."

She again didn't take the opportunity to tell him the rest of her name. "Can you fend off the love of money in your quest?"

"I believe I am well equipped to avoid the love of money." He'd gotten that evil seed out of his heart and prayed daily, more than daily, that it never returned.

She gave him another smile. She really was the most beautiful woman he'd ever seen. And cultured, and educated. What was she doing out here dressed in servants clothing?

"Would you let me come along to your mission field, Parson Tillman? I'm a woman with no idea where I'm going and a great mission of my own that I need to complete."

They watched each other for a long time. Too long. Finally, he said, "Pray about it. It's no decision to make suddenly."

"I will."

"We will stay in a hotel tonight, and I've money to rent

two rooms, one for the women and one for the men. You'd likely need to sleep on the floor, but you're welcome to the shelter I can provide. Baby Willa sleeps well at night, so you wouldn't be disturbed. And you'd be safe."

And that's what he was really concerned about. He was very afraid that she wasn't safe.

"We set out tomorrow morning to our mission field. We have money enough to buy a horse and wagon and supplies, but you'd have to walk for several days. After you've prayed about it, if you want to join us, you're welcome to come. There will be enough work for many hands."

Laura nodded. "I'll attend my prayers then, Parson. The idea to come with you struck me so suddenly and with such strength. I need time in prayer to see if it's really the voice of God."

Or desperation. She didn't say that, but Caleb heard her unspoken thoughts.

He had some praying to do of his own. Because taking a beautiful young woman to the mission field, a woman he found startlingly attractive, might be an unwise idea.

The love of money might be the root of all evil, but it wasn't the only temptation in the Good Book.

She was another kind entirely.

SEVEN

YOU'RE NOT SUPPOSED TO SPEAK TO ME." Michelle looked over Laura's shoulder and dragged her around the corner of the train station.

"I have to. We debated how to stay together and yet not be three sisters, right?"

"Right." Michelle was watching all around her. "We agreed it would be safer to keep track of each other. Not that easy when you're hiding."

"What's going on?"

Michelle squeaked and jumped. Jilly had sneaked up behind Michelle.

Good, Laura needed to talk to both of them. "I've found a way for us to stay together while we"—Laura's voice dropped to an even lower whisper—"find husbands."

"What's that?" Jilly would listen, then analyze.

Michelle would listen, criticize, and organize.

Papa's will gave them ownership when they turned twenty-five or when they married. He'd discussed it with them, and he'd wanted to give them time to mature and put aside all childish things before they had the weight of the company on their shoulders.

But with Edgar now in their home with evil plans to marry them off, twenty-five was too long to wait. Michelle, the oldest, was only twenty-one. Jilly twenty, Laura nineteen. They wouldn't survive to reach twenty-five, not without acquiring loathsome husbands, if Edgar got to choose.

"I'm joining a group of missionaries heading for some terribly impoverished part of the gold mines."

"You're what?" Michelle tried to stay quiet and shriek at the same time. She almost strangled herself. "No, you're not. We can't find husbands in a goldfield."

"An impoverished gold mining area might have men in it who'd be willing to marry wealthy young women," Laura said. "Of course, many of them are probably half-mad with gold fever. And we don't want *them* for husbands. But surely we can ferret out one or two nice ones from the howling mob of madmen."

Laura let them analyze and criticize inside their heads for a moment, figuring they would get there almost as fast as she had.

Michelle sighed.

Jilly crossed her arms and looked into the distance as if she were adding and subtracting, and probably multiplying and dividing, with some advanced calculus thrown in and brought to bear on what seemed like a simple, obvious, and great idea to Laura.

Then Laura added the screw that would stab them until they agreed with her plan. "I'm going with them. We thought it would be best to stick together, or at least know how to contact each other, but if we can't agree, that's fine. I'm going. I'll meet you back on the mountain in one month. Bring a husband."

Laura turned, and Michelle grabbed her arm and turned her right back.

Grinning at her big sister in the deep shadows cast by the depot, she waited.

Then she remembered another detail. "Parson Caleb Tillman said he'd rent two rooms tonight. One for me and the other women on his mission, and one for him and one of the women's husband. So that means we won't be three women together, at least not tonight. If all three of us join on this trip with Parson Tillman and do it in the morning, immediately before he leaves, then that will be our only moment when we might be remembered here in town as three women doing something together. And there are three more women with the mission group. I think we should all go."

Michelle looked like she was doing her best to process this wildly sudden development.

A glance at Jilly told Laura she was picking through details.

"How are they traveling?" Jilly asked.

"He told me they are buying supplies, a wagon, and a horse and heading out at dawn."

"Will three more fit?" Michelle asked, likely trying to organize the seating on a small wagon.

"It'd be worth walking just to get out of this town before anyone recognizes us," Laura said. "We're actually fortunate that Parson Tillman came in on this train with a group of strangers. No one will give it a thought if someone comes around asking about three sisters. We'll blend right in with the other women."

"We've already been swept a long way from home on that river. How much farther is this mission field?" Jilly asked.

Laura shrugged. "I guess we'll find out when we get there. I don't mind putting more miles between us and Edgar."

"Find a moment to speak to the parson alone and ask if we can come." Michelle looked serious. "I'm going to sleep outside. I'll buy some supplies in the morning, maybe a horse to carry them, then I'll follow you and join the group away from town. You said he's buying supplies?"

"Yes, as many as he has money left to buy."

"I'll get enough to make sure we don't add hardship to the group."

Frowning, Laura said, "More supplies would be good. But it will add to your chances of being remembered in town, and it'll make the mission group wonder what's going on."

The three of them exchanged long looks, all of them full of doubts.

"What other choice do we have? Do we get back on the train and ride to San Francisco? Do we split up?" Laura asked. "If we join the mission work, we can always leave whenever we care to. I'm sure the parson already thinks I'm in some kind of trouble, just by the way he talked to me. I believe he'll accept that we're with him for our own reasons. As long as we support their mission and their faith, he'll probably let us join in. And I do support his mission and his faith, and I'm sure you both do, too."

Laura dropped her voice. "There are married men and families at the place he's going, but there have to be some single men, too. We'll probably have to beat the marriage offers back with a stick." She grinned at her sisters.

Michelle rolled her eyes. Jilly shook her head, a faint look of unease on her face.

"I wonder where I could buy a horse and supplies." Michelle looked around the darkened town.

"Don't flash money around." Jilly really should give Michelle credit for more sense.

Nodding, Michelle said, "I'll be careful. But supplies and an extra horse might take some of the weight off the wagon, in case the presence of three extra people adds a harsh burden."

"Parson Tillman told me that I'd have to walk. I have no idea how far it is from here."

Michelle rubbed her chin and glanced around again at the small frontier town. There was a livery stable at the end of the single street. A corral of horses grazed behind the stable.

Laura saw Parson Tillman heading for the hotel. He wasn't overly tall but tall enough. His dark blond hair shone in the light out front of the hotel. She remembered how his eyes had nearly matched his hair. They were a light hazel, almost golden brown, striped with darker brown. Mostly she'd noticed his kindness. She watched him walk up the steps to the hotel with the others in his mission group ahead of him. She had to join them now or wait until morning.

The town was the last stop on a spur coming off the transcontinental railroad, and there were hundreds of spurs growing out of that line. Linking every city possible to the train.

Papa's dream had been to build a spur all the way up to his forest, maybe follow the flume as closely as possible so he could ship logs down and supplies up with far less difficulty. That's why he'd trained his daughters to be engineers. He'd been especially enthused when he saw the education he arranged suited them.

If he'd wanted sons, he'd never said such a thing. In Laura's life, she'd never been treated as anything but greatly loved. And he'd set his girls up to inherit and run the dynasty he built.

A daughter who could blast holes in mountains.

A daughter who could build trestles across vast and rugged mountain gorges.

A daughter who could build and maintain the machines, as well as survey the land, route the course, and organize all the aspects of building a train track and roads. Eventually putting up homes for his lumberjacks, even building towns.

They'd shared an education so they could all do every job. But they'd each found their strengths. They'd found which jobs gave them pleasure and developed unique skills.

"I've got to go. I told the parson I'd sleep in the room he rented for the women of his group. I think he's looking around for me."

"Talk to him alone if you get a chance," Michelle instructed. "Don't mention we're sisters, but ask if two more women of faith can join his mission group."

"I will." Laura waited until the parson stopped scanning the street and turned away from her, then she hurried out to cross the only true street in town. When she got close enough, he must have heard her because he turned around. The others in his group went on ahead.

This was her chance for a private word.

When she reached him, she said in a low voice, "I have some trouble behind me, Parson."

His eyes widened, and she could almost read his mind.

"Not with the law." She rested one hand on his wrist, then quickly stopped touching him. What was she thinking to touch him like that? "I—I'm afraid of a man, and I don't want him to know where I've gone. I would join your mission group if you'd have me. I'd work hard for you and share my faith with others."

"If you're sure," Parson Tillman said.

"I am sure. And I know two others who would join you and work alongside you, if you're willing. They were on the train."

"The woman who came to get a drink of water and interrupted your talk with Harriet and Nora? After which you pretended to sleep?"

Laura covered a small gasp. For the first time, she realized that she really wasn't very good at lying, though she feared she'd gotten better at it since Mama had remarried.

But clearly she wasn't as good at it as she'd hoped.

"Yes, her and one other. They've got accommodations for tonight, but I told them we were leaving at first light. They'll meet us in the morning. One of them told me we shouldn't wait, but she'll catch up."

Parson Tillman gave her a long look. The man seemed to be searching for the truth and not finding it. He did need to decide who was right for his mission group. Laura understood that.

"Pray about it tonight, Parson. See if the Lord gives you peace about letting us come along." She smiled and barely resisted touching his wrist again.

"And that, Miss Laura, is why I'll say yes. Yes, you can join our group, and we'll look forward to including the other women tomorrow. Thank you. You'll find ample work and many opportunities to reach the lost. And most mission workers feel they get more than they give. So you're about to be blessed, you and your friends."

"Thank you, Parson."

"Let's go in and get you ladies settled."

They shared a smile in the quiet of the little town, then went inside together.

EIGHT

L AURA SAID WE'D BE WALKING, but she didn't mention sleeping on the ground, and I had no idea it'd be for a week!"

Jilly was not handling mission work well.

She kept her hair bound, completely covered, hiding the vivid red. Her brows were tinted dark brown, her lashes were also stained to cover the red of them.

And she'd been faithful about it. Laura had never seen a single hair slip free. Jilly sneaked away to tend her lashes and brows every morning before she saw anyone.

Michelle had her horse, and she'd shown up with a packhorse, too. Before the first day was past, she'd managed to get Nora and Harriet Hogan up on horseback. And she was walking along with Laura and Jilly. Along with Caleb, too. Rick drove the wagon, and his wife, Gretel, and the baby rode beside him.

It had been four days, and if they weren't hopelessly lost, three more to go until they reached their mission field.

"I'm enjoying the evening talks," Laura whispered. Caleb

led them all in prayer and spoke a meditation every night. He'd talk about the mission before them. Sometimes they'd sing.

Laura and her sisters had traveled little in their lives. They lived the winters in San Francisco and the spring, summer, and fall in their house on the mountain, deep in the forest.

Until Mama had remarried.

Shortly after the wedding, they'd all been consigned to the mountain house for good. Edgar seemed to think a city gave a girl too many opportunities. And thinking was hard on the female brain. So to keep them from developing . . . what, brain fever? Laura quietly snorted. He'd moved them to the remote Stiles mansion, and there they'd stayed.

The truth was simple. They were prisoners in their home. And they'd broken out and were on the run. Escaped prisoners. She shuddered deeply to think of Mama at Edgar's mercy.

MARGARET STILES BEAUMONT SOAKED in the slipper tub, the water perfumed, her hair in a knot on top of her head. Edgar hadn't come back the day he'd ridden off, but she'd maintained the ruse of measles for her servants. No new poison-ivy treatment had been required. That was to say she didn't have to rub poison ivy on her skin again. It had taken a week for the rash to fade, and it would still bloom a bit if she forgot and scratched.

Now she was just enjoying the solitude. But only in moments.

The rest of the time she felt on the verge of panic.

Where were the girls? Had they made it down that dreadful flume and gotten to the train and headed for parts unknown?

They'd talked and plotted and planned until they couldn't plan anymore. And all the while knowing the girls might end up anywhere. It would depend on whether they reached the train, and then whether they took a train heading east, west, north, or south. Whether they stuck together or split up.

The plan was to head for a city. They'd studied the maps in Liam's library. . . . Well, it was all of the family's library, but Margaret felt her memories of Liam most strongly in there.

They'd studied water routes, cities, what train information they could find from old newspapers, and other information they'd gleaned.

Edgar had cut off book purchases and newspaper subscriptions after he'd moved them permanently to the deep woods.

They'd hoped to reach Sacramento or possibly San Francisco, but they might be recognized there. The world was a dangerous place for a woman alone, or even three women unaccompanied. That added to Margaret's panic. And that all assumed the girls survived their escape.

If they hadn't survived, Margaret felt sure she would have heard. Men worked the bottom of the flume, and they'd have been found.

Because Margaret hadn't heard of her girls being found, she had to believe they'd made it through that and gotten away down the river. And her girls were proper geniuses. If they had trouble, they'd use the fine brains God had blessed them with, and they'd handle whatever came their way.

She would also panic if she wondered when Edgar would

come home. Assuming he wasn't even aware the girls were gone, he might stay away another two weeks. Margaret had worked two weeks of illness, maybe three, into her announcement to him that the girls were ill.

She'd forbidden the maids to enter the room she "shared" with the girls, this one, with its nice-sized water closet and pipes that brought in hot and cold water. She'd emptied the chamber pots herself, mostly to hide all the food she'd thrown away.

But she was fairly sure some of them suspected by now. She only hoped no one wired Edgar to tell him the girls were gone.

It didn't matter. The moment would come when he'd find out, and he'd be furious. And if he was furious, he wasn't above giving her the back of his hand.

She was prepared to face whatever needed facing. There was little choice. She knew the girls needed time to hide. And if it meant her life to give them that time, she'd willingly lay her life down.

Thinking about it ended her lolling in the tub though. She was too frightened.

As she dressed, she prayed. And prayed and prayed.

Help them find a hiding place, Lord. If you keep them safe, even if they never return, I'll sing your praises every day.

"DO YOU KNOW HOW TO WASH CLOTHES?" Jilly whispered to Laura.

Parson Tillman had assigned them each a task.

"No, but how hard can it be?"

Jilly pointed to a tidy little mountain of clothes. They were next to a small stream babbling along over rocks. "He wants it all washed because we'll be arriving at his mission field tomorrow, and he doesn't want us coming in filthy. We need to wash our clothes, too. But we only have one set of dresses."

"I guess you just get them wet and the dirt washes away?" Laura sighed. "I envy you. I'm supposed to cook supper."

"What food do you have?"

Laura pointed to . . . something. "I'm guessing it's the hind leg of a deer or antelope maybe. I was embarrassed to ask. It might be a pig."

The haunch of meat was skinned, and to Laura it was unrecognizable as any particular animal. Which, considering looking at it turned her stomach, was probably just as well.

"Hack it into small pieces and hold them over the fire to cook. Not much else makes sense," Jilly said.

"There are pans." Laura pointed. "But not big enough for the whole thing. And besides, there are potatoes, so at least one of the pans might be for them."

"I know the peelings come off, and the potatoes go in water. So that's probably right."

Michelle came up beside them. "Have any of you ever mended torn clothes?" She had a bundle of clothes in her hands. Shirts, pants, skirts, underthings, who knew what all.

"You know how to thread a needle. We embroider," Laura said.

"But I've never been very good at it."

Jilly shook her head. "I never could see the sense in coloring up cloth with pretty thread. What is the point of such a pastime?"

Embroidery was one of their few feminine skills. None of them had developed any real talent for it.

"It's decorative," Laura said, thinking of some womanly skills she actually preferred to blowing things up. But she didn't admit it out loud. She'd heard enough comments about the fussy baby sister to last a lifetime. To shut her mouth for a lifetime.

"But sewing patches on clothes." Michelle shrugged one shoulder sheepishly. "We have always had plenty of money and servants. But for many women, sewing clothes is a very serious, important, and, yes, crucial use of her time, since she has to make clothes for her whole family. I've always taken pride in our education. But now I realize that unless we're being waited on by servants"—she tugged on the drab collar of her dress— "there are some serious holes in it."

"Which makes us well-educated, entitled snobs," Laura said. "Unless Parson Tillman wants us to build a train track or blow up a tree stump, we're useless. Our education is useless."

Her sisters looked at her, and she braced herself to be called a baby or spoiled or a whiner. Instead, they looked sheepish. Maybe even a little ashamed of their years of arrogant dismissal of something that was now vital to survival.

"Just use your heads, both of you. Michelle, use a threaded needle to pull the holes together. Jilly, let the water rinse the dirt away. If you fail, Michelle, someone's knee may show. Jilly, if you fail, people might wear dirty clothes. Me? If I fail, I just might poison or starve the entire mission group. I think things are more serious for me."

Parson Tillman came striding up, smiling. He really was the nicest man. Laura was tempted to just admit they needed help. They were educated women. They knew math and chemicals. They could survey gorges and mountains and design a span to carry a train across. But God help her cook a haunch of venison . . . or whatever it was.

But they were dressed as servants. To admit they didn't know these basic chores was to admit to the whole pack of lies.

And she was a little afraid he'd . . . what? He was a nice man. He wouldn't just abandon them along the trail.

Would he?

THOSE THREE WERE UP TO SOMETHING.

As a man who'd spent his youth sneaking, lying, and worse, Caleb recognized deceit when he came upon it.

He had to decide if they just didn't have anywhere else to go and had joined his mission team in desperation. Or were they . . . preparing to steal the mission purse?

Well, the mission purse, badly depleted after their cross-country travels and the purchase of supplies, wouldn't get them far, so that wasn't a big worry.

In fact, the one, Michelle, had shown up riding a horse and leading a packhorse loaded with supplies.

She'd brought more to the group than she'd ever take. If they were thieves, they weren't good at it.

And all three were friendly and seemed to enjoy talking, knew their Bible. Joined in solemnly with prayers.

Caleb had a good ear for a phony minister or believer whose faith wasn't real. Or maybe just a confused believer or one new to the faith. But these women knew their Bible.

Not just a few well-known verses, they really listened and contributed when they talked of faith.

But they were certainly up to something.

He wondered what it would take for them to reveal whatever had driven them into some kind of desperate run from somebody.

"Can I help you with your chores?" Caleb had a lot to do on his own, but there was something about their whispering and the glances they'd stolen at the pile of laundry and the cook pots and haunch of venison, from one of three deer he and Rick had shot to stock up on their meat supply before they arrived at the settlement.

Rick was presently butchering all of them and preparing them to be smoked. The hides were in the capable hands of Harriet and Nora.

And Gretel was traipsing through the surrounding woods searching for firewood while the baby slept in a sling on her chest. A job Caleb should help her with. Or he could take over the butchering and let Rick hunt wood with his wife. But Rick was better at the butchering.

Laura clapped her hands in a way that struck Caleb as falsely cheerful. "No, we're wasting time talking when there's work to be done. Let's get to it, ladies."

Laura strode toward the meat, her steps determined. Jilly went to the pile of laundry. Michelle picked up a bundle of mending and carried it to a log, sat down, and must have realized she didn't have a needle because she went to fetch one. Then got back without thread and went to get that.

Jilly spread a stained, sweat-soaked shirt on top of the flowing stream and just watched it get wet. She held it there a while, then draped it over a rock and reached for a pair of pants, not even looking at the small cake of soap or the washboard that sat nearby.

He turned to watch Laura pick up a knife and approach the haunch of venison as if she were in for a fight.

But then he'd known they weren't servants, hadn't he? They spoke and moved and sat like refined ladies. Fine ladies disguised as servants and on the run.

He really needed to help Gretel gather wood. But for now, he went to Jilly, knelt beside her, and talked quietly of soap and a washboard. He even demonstrated. She watched with sharp eyes, glancing at him with a furrowed brow occasionally. As if she didn't like it that he'd seen through her incompetence, but she also was listening and learning. If she was a refined lady who'd fallen on hard times and needed to work as a servant, it gave him some satisfaction to know he was teaching her a life skill.

He went to Michelle and lifted the pair of trousers—his own as a matter of fact, with a tear in the knee.

He lifted it up to find she'd sown it to her skirt.

"Um, I'm fine, Parson. I'm sure I can . . ."

"This needs a patch." He took the scissors from mending supplies and clipped the trousers loose from her skirt.

She looked up at him, her cheeks pink with a blush. Then he lifted up a swatch of fabric from the rags. "Use this to patch. Cut out a square. But first you're going to have to trim the frayed threads on the hole." He demonstrated. "Then you'll need to turn the edges of the hole back like this and hem them or the patch won't hold."

That same intent listening. That same sharp intelligence in her eyes. He suspected that after telling her something once, she'd be able to copy it and do a fine job.

It took a few minutes for him to hem the hole and sew on the patch. He sifted through the clothes—it wasn't a large bundle—and found another worn-out knee.

"Not all of these need a hole patched. Some have ripped seams, some are . . ." He finished with his lesson in about fifteen minutes and went to rescue supper.

"Let me show you how we cut venison into steaks and put them on a spit to roast over the fire." He took a few minutes to sharpen the dull butcher knife, talking to Laura as he demonstrated. She had that same keen focus.

He finished the sharpening, then sliced two steaks, showing her how thick and telling her what to do with the scraps of meat.

"While you finish cutting the steaks, I'll show you how to peel and cook the potatoes."

Once he turned his attention to the potatoes, Laura looked up from her stern focus on the work. With a quick glance at the two other women, she said quietly, "I'd like to tell you why we're here, but it has to remain confidential. We aren't good at household chores, but we are women of faith, and we intend to work hard for you at your mission field. I hope you can believe that."

"Of course, I can, Laura. I've, that is, *we've* all got things in our past that are hard to discuss. In many ways, all of life is a mission field, no matter where you are." He talked quietly of potatoes and faith while she sliced and he peeled.

He'd talked with all three of them. They looked very little alike. Jilly, with her decent but not-good-enough disguise was a redhead. Her brows and lashes had been touched with something, charcoal maybe. Her hair was always bound, but he'd seen enough wisps escaping to know. Laura was blond and fair with blue eyes. Michelle had dark blue eyes but not the same shade as Laura's. Even so, there was a way about them. The bright intelligence shining in their eyes. The way they tilted their chins. Jilly had the same nose as Michelle. Laura's smile matched Jilly's. They all had the same curve of their chins.

Caleb was more certain than not they were family, most likely sisters. And well-off, genteel sisters, not born to be servants, and yet, here they were, willing to work as servants and serve the Lord.

"When you feel ready to talk, I'll be ready to listen. You'll find only kindness and acceptance among our group, and if you only want to talk to me, I'll promise to keep your words private."

Nodding, Laura said, "Thank you. And thank you for the help."

"Please don't be afraid to ask." What he really wanted to say was *please ask for help before you destroy a meal* or whatever else these women might get up to.

He saw Michelle staring blankly at a sock with a hole in the heel. He really didn't have time to teach her to darn.

Going to her, he said, "Gretel is really struggling to find wood and carry the baby at the same time. Do you mind helping her?"

Michelle looked up at him and arched one brow. He almost laughed. She wasn't fooled for a second that he was trying to get the mending away from her.

Since she was being very frank in the way she glared at him, he figured he'd return the favor. "I don't have time to teach you how to darn socks. But you can pick up wood. Please."

He didn't tell her to send Gretel over to work on the mending as he normally would have. He wasn't absolutely positive Michelle knew how to pick up pieces of wood.

She nodded. He was afraid she might be hurt or angry, but again he was pleased to see that intelligence in her eyes, and with it, just plain good sense. She set the mending aside and headed in the direction Gretel had gone.

"PARSON TILLMAN SAID we'll arrive at the mission field tomorrow." Michelle rolled onto her back.

Laura rolled onto her side and whispered, "Sleeping on the ground is awful."

"Shut up, both of you." Jilly sat up, fluffed the satchel she'd brought along and was now using for a pillow. "Go to sleep."

As if Jilly had been asleep.

"He knew we couldn't do the jobs we were assigned." Laura was careful to keep her voice low. The Steinmeyer family slept in the wagon. The Hogan sisters slept under the wagon. Parson Tillman slept on the far side of the fire across from Laura and her sisters. They weren't exactly near anyone. But the night was so quiet that she was very careful.

"Maybe we should help out for a while." Jilly punched her satchel, but no amount of fluffing was going to make that thing a pillow. "Then as soon as we can find a way, head for Sacramento. Or somewhere."

"Day by day, sisters." Laura thought she was best suited to this. Michelle especially didn't like dealing with things as they came along. She liked to plan.

76

Well, as soon as anyone could think of a plan, Laura would be glad to let Michelle organize it. But for right now . . . "Day by day."

She fell asleep praying for her mother. And thanking God she hadn't poisoned anyone.

NINE

T HAT'S THE MISSION?" Somehow Laura had expected a mission to be like a church, a building. She'd read books about the Alamo.

"We're here." The parson was driving the wagon. Gretel rode in the back with the baby. The Hogan sisters rode Michelle's two horses. Rick, along with Laura and her sisters, walked behind the wagon.

Laura had about fifty questions, and she didn't ask a one of them. Children of all ages sat around, the older ones lolling on boulders and the little ones building mounds of rocks and piling up dirt. There was one older girl and no older boys.

Women stepped out of ramshackle cabins that didn't look fit to keep the rain off anyone's head. And Laura knew enough about land at this altitude to know it did rain, and what's more, even this late in the spring, it could snow.

The settlement clung to the side of a mountain. The ground was steep in places, but right here there was a rugged but generally level stretch of land about a quarter of a mile long and half that wide. The houses—or more accurately shanties, maybe hovels—whatever they were, they stood as far apart as space would allow, which was to say, they were really close together. She counted ten cabins, though two of them had no roof, and one had fallen completely into a heap. Women had stepped out of half of them. Five adult women. Who lived in the other cabins?

There was a trickle of water from a spring. There were no gardens. The ground was more stone than dirt, with scattered boulders. Trees grew all around the little clearing. Down the slope, more trees fought their way up between rocks. Scrubby grass grew in clumps here and there. Then at the bottom of the hill was grass, lush green grass, deep enough to brush the bellies of the herd of Hereford cattle that grazed all around.

The cows were a whole lot fatter and healthier looking than the people up here.

Laura drew her eyes back to the people, and her stomach twisted to see their grim condition. The adult women stood, staring, not a waved hand or a hello to be heard. The children sat and stared. Silently. All of them were almost skeletally thin. They were filthy. Their clothes were worn down until they were nearly transparent, and one couldn't guess what color they'd been because they'd all faded to a drab grayish tone, touched by filth.

Most all of them were barefoot.

"We'll have plenty to do," Parson Tillman said under his breath as he drew his team to a halt.

Laura, walking alongside her sisters, and Rick stopped as the wagon did. The Hogan sisters reined their mounts to a halt. All of them were at a loss for words.

The older girl rose, watching them. There was something in her eyes Laura couldn't quite define. What came to her mind was feral. The girl looked at them like a wolf would. A hungry wolf. She had fear in her eyes, but also something calculating. Laura thought of the money in the pouch around her neck.

Part of her wanted to fold her hands tightly around it, and part of her wanted to just hand it over.

Parson Tillman stepped down from the wagon and lifted his voice. "We've come to settle here. I hope to hold church services. And we've brought supplies. I'm going to start unloading them over here, and we got a deer yesterday. We'll have a big pot of stew ready in an hour or so."

The wagon stopped just before the row of cabins began.

He gave Nora Hogan a quick look, then another at Heinrich Steinmeyer. To establish some rapport, they'd planned on making a good meal and sharing it. They'd even brought along firewood. Parson Tillman had said he wanted to make a meal when they got here and ask for nothing, not even wood. That was before they'd seen any of these folks and how terribly hungry they looked. The plan was the same, but now there was an urgency. A need to get food for this settlement fast.

Nora swung off her horse, Harriet only a moment behind her. Rick immediately gathered the firewood they had in the back of the wagon while the women fetched bags and a small crate full of potatoes and a large pot.

It occurred to Laura as she watched Rick swiftly start a small blaze that even the ground around here would be picked clean. The woods might be hunted out for firewood right along with the wildlife.

Finding wood might be as big a problem as finding food.

The hungry wolf-girl sidled to Laura's left. Laura noticed the other children and one of the adult women move as if they were spreading out to circle the mission group. She saw the girl smoothly swing an arm down and pick up a fist-sized rock.

It would make a likely weapon.

Parson Tillman might've noticed, too. He suddenly reached into the back of the wagon and produced a burlap bag full of deer meat cut into strips and turned into jerky just yesterday. He pulled it open and strode straight into the middle of what could be a dangerous situation.

"We've brought food. We heard times were hard in this settlement. Would anyone like venison? There's enough for everyone to have a bit of jerky while we make a stew."

Laura saw the rock drop out of the girl's hand. She stopped sidling to get behind them and walked toward the food. Her eyes were suspicious, but hunger urged her on.

Another woman came closer, her hand on her belly. A child on the way, another toddler on her hip. The woman was so thin, except for her rounded belly, that Laura felt alarm for the coming child and the mother's chances to deliver the baby and survive herself.

Then the children all came faster.

Rick had a fire going with the warm crackle as it burned. The smell of woodsmoke swirled around them in the gentle breeze. He stepped back from the growing fire and took Willa so Gretel could have both hands free.

Nora had plucked all the canteens out of the back of the wagon—no, they didn't even ask for water—and poured them into their biggest cauldron. Harriet sliced potatoes into the cold water while Rick set up the cast-iron hanger for the pot. They had onions and carrots splashing into the water. Gretel was soon at work making biscuits.

Regretting she was such poor help, Laura went to the cook pot, and Nora gave her the job of cutting more of the cooked-yesterday deer meat into bite-sized chunks. Laura's main goal tonight was not to cut her finger off.

Michelle and Jilly threw in by dragging a stack of tin plates out of the back of the wagon. The parson didn't have enough of those for everyone. But it was hoped that the people who lived here had their own.

Soon the stew was simmering. With the meat already cooked, it was a fast meal. The time it took for the pot to come to a boil and the vegetables to soften would be short.

Over their quick and quiet work, Laura heard the parson's kind voice. He asked questions, offered the bag of jerky, and made a few promises that Laura hoped they were capable of keeping. With the stew sending out its rich, meaty smell, the biscuits browning in the covered baking sheet, and coffee boiling away, the parson called his mission group over for introductions.

Rick got the horses unhitched and staked out on the meager grass.

They all went to the strangers except Gretel, who stayed to tend the meal. Laura prayed as she walked toward the people. They were still quiet, still filthy, still emaciated. But not quite so wary as before.

"Tomorrow, our group is going to build a church," Parson Tillman said. "We'll start by finding a sturdy rock I can rest my Bible on while I say prayers for you all and for ourselves

that we'll serve you as Jesus would. Rick is our best hunter.
I hope he'll keep us in food."

"None of us have a gun. And for small game, rabbits and
birds, the area's hunted out." The woman with the rounded
belly sounded dejected.

"He'll have to go far afield then."

Heinrich nodded his head. "I'm Heinrich, please call me
Rick." He spoke with a heavy German accent. "My wife,
Gretel, is cooking." He went on to talk a bit about himself.

Each member of the mission group in turn said their
names, and the parson encouraged the women and children
to speak a bit.

It was awkward, but Laura studied all the folks here. Most
of the feral look had gone out of everyone's eyes.

"When do your men come home? In time for supper?"
There'd been no mention of men, but surely the men and
the older boys were gone to the mines.

"They take off early Monday mornin', and we don't see
'em again till Saturday night." The woman, named Janine,
watched them with hostile eyes, her arms crossed, but the
stew was keeping her nearby. "We live too far out from the
mining town, Dorada Rio, for 'em to git home from work
every night."

The stew was ready, and the families did have their own
tin plates, plus a drink of water from the nearby stream.

It was a shame there wasn't a cow anywhere to give these
children a drink of milk. Laura's eyes wandered down the
wooded slope to that lush pasture brimming with cows. All
sorts of milk down there.

And here she stood with coins in a pouch under her dress.

Something could be worked out.

JILLY WAITED until everyone had a good serving of stew, then she tugged on Parson Tillman's arm.

"You're building a church?" She grinned. Finally, something she could help with. Building a church would be simple, and she'd get to use her architectural and engineering skills out in the world, not on some sketch pad.

She'd build it with natural material. This place with rocks and lumber everywhere was rich in building material. And on the side of a mountain, or almost the side. She'd use skills she'd been trained for, but now instead of theory, she'd have reality. She could do it a lot better than she washed trousers.

"Yes. It's not our first priority. A building I mean. You don't need a building for a church. You just need believers gathered together to worship. That's what I meant when I said I'd start out with a rock to rest my Bible on while I shared my message and prayers."

Jilly quit listening and looked at the decrepit shacks and lean-tos.

These women, one expecting a baby. The rest most likely the mothers of the various children. They needed better shelter than they had. She could build each of them a cabin.

"I know how to build a church. We even have some tools."

"I brought along an ax for me and one for Rick."

"Good, you do the chopping. I'll make up the design for the church."

"It has to be simple, I—"

"Simple, sure. I can't exactly plan on stained glass windows. I'll control myself about flying buttresses." She smirked at him.

"Uh, flying buttresses?" He sounded a little dazed. "Like the ones in Notre-Dame Cathedral in Paris?"

"Yep, we'll skip those." She crossed her eyes at him and grinned. "I understand simple, Parson. I know what the word *simple* means, and I understand why an ornate church could actually alienate these people from God when they have so little. I'll build a log cabin. If we have the right tools, I can put a steeple on it, but that won't be a requirement. Some benches inside. I'll keep windows to a minimum both for ease of construction and to keep the building warm in winter. Hmmm . . . heat. A fireplace." She was already calculating the square footage. "Do we need a fireplace?"

"Um, I haven't thought of it. The work can't be too heavy, Jilly. There are only two men to—"

"Heavy's not a problem. 'Give me a lever long enough and a fulcrum on which to place it, and I shall move the world.'"

The parson gave her a look through eyes so narrow and suspicious she wished she had skipped the quote.

"You're not, nor have you ever been, a servant, have you, Jilly?"

Nope, she probably shouldn't be quoting Archimedes. She clamped her mouth shut. Ignoring his question, she said, "I'm going to do some planning."

She needed to get away from him, but before she did, she rested one hand on his arm. "It would give me the greatest pleasure to help build a church for these folks. Something simple that won't offend or hurt a group of people who don't have much of a roof over their heads. And then I'll repair their cabins to keep the rain and snow out."

She said *repair*, but in her head, she was already building them each a new cabin. Michelle had included some tools in the supplies she'd bought. Jilly hadn't given her a list, but Michelle was smart. She'd have what they needed.

Jilly wondered when she'd have time to find a husband in the middle of all this work.

Mama. What about Mama? Praying, she went to the supplies Michelle had bought, looking for writing material.

TEN

C ALEB SHOULD HAVE ADDED, "And neither were your sisters," when he'd confronted Jilly about never being a servant.

He'd caught her off guard. She'd controlled her mouth, but she hadn't quite controlled her expression. Caleb knew how to read people. And not because he was such an experienced and sensitive parson. No, it was a skill developed when he'd swindled people. He'd gotten very good at figuring out what they wanted and giving it to them in exchange for their trust and, eventually, their money.

Well, there'd be another chance to question these women. And Rick had built a log cabin before, well, helped build one. He knew how it was done. But maybe they'd found a job one of their new missionaries could do. He suspected they were all skilled at something. He just hadn't found it yet. And when he did, would it be a skill useful for running a mission? Honestly, if Jilly really could build a church and make cabin repairs for his flock, she'd be very helpful.

And flying buttresses? How had . . . "Oh, forget it."

He'd strain his brain trying to imagine answers to everything.

The woman expecting a baby looked like she was going to split kindling for the fire. Caleb hurried to help her. Maybe if he worked hard in her stead, she might smile or even tell him her name. She'd eaten the food he'd offered. He thought she was too hungry not to. But she was far from friendly.

His flock. Maybe a flock of angry badgers . . . if those came in flocks.

He'd do his best to reach out to them and get to know them and serve them.

He heard an ax swing behind him and turned to see Rick, a few yards into the rocky, uneven woods behind the settlement. Jilly was pointing and talking between chops.

Michelle was studying a sheet of paper. Laura was walking just uphill of the wagon. Her long strides told him she was measuring off paces. Planning the foundation of the church.

The Hogan sisters were standing by, looking a little shocked but still ready and willing to take orders.

Only Gretel and baby Willa had been spared . . . and Gretel was cooking dinner for about twenty people.

Huh, maybe he'd have his church built before nightfall.

Caleb looked around. The women and children had all gone back inside. He'd heard one of them call the settlement Purgatory. He should urge them to change the name.

He'd talked of being called here by God. He tried to share his faith with them while they grabbed chunks of venison. They'd hear more before he was done.

And he'd make this a better place before he left. Better in spirit and in truth . . . and in cabins.

Laura came to his side.

"Can I go door-to-door with you to talk to each family? I'd like to learn the names of these folks and see inside their cabins, if they'll allow it. See what their needs are. I have a bit of cash money, and if I could find a settlement with a general store, I might be able to buy fabric for clothing, and maybe some supplies, some canned goods, so they'd have the food in their own cabins."

Caleb studied her. Oh, he had so many questions. But Jilly was building him a church. And Laura wanted to buy food and clothing with her own money. And how she had any money, he'd like to know.

"The usual way of things near a goldfield is that the price of supplies is sky high. The shopkeepers do their very best to charge the miners every ounce of gold dust they dig out," Caleb said. "I stocked up to the extent I was able. And if Rick and I deem it safe to leave you here, we'll go hunting to get food. Maybe we can go far enough afield to find supplies sold for a reasonable price. But I doubt Rick is willing to be gone overnight, and the fact of the matter is, I'm unwilling, too."

She watched him. Listened in that acute way she shared with her sisters. As if every word was to be understood and memorized.

"You three are sisters. I know that. You may not realize it, but you resemble each other."

Laura studied him. She looked past his shoulder to the cabins. Caleb glanced back. No one outside.

Then she looked over her shoulder. Jilly and Michelle were busy.

"It was Jilly, wasn't it? No discipline, that girl."

"I take that as a yes."

Laura shrugged one shoulder. Her blue eyes shone with

intelligence and a bit of guilt. But humor, too. As if she wasn't really all that worried about him finding out they were sisters.

"I trust you, Caleb."

A warm shiver went up Caleb's spine. No one had called him Caleb for months. He was always Parson or Parson Tillman, occasionally Parson Caleb. He realized that while the title parson was an honor and he appreciated it, it was always, in some ways, a barrier between him and others. They weren't true friends as long as he was their parson. Could he be friends with Laura?

"What's your last name?"

"I'm unwilling to tell you that because there is someone searching for us. Someone who means us harm."

Those busy eyes shifted to something else . . . something that made his shiver rush a bit faster and get a bit warmer.

"The way to be safe for all of us is to marry. That puts us beyond the reach of the one who would harm us."

"A parent? Your father?"

"Another question I'm unwilling to answer. I hope you can abide that." She focused her eyes on him and said, "I don't suppose you'd like to marry me?"

He staggered back and was only vaguely aware Laura caught him, steadied him. Honestly, kept him on his feet. Because, God save him, in that moment, there really wasn't much he'd like more than to marry her.

"Are you all right?" Laura's voice came through the buzzing in his ears. He inhaled so hard he started coughing.

She patted him on his back a little too hard. He considered that maybe his reaction to a completely inappropriate, shocking question insulted her, but "I'm sorry" was a bit beyond him right now.

"I-I'd only m-marry you if I thought you were the one woman ch-chosen for me by God."

She grimaced. "What if God brought me here, right to your side, over hundreds of miles, for just that purpose?" She didn't sound like she considered it absolutely out of the question.

And he didn't, either. Though neither did he think a woman who wasn't willing to reveal her last name should be proposing on a week's acquaintance.

Even God might be confused right now.

"I think we should check the cabins."

"Good idea." Laura hooked a hand around the crook of his elbow. "We need to get to know each other better while we search for God's will, isn't that right?"

"That is exactly right." Mentally he added that the true right thing for him might be to run for the hills.

"So where did you grow up, Caleb?"

That same warm feeling to hear his name. "I don't suppose any of this 'getting to know each other' includes *you*, since you won't even tell me your last name?"

He sounded snappish and caught himself. He didn't sound like a loving parson at all. He really didn't know how to treat a woman, he realized. Not as a Christian. There had been some unfortunate dealings with women in his former life, but since he'd been called to the ministry, he'd never tried to get beyond parson, not with women. He'd treated them as children of God. Confusing children of God.

"I'll tell you about myself some." Laura nodded. "That's only fair. I've had a wonderful life, and only in the last little while have things turned really bad for us. And now we're— we're—" She gave him a look like she really wasn't sure she should confide in him. "Well, the truth is, we're on the run. But for our own safety. We aren't running from the law."

"Is the man you're running from dangerous to the others here? Dangerous to these folks from Purgatory? Or the rest of my mission team?"

"No, I can't see how. Unless somehow he finds us here, and you try and save me from being dragged off to a life of misery and horror. That could be dangerous for you." She smiled.

The little minx was torturing him, and she knew it.

"Something I could be spared from if I was married." Her smile faded. "But then he'd just try and drag off Michelle and Jilly. We need to get them married, too."

"You've come to the wrong place for that. All the men here, assuming there *are* men here, are married."

"Except you."

"Yes, except me." He sighed. This conversation felt like a game—and he was losing.

"You could be wrong about that. There are women in only about half the cabins. Maybe single men live in the other ones."

"It's a good bet that anyone living up here is in dire straits. These are cabins that stand empty, that people choose when they've come to the end of the trail. That's why they need God. That's why they need a parson to bring them the story of Jesus. They're not here, or most likely not, because their men have yet to strike it rich. They're here because their men drink up every speck of gold dust they find. Or gamble it away. Or they were robbed or cheated out of what money they had. These folks have lost their way, and if a few single men *do* come up here to sleep, you can be sure there will be no decent men to choose among them. And surely you intend to marry at least a decent man? You wouldn't wed your sisters to drunks and gamblers, would you?"

Nodding, Laura thought all the way through everything, or at least that's what Caleb imagined was going through her head. Because she was quiet too long while she stared at him, or maybe better to say *through* him.

At last, she gave him a bracing pat on the shoulder, as if to keep his spirits up. "We may need to branch out to find husbands. But we'll build the church first. Now let's talk to these families."

Whatever decision she'd come to was probably perfectly reasonable to her. But he wasn't sure what had gone through her head, and he was afraid to ask more questions because serving the people of Purgatory was his prime objective. "Let's go."

She took his arm again. Not unlike how a woman takes the arm of a man to walk down the aisle.

That shiver was back.

"HE'S BACK, MA'AM."

Margaret knew some of the servants were disloyal to her. But many, and especially her longtime personal maid, Sarah, could be trusted.

"Just now?" Margaret felt herself tense.

He'd come. He always came to her when he'd been away. She'd become a master at headaches and other such things.

He'd stayed away long enough for them to all be well from their measles. But it was inevitable that he return. She was glad she hadn't prepared yet for bed, so she wouldn't have to dress. She wasn't going to see him in her nightclothes. The days were growing longer, and she'd been lingering in her room.

"Yes. He's asking for you, ma'am. Summoned you to his study."

Margaret controlled a snort. Her new husband had claimed it as his. But to Margaret all she owned still belonged to her precious Liam. And if not him, then to her daughters. But Edgar liked to lay claim to all he could.

"I'll be right down. No need to tell him. I'll present myself." She dreaded this moment. She'd felt the back of Edgar's hand too often in her marriage. He'd struck her hard enough to knock her to the floor. But mostly it was just a single blow. He'd even taken to striking her in the stomach so bruises didn't show.

That was going to stop tonight. She'd see to it.

Edgar didn't understand how things were in this house, especially as it concerned Liam's will. It was high time he learned.

It would come as an ugly surprise.

Swinging the door open to Liam's study and the usurper behind Liam's desk, Margaret entered.

He glanced up at her. "You're well. High time."

He held amber liquor in a short crystal glass. He took a long sip. "I'll send a wire to San Francisco. The men who have gained my permission for my daughters' hands in marriage will soon be here."

Margaret approached the desk as he spoke. She wanted the desk between them so she would be out of arm's reach.

Edgar took another long drink.

"The girls are gone."

He spit liquor all across the desk. Margaret had stayed back far enough.

"Gone?" He slammed his glass on the desk and lunged to his feet. "What does that mean? Gone where?"

Margaret needed Edgar to understand a few things, and understand them fast.

"I didn't inherit Liam's company, did you know that?"

Edgar took one long stride to round the desk, but that brought him to a sudden halt. "Of course you inherited the business. Everyone knows that a wife comes into her husband's property upon his death, and when she remarries, that property becomes the property of her new husband."

"That's true, unless the will is very carefully structured. I have the use of the income from the company, but I don't have any ownership. The girls do. If anything should happen to me, then the income goes directly to the girls, and you'd be cut out completely." Margaret didn't want to tell him too much. Just enough he'd know he didn't dare kill her. "They've run off, and they will soon return to claim ownership and throw you out. The company is not mine nor is it yours. It belongs to my daughters."

Edgar's face turned red. He resumed rounding the desk, and Margaret, having thought this through, rounded away from him. When she reached the fireplace with its cozy flame, she backed up to the rack that held her fireplace tools. Careful not to move suddenly, she slid one hand behind her and took a firm hold of an iron poker. Making sure it wouldn't hang up on the rack, she braced herself. She was counting on the element of surprise because she'd never fought back.

And why not, she wondered? Why had it taken her so long to realize she didn't just have to stand still and take Edgar's abuse? Then she remembered his threats against her girls and knew exactly why she'd never fought back.

He stormed across the room until he stood face-to-face with her.

A handsome man when his face wasn't burning red with temper.

"Tell me where they went."

"I don't know, but if I did, I'd never tell you. I lied about the measles to give them time to put a lot of distance between you and them. They've been running far and fast for weeks. And my girls are smart. They won't leave a trail. But they won't run forever. They'll be back soon." Her voice rose with every word until she was shouting. "They'll come with the law to throw you out of this house. And out of our lives. How could you have chosen such vile men for my daughters? How could you . . ."

She kept yelling as she watched his hand draw back. She wanted his attention on her. Besides she'd wanted to say some very harsh things to Edgar for a long time. Picking her moment, right before he brought his hand forward, she swung the poker with all her strength and slammed it into the side of his knee.

He cried out and bent down to clutch his leg. She brought the poker around again and hit him on the side of the head. He toppled to the floor, roaring in pain.

He was noisy enough that he couldn't be too badly hurt. She hadn't hit him hard enough to kill him.

She didn't think.

She had no plans to turn murderess.

As he lurched to his feet, she drew the poker back to swing. He took a single step, and his knee gave out. He collapsed again. He had a vivid red line across his cheek where the poker had struck. Blood trickled down the side of his face.

Leaning over him, but staying well back, Margaret said, "My girls are gone. And if you try to kill me as some sort of revenge, then you'll be done with everything to do with Stiles Lumber. When they return, you'll have to slink back into whatever gutter you crawled out of."

She stormed out of the room and took the poker with her.

ELEVEN

Y OU TOLD HIM?" Jilly sat up so fast that Laura was
relieved they didn't sleep under the wagon. Jilly
would have bashed her brains in.

"Shhhh!" Laura put her finger to her lips, but the night
was quiet, so if anyone was still awake, they could hear.

Jilly clapped her mouth shut. She was way too slow
doing that. Jilly, more than any of them, was very blunt and
straightforward. Maybe she'd get better at being a sneaky
liar over time.

Michelle grabbed Laura's arm.

From the way Jilly squeaked, Laura guessed her arm was
in the same vise. Since Laura slept in the middle, that meant
Michelle had a long reach.

"Hush." Michelle's voice was quiet enough not even a
church mouse would have paused to listen.

"We'll talk in the morning." Laura spoke as quietly as she
could. The vise tightened for a count of three, then Michelle
released them both . . . or Laura assumed she let Jilly go, too.

"Sleep." Michelle lay back down.

It had been one of the hardest working days of her life, Laura thought as she lay down between her sisters, which was a habit now. Soon after Mama had married Edgar and he'd banished them to the mansion in the mountains, they'd moved into the same room and slept together. It had been Jilly's idea, but they'd all agreed and done it quickly, making no mention of it, as if they'd always shared a room and a bed. In a mansion.

But none of them ever wanted Edgar to catch them alone.

Laura felt the beginnings of the mental turmoil that sometimes brought on a sleepless night.

On her right, Michelle rested one hand on her wrist. Jilly, who preferred to sleep on her side, on Laura's left, rested one hand on her shoulder. They knew each other so well. Her sisters felt her tension and knew what followed. And knew that a reminder she wasn't alone helped.

The hard travel.

The distress of seeing the crying need of these people from Purgatory.

The hard work of beginning a church.

All of it overrode the turmoil. She blinked her eyes in the dark and opened them to the light. An entire night passed without her being aware.

Michelle was gone. Laura looked and saw her working with Gretel on breakfast. Jilly sat up beside her, smiling as she stretched, then the smile vanished, and she leaned close to Laura's ear. "I can't believe you told him."

Laura looked Jilly in the eye. She might be the youngest, but she was clever, she had a lot of highly regarded skills, and she demanded respect.

The only one who could know Laura for long and not respect her was a fool.

That thought gave her pause. Her sisters had known her all her life, and yet they had no idea of all that went on inside her. All the doubts about the future that had been laid out for her. No one really knew her at all. It struck her as the loneliest feeling in the world.

She gave Jilly the coldest, haughtiest expression she could muster. And it was a good one. "I had reason, and once I explain my reasons to you, you'll agree I did the right thing. Now, you get to work on that church. I have another idea. I'm going to find out who owns those cows, buy a few, and herd them up here. That will be a steady source of milk for these people."

Jilly straightened away from her, then stood. "That's a good idea. I'll get to work on the church and fix these cabins, then we have to find husbands and get back to Mama."

"I'll tell Parson Caleb my intentions and see if he or Rick wants to ride with me. I probably shouldn't go off alone."

"See if the man's got chickens to spare. Eggs would come in handy, too."

"Good thought." Laura was up, and since she slept in her increasingly dowdy servants dress and apron—she didn't have a nightgown—she was dressed and ready for the day. She did comb her hair and find the spring to brush her teeth, but that was the work of minutes. Then she set off to find Caleb.

NORA AND GRETEL had stew ready for breakfast. As long as there were no eggs nor a ready source of milk, meals would be very simple. There was sourdough and plenty of flour, which would keep them in biscuits. They could survive on that, but to thrive they had to do a lot better.

Laura explained her plan to Caleb.

He turned to stare through the trees down at the pasture full of cattle. "You really have enough money to buy a cow?"

Laura had enough money to buy the whole stinking herd. Although, she didn't really know what a cow cost. Her true intention was to buy two or three cows. She thought the settlement here needed that much milk. Of course, she didn't really know how much milk a single cow gave, either.

They'd need a corral before they got the church built, but Jilly was aware of that and could build a sturdy corral in no time.

"Yes. Let's go," Laura said.

An ax thudded into a tree. Jilly, chopping down trees uphill on the east side of the Purgatory settlement where the church would stand. Another ax thudded. Rick helping her. Michelle could swing an ax, too. And Laura would get to work as soon as she was back with the cow.

They knew all about the lumber business, and that included how to chop down a tree and let the ax do the bulk of the work.

Laura headed for the horses and was dragging a saddle onto the closest one when Caleb lifted it up for her.

She smiled. "Thank you." Then stared as he continued to tighten the cinch, before shifting around to bridle the pretty brown mustang.

Shaking off the strange fascination with Caleb doing the chore for her, she turned to the next saddle and swung it onto the pinto Michelle had bought.

"Hey," Jilly called from the edge of the forest. "You're leaving me at least one horse, aren't you?"

"Yes. We'll leave the black one." The black gelding was Caleb's, and it had pulled the wagon.

"Good, I need horsepower." Jilly headed on into the woods.

"Horsepower?" Caleb asked as he finished bridling the chestnut and took over tightening the cinch on Laura's horse.

She let him work and got busy with the bridle.

"Laura, you should let me handle this." Caleb drew her attention from thoughts of Jilly and corrals and milk cows.

"Handle what?" Laura gave him a look, trying to think what he could mean.

"Men's work. You should let me handle the saddle and bridle." His hazel eyes were solemn, sincere. She studied him over the back of her horse and wondered how to tell him men's work, women's work, not much of it mattered to a woman whose whole life was all laid out for her, and it included blasting holes in mountains.

"Um . . ." She knew she'd been raised strangely. She'd been raised to take the reins of a huge business. Her father had schooled her in leadership—leadership in business dealings with strong, independent men. Beyond her intensive studies in physics, science, and mathematics, she'd also learned logging, railroads, banking, and chemical engineering, which was a field opening wide in this industrial age. And she'd definitely been raised to saddle her own horse.

She was a little uncertain, a feeling she rarely had. Should she feign helplessness to better fit into the world away from her father's enterprises? Was that part of wearing a disguise? Then once she was back home, set all this helplessness aside and take charge again?

Caleb seemed to think there was men's work and women's work and being a helpless woman should come naturally to her, but it had been educated out of her.

She'd noticed Rick looking at Michelle strangely when she slung an ax over her shoulder and headed up the slope into the forest to join him and Jilly.

If they did pretend a more feminine helplessness, then this whole business of building a church and setting these folks up to survive was going to take a lot longer, and they didn't have time. They needed to get back to Mama.

"Laura, come on back now." Caleb was watching her, grinning.

"What's so funny?"

His grin widened to a smile. "I can see wheels spinning in your head as you consider a long list of possible ways to react to me. The horses are saddled, and I'll admit I'm about half-mad with curiosity to see how you go about talking that rancher, assuming we can find him, out of his cows."

"You can see the wheels turning?"

He didn't respond to that. Instead, he put his hands around her waist and lifted her up. This was no way to get on a horse. But she caught the saddle horn, got her foot in the stirrup and swung her leg over.

Caleb mounted up. "You can think while we ride."

The small level stretch where they'd found Purgatory was tucked in the middle of a rugged mountain. It loomed high above the ledge, thick with oak and pines of every color and height. Laura and her sisters had identified almost all the trees while they rode through the woods to get here. Their greatest knowledge, after all, was trees. Beyond the usual redwoods, pine, and oak, there were mahogany trees, mountain laurel, and some beautiful little flowering dogwood trees. And so many more that Laura didn't try to list them.

Then there was this level, treeless spot, rugged with rocks and little grass. Land that was useless for much of anything— which was why no trees grew here and wretched little cabins did. After the ledge with the cabins, the mission camp, and the soon-to-be church, the mountain turned downward and was again forest. Laura had looked around a bit last night while she was planning how to get a cow for the settlement. Now she walked her horse along the ledge, past the cabins, to a trail she'd found. She turned and entered the forest, and the trail sloped sharply down, but not so badly their horses couldn't handle it.

It was a beautiful ride with the scents of the forest and the dappled sunlight. The horses were calm and did most of the thinking, so Laura could consider whether being ladylike was more trouble than it was worth. What would help her reach her goal of finding a husband?

She was most of the way down the trail when she started to see through the thinning woods to the large pasture with the calmly grazing cattle. Herefords, she knew. Red cows with white faces. They were beautiful against the green grass. She gave up thinking of how to snare a husband and pondered how to find the owner of the cattle. Trails. Find a trail, follow it. And there was a big herd in this meadow. They'd have left a trail.

It'd be nice if they didn't have to go far.

IF CALEB HAD KNOWN they'd be riding for so long, he'd've packed a lunch.

"So you were born in West Virginia?" Laura wasn't so much talking with him as interviewing him. Or maybe she was questioning a witness in the courtroom.

"Enough about me, you're repeating yourself, and I think you are smart enough to remember every word I've said." Spring calves gamboled around their mothers. Some gathered into groups and almost seemed to be playing games.

When Laura and Caleb rode through, the babies abandoned their games and rushed to their mothers' sides. A big old bull watched them but didn't approach, for which Caleb was grateful.

Glancing at him with a sheepish grin, she said, "Sorry, I *am* covering the same ground. I'm very reluctant to tell you about myself. I trust you, Caleb. I do. But what if I tell you my name, and you say it to someone while you're introducing me, something like that. It's an easy slip, and it could bring danger to my sisters and me."

Solemnly, Caleb said, "I understand your fears. I'm very good at keeping the confidences of people who come to me and share sins that burden them." Not to mention secrets of his own that he kept with great skill.

"Like confession?"

"Well, our group has no membership in any church. We aren't Catholic nor Baptist nor Presbyterian, Lutheran, or Methodist, though I was raised Lutheran. I don't embrace confession as Catholics understand it. But I do believe it's a sacred duty to keep confidences people share with me." He looked at her steadily as they rode. They'd crossed the wide pasture full of grazing cows, who hardly bothered to stop grazing and look up at them as they passed before going back to eating as soon as they went on.

Then Laura found a wide trail that even Caleb could see, and he possessed no skill at following trails.

"My sisters and I are on the run from our stepfather. We intended to bring our mother with us, but she fell the night we were running away, hurt her ankle too badly to continue on, and had to go back."

Caleb heard the fear in Laura's voice, the dread. He had plenty of questions already, but he left her to tell her story first.

By the time he'd heard the provisions of the will, he understood why she'd proposed to him last night.

A twist of fear had him wondering just how particular the sisters would be about picking men. They were intelligent women, but he had to wonder if they had much common sense.

They certainly had no regular . . . what he would call female skills.

"You really rode down a flume? I've seen one. I saw logs tearing down the side of a mountain on it."

"The flume was the fastest way off the mountain, and we needed to get far away as fast as we could."

"And the men he had arranged for you to marry?"

"You have to understand. Edgar didn't just charm Mama, he charmed us all. He was . . . well, the easiest way to say it is . . . he was everything any of us could dream a man to be. He was a skilled liar and a very talented trickster. Mama fell madly in love with him and, to an extent, all three of us did, too."

That stopped Caleb's brain from working. A "talented trickster" described him in his old life very well.

"And then he got into the family, and he changed. He changed back into himself."

They'd found another open stretch between two mountains, and Caleb could look to his left and see the mountains rising and rising, so these must be foothills. In the open stretch were dozens, maybe hundreds of Herefords. Too many to think of counting.

"I would have hated it if he'd come in to steal all the money and cheat all of us, as many swindlers do. But he was cruel on top of it. Cruel to Mama especially. I've never known him to strike her, but a few things she said when she fell and urged us to leave her made us all sure he does.

"After the wedding last spring, he moved us from San Francisco, where we spent winters, up to our mountain house, and we've never left it. We were as good as prisoners there. And by the time we got there, we knew we'd never want to be caught alone with Edgar. He's cruel with words and capable of violence, and after how wonderful and wise and kind Papa was, we clung together to protect each other."

"And you inherit a third of the lumber business when you marry?"

"Yes, that's right. We inherit outright, without marriages, when we turn twenty-five, but that is too long." Laura shuddered. "Edgar has arranged marriages for us but without knowledge of the will. Mama has control of it until we marry, and since she remarried, Edgar has taken control of it. With one wedding, he'd be down to two-thirds control, then a second wedding would give him one-third control, and so on, until we three owned it all. If Mama dies, then we all inherit immediately. I don't think Edgar knows the details. He just thinks it's all his. Mama said she's going to make sure he knows killing her—" Laura's voice broke.

They were on a trail just wide enough for them both.

Caleb reached across and rested one hand on hers, where she gripped the saddle horn. The trail wound through a rugged stretch around the side of the mountain. Then through land so heavily wooded they couldn't ride side by side. Still, Caleb could see that the cattle had come this way.

"We'll think of something, and we'll do it fast, Laura. You need help, and your mother definitely needs help and soon."

"So you'll marry me?"

Before Caleb could gather enough thoughts to respond, Laura pointed to a smudge of gray rising from behind another roll of land.

"That's from a chimney. I think we've found the man who owns all these cattle." She kicked her horse into a gallop, and as she dashed ahead, Caleb recognized a truly skilled rider.

As he hurried after her, he thought of the way she'd saddled the horse, the way she'd found the trail down that mountainside. Now the way she rode, her back straight, but leaned forward until her body ran parallel to the horse's neck. And so smooth and graceful. It was as if she and the horse were a single creature.

But marry her?

God, I want to say yes so badly it must be a sin. I'm being lured in by how pretty she is and how likeable and how badly she needs help.

These are not true reasons to marry a woman.

He was a praying man. A man of strong, deep faith.

When he prayed, he listened. Not necessarily for a voice from a burning bush. Not a thunderous answer from his Creator. Not even a still small voice. God could speak in that way, but for him, God communicated in ideas. The ideas that came as he prayed he paid close attention to, because he realized God spoke to him in just that way.

Now his ideas were all about Laura. All about helping her. Was he inspired to help a damsel in distress?

Had he drowned out the ideas sent from God because he had his own ideas?

He didn't know. For now, he prayed and chased after the most beautiful woman he'd ever seen. Possibly the nicest and smartest, too. And, it seemed to him, a woman of strong faith.

The only ideas he got were catching her and keeping her. Rescuing her and her mama. And never letting her know that there was a time she'd've distrusted him completely. A time she'd have thought he was the same kind of man as her hated Edgar.

Caleb was sorely afraid that God was going to have to speak to him out of a burning bush to stop him from ending up a married man.

A very happily married man.

He'd pray and listen, but God had better give him some clear direction, and He'd better do it fast if Caleb was heading down the wrong path.

TWELVE

RIDERS COMING IN FAST, ZANE."

Zane Hart stood from his desk, leaving his meticulous account books open.

Shad Donovan didn't close the door, didn't even come in. "Two riders coming from the north, riding hard."

Zane strode past him. They didn't get that many strangers out here. And usually, with the madness still lingering from the goldfields and now new madness from the fast-growing city of Sacramento, most strangers were trouble.

Nick, a new wrangler with oddly colored eyes, swung the front door open as Zane kept moving. "One of 'em's a woman, Boss."

Zane rushed forward and almost staggered back at the same time. It amounted to him stumbling for a few steps before he got control of his feet. A woman?

Curiosity drove him forward. The two riders were a far piece yet. But the rider in front on the little pinto was definitely a woman. She wore a bonnet that blew back off her head, but it was tied with strings so she didn't lose it. Her hair broke free of whatever had bound it, and he saw a yard of golden blond.

He stumbled again and grabbed a post on his front porch to keep himself upright.

He could honestly say he hadn't seen a woman since the last cattle drive about six months ago. And then he avoided them unless they were serving him food. He'd lived in an all-male world the last few years after one sister had married, a second went to school in San Francisco, and his ma had died. He'd had a big family at one time, but one by one, they'd left. His brother, Josh, had gone to sea, and Zane had been running the place alone since Pa had died a couple of years back.

There wasn't a woman on the place, and Zane liked it that way. Or at least, he hadn't considered changing anything.

Driving the scattered thoughts to the back of his mind, he forced himself to look at the second rider. And he had to admit, he only managed it because he wondered if it might be two women. But nope.

The rider behind . . . Zane's head tilted as he saw . . . a parson's collar?

He didn't see many of those out here, either.

"Reckon we're in for a strange visit, Zane." Shad had been with Two Harts Ranch since Zane was too young to sit a horse. Shad and his pa had been a good team. Several of the twenty or so men who worked for him had been hired by Pa. They worked for Zane, but they were old friends, too.

Zane had no hankering for gold, probably because he had plenty of cash on the hoof. So instead, he followed his prosperous father's inclinations and raised cows. And with all the people roaring west to live, prices were sky-high, and cattle herds driven into Sacramento or San Francisco made him a fine profit.

He used the money to buy more land and keep expanding his herd because owning land was the goal, the aim of his life. His deepest pleasure.

He watched the woman ride up and *what a rider*. He had longtime cowhands that didn't sit a horse better.

Here was a pleasure he didn't have much practice with. He enjoyed the moment and sure enough hoped he wasn't looking straight at trouble.

CALEB SAW THE RANCH YARD AHEAD and was so stunned he pulled the reins back on his horse.

Shocked honestly.

This place was beautiful. Money and skill had been lavished on it. And it had a settled look, like it had always been there, had grown out of the mountain that rose up behind the ranch house, the corrals, the barn, the bunkhouse, so many buildings.

The shock was from comparing it to the place he'd just come from.

Then he realized Laura hadn't slowed, and she was riding right into a crowd of who-knew-what-kind-of-men. Alone.

He kicked his brown mustang—he only knew it was a mustang because someone had called it that. It looked like every other horse to him. Bending low, he got the most speed out of his horse he could.

Laura reached the crowd of men, who started walking toward her, including three coming down off the porch steps of the massive ranch house made of lumber and stone with a white wooden porch lining the front of it.

Caleb had always heard that men in the West were decent to women, even if the men themselves weren't decent. A woman was a rare and fine thing, and it was a rare man who'd abuse one of them. In fact, it was said outright villains in the act of committing a crime would draw the line at harming a woman and would even switch sides to protect her if anyone in his band of outlaws looked set on harming her.

Caleb sure hoped it was true because Laura was surrounded, and he wasn't getting there fast enough.

The tallest man, who'd descended from the porch first, came to Laura's side, and she swung off her horse. Even from this distance, Caleb could see the white of her smile. And the blind pleasure every man around her took from watching her.

Then Caleb was there. He brought his poor, winded mustang to a halt, got to the ground, and rushed to Laura's side.

Laura turned and beamed that smile at him. "This is Parson Tillman. Caleb, this is Zane Hart. He says to call him Zane. We came hunting you, Zane, searching for whoever owns the Herefords near where we're living." She told him briefly where they had camped. "We followed the trail left by the cattle. We want to buy some cows."

The dazed look on good old Zane's face melted away like wax in a bonfire.

"HOW MANY LOGS?" Rick paused beside Michelle.

She saw how tired he was. The man didn't know how to

chop down a tree. He was keeping up with her and Jilly but working far harder than either of them.

He also knew they didn't have near enough trees after only six hours of chopping. He took a long drink from his canteen, and she suspected he'd just stopped to ask as a way to take a break.

A gunshot turned them both to face the collection of shanties, shacks, lean-tos . . . Michelle didn't know exactly what to call those wretched houses. *Cabins* was probably best, but it wasn't a fair description. It was far too fancy a name.

A man came staggering out of the woods, gun pointed to the sky. He laughed as if the joy couldn't be contained.

"I struck it rich. Emma Kate, get out here. We're movin' to better digs."

Emma Kate, the pregnant woman, with a child on her hip emerged smiling. "Let me pack up, and we'll go, Charlie."

They were on foot, so Michelle wasn't exactly sure where they intended to go. She knew the men left well before dawn on Monday morning, hiked a long way to a point where a wagon picked up dozens of men to take them to the mines, and returned Saturday night.

Others came out of their cabins, including a few children who clung to their mothers, acting more frightened than they had last night.

"Leave it all, little mama. We're buyin' new. You're gonna dress in silk after today. C'mon."

Emma Kate ducked inside but was back fast with an armful of something.

"I told you to leave everything." He charged straight for her and slapped the bundle out of her arms, knocking her sideways as the slap hit her arm.

114

"We'll need diapers, Charlie."

He reeled around, drunk as a sow. "Bring 'em then, but let's skeeee-daddle."

Emma Kate giggled, grabbed up what she'd dropped, and rushed after the man who'd just slapped her. She and her husband walked out of sight in the direction he'd come from.

Michelle said quietly to Rick, "I suppose no one stays here if they can afford anything else."

One of the women, Michelle thought her name was Janine, looked at her and said furiously, "This is only for now. My man'll make a good strike, and we'll get on. These cabins turn over alla time. We've only come because we fell on hard times, and everyone knows there are abandoned cabins up here. My man'll get a bit of gold dust, and we'll be gone."

She whirled and went into her cabin. The other women scowled at Michelle, then herded their children inside like they needed to be protected from her.

"Um, I hope I haven't made things harder for Parson Caleb."

Rick shook his head. In his heavy accent, he said, "You said one quiet vord. If that turns folks away from the path of righteousness, then they vere likely traveling hard down the wrong road. Real hard to turn them aside to a new path."

He pulled a handkerchief from his pocket and mopped the back of his neck. "Now how many logs did you say you need?"

Michelle took pity on the poor man. A hardworking, decent man who loved his wife and child. "Let me show you how to chop in a way that lets the ax do the work."

"Timber!" Jilly yelled, and a tree came down a distance into the woods.

"Let's go," Michelle said. "It's a good time to get in there before she chops down another one."

THIRTEEN

I KNOW RIGHT WHERE YOU'RE STAYING. Those cabins are on my land. Shad, you take Nick and Bo and drive those squatters out of there. This time burn down those cabins."

"You men stay right where you are." Laura rapped out the order as fiercely as Zane. The three stopped dead in their tracks.

Well, four counting Zane.

Laura fought to keep the smile off her face.

Zane's eyes narrowed, his arms crossed. "No one gives orders on my land to my men but me."

"You don't want that land." Laura tried to be calm in the face of Zane's grouchy expression. "It doesn't grow grass enough for cattle. It's on a mountainside. It's obvious you're not using it."

"But they settle on that mountain, then they start creeping downhill. We've had people building cabins on my grassland before I put a stop to it."

"Mr. Hart, those people have nothing. There are women

and children in those cabins. The only roof they have over their heads are those hovels. And the land they're on is wasteland. We'll be hard-pressed to find grazing for a couple of cows. No one is on your grassland."

Zane glowered at her. He was a lot taller than her, and he practically loomed over her.

Speaking more gently, hoping the man could be affected by reason, Laura said, "Please don't do anything to harm those people."

He seemed intelligent, but how greedy to have so much and deny the poorest folks she'd ever seen in those ramshackle buildings.

"I came to buy cows from you."

"Not possible."

"Of course, it's possible. Selling cows is what you do for a living."

"I don't sell them to people who are squatting on my land."

"I'd like you to do just that. And we'd like tame cows. We plan to milk them to provide food to the terribly thin children who live up there." She leaned close, held his gaze. "Skeletally thin. It's horrible to see."

Caleb came up behind her, put both of his hands on her shoulders, and shifted her aside. She looked over her shoulder to glare at him, and he smiled.

Bristling, she stepped out from between Zane and Caleb. She knew what it felt like to be treated like a rather dim woman, who couldn't be allowed to take charge of anything.

Most of her growing up years, she hadn't known what that was like because her father had never treated her and her sisters like that, and beyond him and tutors, they hadn't known many men, at least not outside their father's circle of friends, and they'd always been respectful.

But Edgar had taught her well.

Caleb seemed ready to pat her on the head and tell her to run along and let the big, strong men talk.

It didn't suit her, but maybe Caleb could do something with this stubborn, greedy oaf. He shifted so he stood right in front of her.

"Mr. Hart—"

"Call me Zane." The snap in his voice made Laura wonder how many men he'd employed over the years. He certainly seemed experienced with giving orders.

"Zane, I'm Caleb Tillman. The land these folks are on is useless to you. And it's not a big group of people. Several cabins are empty, so it's not like the settlement is overflowing and spreading. I'm a parson"—Caleb touched his collar in a gesture Laura suspected wasn't planned—"I felt called to minister to those people. They are in dire straits. Hungry beyond what you can believe. They are—"

"The people up there," Zane cut him off, "are the ones whose husbands buy whiskey with every drop of gold they dig out of the ground. Or gamble it away as fast as they make it. Even the unlucky miners scratch out enough color to live decent lives and put food on the table. There are married men in Sacramento and a bunch of little towns from Dorada Rio and all the way to San Francisco. They live humbly but are by no means starving. And they have no better luck than those men up there."

"Whatever their menfolk are doing doesn't change the conditions the women and children are living in." Caleb took a step closer to Zane. "It is simple decency to let me feed them and simple Christianity for you to aid me in feeding them. 'For I was hungered and you gave me meat.'"

"Don't start quoting Scripture to me."

"You recognized it. I take that as a hopeful sign. 'Inasmuch as ye have done it unto one of the least of these, my brethren, ye have done it unto me.'"

Zane scowled but didn't complain about the Bible quoting.

"This is your chance to be the hands and feet of Jesus here on earth. Let us buy, at a fair market price, two cows. Milk cows if at all possible because I know the usual cattle are wild and will be almost impossible to milk. I'm setting up a mission field there. Let me serve these people. *Help* me serve these people. They are desperate."

Caleb stopped.

Zane glared.

Laura prayed. And she might not be the only one.

Finally, Zane turned to a young man with unusual eyes, standing on the porch behind him. "Nick, go round up two of the milk cows. Shad, saddle three horses."

"Oh, thank you, Zane." Laura clasped his right wrist with two hands.

He gave her a startled look, and she snatched her hands back.

"You don't have to come. We appreciate it, but Caleb, that is, Parson Tillman and I can take the cows."

"I'm not coming to be helpful. I want to see what that settlement looks like by now. I haven't been over there in months. I'm coming, and my men will help me get the cows to Purgatory."

He turned to the men gathered round, men who, in Laura's

estimation, mainly wanted to stand close to her. "The rest of you quit gawking and get back to work."

To a man they all grinned, then doffed their hats and walked away.

"Thank you, Mr. Hart." Laura didn't approach him. She didn't want Caleb to tuck her behind him again. She wasn't sure why, but she knew it wasn't a good idea to upset Caleb right now.

"How much do we owe you?" she asked.

"I'm making a donation to the poor. If I take money for it, God'll give you credit and not me."

Laura giggled.

Caleb turned to her and arched a brow.

"Wait here. I'll help saddle the horses and be back with two cows." Zane turned and strode toward the barn.

He shouted at one man still lingering too close. "Pack up some potatoes from the cellar, plenty of them. And see what we've got for flour and yeast."

Then he was gone into the huge log barn.

Caleb turned to look fully at Laura, his eyes alight with pleasure.

"He's really going to help us." Laura rested her hands on Caleb's shoulders this time. "You said just the right thing. The true thing. You inspire me, Caleb."

He stood there, her hands on him for too long. At last he said, "I suppose he's the kind of man you should marry. Tough, rich, strong enough to protect you."

Laura gasped, then felt a smile spread wide on her face. "That's a terrific idea."

Caleb stepped back, frowning, sad, maybe hurt.

"No, I don't mean for me. I'm still planning to marry you

as soon as you figure God's in favor of it. But Zane would be perfect for one of my sisters."

"Let's get moving." Zane came out of the barn astride a shining buckskin stallion. He had bulging saddlebags, and behind him, Shad had something hanging from his saddle horn. But Laura quit looking at that when she saw the younger cowhand, Nick, lead out two very calm-looking Hereford cows by the rope around their short, curved horns.

Laura and Caleb mounted up.

The third man he'd given orders to came from behind the cabin with a gunnysack loaded with what was most likely potatoes and a bulging cloth bag, possibly an old flour sack that probably contained flour and yeast.

The man hoisted the gunnysack up to Zane, who settled it in front of him. As he handed up the flour sack, Caleb rode over. "Let me carry that."

The man looked at Zane. When his boss nodded, he handed the smaller sack to Caleb.

"Thank you." Caleb said to the man, then turned and repeated it to Zane. "Thank you most sincerely, Zane. You've got a friend in that settlement. I've little to offer, but if you need a parson's care, come for me."

Zane grunted and said, "Let's ride."

JILLY DRAGGED THE CHURCH'S FOUNDATION LOG into place using a chain hitched to the horse.

She'd notched both ends and, after some serious consideration, left the logs rounded on all sides. She'd seen it done this way, and she'd seen them built with the logs squared off.

Squared-off logs definitely created a much tighter wall and a much warmer building that was easier to heat. But it took a lot of time. And the church wasn't going to have people living in it.

It needed to be bearable for services on Sunday mornings and maybe a few other meeting times a week. Add to that, the weather was more temperate here, if she'd judged the altitude and the latitude and longitude correctly—and she had.

Anyway, she'd made multiple calculations and decided to save the hard labor of squaring off the logs. She might do it for the cabins when she got to them.

She'd decided against a fireplace and windows, too.

The trees were sixty feet tall or more, so she was cutting them in not quite thirds, figuring a thirty by twenty-foot building, allowing for the thickness of the logs, of course. She'd gotten one log done—stripped of its branches, cut in thirds, and notched at the ends—to start the walls. But it was a big job. She'd use the bottom section of the tree on the longer side walls, and the middle section on the narrower front and back walls, the top section, she'd use for the roof.

She, Michelle, and Rick had been chopping all day. They each brought down about one tree an hour. She thought she needed about twenty trees. The three of them, working eight hours today, had twenty-four trees down. Enough. Any extra would be used on the houses, but they'd done enough chopping for one day.

She'd consulted with Rick, and he decided to chop a few more down, thinking to the cabins they needed to build. The man was all in, and he'd hurt like the dickens tomorrow, but Jilly admired his dedication.

Michelle dragged a downed tree in from the woods, un-hooked it for Jilly to work on, then led the horse back for the next log. When Jilly set down her ax, she talked the Hogan sisters through notching logs.

"Chopping a tree is heavy work." Nora clutched the front of her dress.

Not much stopped Nora and Harriet, so Jilly patted her on the arm. "I'm not saying it's not hard labor, but there are ways to let the ax do most of the work. Here, let me show you."

Soon Michelle was dragging logs, Jilly was stripping limbs, and Nora and Harriet were taking turns using the one remaining ax to notch.

Mama had told Jilly many times she was a natural teacher.

Michelle came with the next log. The first two on opposite walls were sunk half a log's width into the ground.

"Keep up, Michelle. I'm standing idle while you bring in logs."

Michelle looked up and grinned. "I'll bring you two more, then we're breaking for supper. I've got to stop Rick from chopping while he still has a muscle left unstrained."

Jilly nodded. "We've done good work here today."

"We'll be ready to start the walls by the end of the day tomorrow. The roof will take longer."

"I'm keeping it simple. No windows. One door. Details like that take time. Three solid walls, the fourth wall will have the door in it. Yes, I think we can start on the walls to-morrow. And the roof won't take much longer." Jilly looked at her hands. She'd worn gloves, but her hands were very tender.

"Then the church will be done, and we can start on the cabins."

Jilly looked up. "It's all well and good to build cabins, Michelle, but what about Mama? I can't stand out here, safe and working, even for a good thing, while I imagine her being abused by Edgar. I just can't."

Her voice rose until it was far too close to a wail.

The Hogan sisters turned to look at her, their notching temporarily abandoned.

Jilly clamped her mouth shut and got control of herself. She whispered, "We'll never find husbands in a settlement of women, children, and married men." Her stomach twisted at the thought. After being raised by Papa, then exposed to the cruelty of Edgar, she feared the idea of dragging any man she found to the altar. It had occurred to her that if Laura and Michelle married, they'd have two-thirds of Stiles Lumber. That was controlling interest.

"I know that," Michelle said. "But where are we going to find single men?"

The sound of clomping hooves turned them toward the woods in the direction Laura had gone this morning with Parson Caleb.

A man on a tall, regal buckskin stallion burst out of the woods. He had a large bundle balanced in front of him on his saddle. Next came an older man leading a Hereford cow. Then Laura. Tension flowed out of Jilly that she hadn't known she was feeling.

Parson Tillman was right behind her, then a third man, leading a second cow. This man was young and a little messy. A scruff of beard, hair badly in need of a trim dangling below his Stetson. He wore black trousers and a blue broadcloth shirt. He had eyes that from this distance struck her as weird, but she couldn't say why.

Jilly was surprised to notice how good looking the young man was. She chalked that strange reaction up to her being very tired.

FOURTEEN

AURA SAW HER SISTERS STANDING by the foundation of the church. The Hogan sisters were notching logs. Gretel was working over the fire, and Laura saw her baby lying on a blanket near her.

There was chopping in the woods, and a good-sized scattering of logs visible in the forest. Plenty of work ahead for everyone.

Laura smelled the fresh cut wood as she rode straight for Michelle and Jilly. One of her favorite smells in the world. It reminded her of home.

Smiling at her two sweat-soaked big sisters, she said, "You've already started building?"

The chopping in the woods stopped. Rick emerged looking exhausted, but his eyes went to Laura, then to Caleb. He was visibly relieved to see the parson return.

"Yes, we've got enough logs for the church and some extra." Michelle raised her voice. "Rick, that's all for today."

Rick nodded, dropped his ax right there on the ground and walked, or more correctly trudged, toward Caleb. Shoulders slumped, head down. Each step looked like his feet weighed double what they should.

Laura pointed to the two cows. "Their udders are full of milk after a long hike."

Jilly's eyes lit up, green as pine. Michelle gave a satisfied, if weary, smile.

"You look tired." Laura looked from Michelle to Jilly. "I can't believe you've already started with construction. I'll be here to help tomorrow."

"What you did was important, too." Michelle patted Laura's shoulder.

The three of them were in a small circle a few feet away from everyone else, so Laura leaned close and whispered. "In case you're wondering, all three of the men who came back with me are single. You should pick two of them out and marry them. Probably the younger ones."

Michelle gasped and looked nervously at the men tying the cows to a tree.

Jilly visibly shuddered.

Laura wasn't sure just why, but Jilly had a problem with this whole plan. She'd gone along because honestly there'd been no choice. But getting her married was going to be a chore.

"One's too young and one's too old. Jilly can have the one in the middle years." Michelle leaned closer. "I know enough about the more, um, private side of marriage . . . from a book I once read . . . that makes me sure I can't be marrying some stranger. I know we have to do it to save Mama, but . . . but . . ." Her eyes stole to the three men.

Laura saw Shad pluck a pail off his saddle horn. She hadn't noticed it before. He went to the first cow, crouched beside her, and began milking.

Shad was on this side of the cow with his back to them. The sound of milk zipping into the bucket soon began.

Zane was on this side, too, but he rounded the back end of the cow and went to the first of the ramshackle cabins and pounded his fist on the door. He stepped back.

A woman came to the door, so thin she was more skeleton than woman.

"Come on over here."

Several other women peeked out, children behind them.

Jilly said, "They've all spent most of the day indoors. As if the fuss, the chopping and such, frightened them into their holes. We lured them out to eat a noon meal, but mostly they've stayed inside."

Zane's voice cut through Jilly's talk. "You all need to learn to milk a cow."

He waved his hand at the women. "Your mission parson bought these cows for the settlement. They're from my herd, and I picked gentle ones. Does anyone here know how to milk?"

Three of the women shyly raised their hands.

Caleb said, "There were five of you this morning. Where's Emma Kate?"

Janine, the angriest and boldest, said, "Charlie had a gold strike. He came in and took her and her baby away." The woman sighed as if that was a dream she carried with her.

The older girl came out behind her. Sally Jo, Laura remembered.

Caleb nodded. He said to Zane, "We can milk the cows. I'm here to serve these women. I don't demand labor of them."

The woman stopped approaching the cows and looked uncertainly between Caleb and Zane.

"Nope, that ain't right," Zane said. "You women want to have a hand in caring for yourselves, don't you?"

A couple of them nodded.

Zane turned to Caleb. "It's not right for you to stop them. It takes something from them if they just get food handed to them. Their pride, their sense of being able to fend for themselves. Let them help."

The closest woman nodded. Sally Jo, the one who'd watched them so carefully when they'd come yesterday, stepped out from behind her mother and walked around the cow to Shad's side.

"We had a cow in the place we lived before this. I know the way of milking one."

Shad glanced up at Sally Jo, then pulled the bucket out from under the cow as he stood. There were six inches of foamy milk.

"Let's give the young'uns a drink, maybe there's enough for all of you. But the cow ain't emptied out yet, so we'll empty this bucket, then you can finish with her and get to the other one."

The girl gave him a slight smile. She looked over the cow's back at the group of woman and children. "Run fetch your cups. We'll have us some fresh, warm milk."

One person from each cabin rushed in to get the tin cup each family owned. Only one per family, it seemed.

Then they were back, and there was enough milk for a taste all around, including the missionaries and even Zane and his men.

Zane produced a few tools, including his own ax. "I need to build a corral for the cows. Come and help me."

He gave a come-on wave toward the settlement crowd,

and the women and the oldest of the children walked along with him and his men. Soon there was renewed chopping.

Sally Jo took the empty bucket and hunkered down beside the cow and took right off milking her.

Shad watched for a time, then left to follow Zane.

Laura felt the rightness of it. It did give them pride. Or maybe not pride exactly. Pride was listed among the sins in the Bible. But confidence, an inner lift to the spirit to take a hand in caring for yourself.

Maybe there was a sinful kind of pride and an honorable kind of pride. Laura decided to ask Caleb about it later.

Sally Jo stood from beside the cow, patted her gently but firmly on the rump, then petted her neck and talked quietly to her for a few moments. She served more milk to the younger children, who'd stayed near the cabins, then she went to the second cow.

THE CORRAL WAS SHAPING UP, but there was still a lot to do. Gretel had served stew again. Zane's hired hands had thrown a few carrots and onions in with the potatoes, which made a much tastier stew.

The group ate in shifts, so everyone kept busy.

The sun was setting as everyone set to work finishing the corral.

Caleb came over to Laura and sat beside her on a log to eat.

"I messed up not asking for help." He wasn't sure Laura was the one to come to with his self-doubt. But who then? "A rancher knows how to help people better than I do."

Laura chewed on her meat and vegetables for a spell. When she'd swallowed, she said, "I think we need to just be glad Zane thought of it. I hadn't. I felt like we needed to give them everything we had. The food, the church building, the cows."

"I didn't really intend to build a church right away. I thought we'd worship outdoors while we tried to make their living situation better." He glanced at Laura again. "Is the church building wrong, too? It was kind of hard to stop your sisters once they got the bit in their teeth."

"About as hard as stopping Zane with the corral." Laura smiled at him. "We're in the clutches of some headstrong people, I'd say."

Zane and Nick came over from where the corral was going up. The two of them accepted a plate of food from Gretel and sat on the ground facing Caleb and Laura.

"Laura"—Caleb very gently nudged her with his shoulder— "I think you should tell Zane what's happened to you. They are honorable men. They might be able to help you."

They might be able to marry her. Caleb didn't want any-one marrying her. Not him either, at least not so fast. But for sure not anyone else.

"You got problems, Miss Laura?" Zane ate and watched.

Caleb felt as if Laura nearly vibrated beside him. But she didn't speak.

Quietly, but not so quietly Laura couldn't hear, Caleb said, "It's occurred to me that maybe somehow Zane could get a message to your mother."

Laura gasped and sat up straight.

Michelle must've heard it because she came over. "What's wrong?"

"Can you do that?" Laura sounded near to dropping to her knees to beg Zane to do just that.

"Um, we could get mail to town for you. Send a letter."

"No." Michelle cut him off with a violent sweep of her hand. "There'd have to be a way to slip it past our stepfather. He couldn't know we'd written. He can't know where we are."

Laura clutched her hands together against her chest. Like she was praying . . . or begging. "I guess Michelle just told you the very short version of our troubles." Laura told him of their mother's plight until her voice broke, then she didn't go on.

Caleb rested a hand on her back. He wanted to pull her into his arms and hold her, and let her cry out all her fears.

Michelle pressed a hand to Laura's shoulder on the side away from Caleb. "We feel like we've left her in terrible danger. She might even now be fighting for her life." Michelle paused and rubbed a hand over her mouth.

Laura leaned against her.

"We know our stepfather is capable of violence," Michelle went on. "Though Mama has done her best to keep it from us, I believe he's hit her before."

Zane as good as growled. Nick shot to his feet. His knuckles turned white where he held his plate.

"I think Mama will die before she'll tell him where we are." Michelle's eyes filled with tears. She swiped them away with a rough dash of her sleeve over her eyes. "But she couldn't tell him no matter how harshly he treated her because she doesn't know. We ran off in the night. It was a desperate, dangerous thing to do. We survived it and found the mission group. Parson Tillman allowed us to join, and that took us in a direction we couldn't have planned."

"You took off on your own?" Nick scowled down at them.

"He had terrible plans for us," Laura said in a grim voice. "He sees us as something to sell. He's found wealthy men, terrible men with dreadful reputations, who were ready to pay well to marry us and gain that connection to the industry my father had created and now my stepfather runs."

"But if we could just tell her we're all right. If we could find out if he's hurt her." It was Michelle's turn to stop talking and swallow hard.

"Is it far?" Nick asked.

Laura and Michelle looked at each other just as Jilly, likely sensing something important, came up.

"It's quite a distance," Laura said, "but I can draw you a map. Our house is deep in a heavily forested stretch on a mountaintop."

Jilly interrupted. "Don't tell them our names. It's not safe."

Silence fell as the three sisters studied each other.

This part Caleb couldn't tell, because he didn't know their last name either, and he wouldn't have if he did know. This was their secret to tell.

"All our lives, we've spent summer in the mountains and winter in San Francisco," Laura said. "But when our stepfather took us up to that mountain mansion that we loved so much, it wasn't for the summer. There we've stayed, as good as prisoners in our home."

"Are you the daughters of Liam Stiles?" Nick asked softly.

Laura's eyes went wide with fear. Caleb tore his gaze from her and saw Michelle and Jilly had expressions to match.

"You can't tell him where we are." Jilly clamped her hand on to the front of Nick's shirt.

He faced her, wincing when the clamp tightened. She

must have some hair. "I would die before I let such a terrible man harm you. Your secret is safe," Nick said as if a vow to God.

Jilly's fear faded slightly. She let go of Nick.

"Can you help us? Can you or Zane or someone go, sneak in, get to Mama, tell her—t-tell her—" Laura's voice broke.

Caleb wrapped an arm around her shoulders and pulled her close.

"I worked for Stiles Lumber last summer," Nick said. "I know lumbering from working in camps in Michigan and Minnesota."

Jilly's forehead furrowed. "You look like a boy."

"I'm older than you, and here you are building a church." With narrowed eyes, Nick said, "I've been working, wandering, most of my life. I started in lumber, running errands when I was thirteen. Then as a lumberjack when I was sixteen. I'm twenty-four years old."

Jilly jerked one shoulder sheepishly. "I'm twenty. We're three years in a row, my sisters and I. Michelle twenty-one, Laura nineteen. And then there were never any more babies."

"None that lived, not after me," Laura said quietly. "It's why Papa and Mama raised us to take over the company. They knew there'd be no more babies."

Caleb rubbed her back between her shoulder blades.

Nick spoke more gently now. "I never met your father, but I heard the talk of the new owner and how much worse the company was run since your pa's time. And the talk of you girls. Those lumberjacks would've died for you. They can't know your ma is being harmed, or they'd be in that house standing guard around her, around all of you, day and night."

Laura and her sisters sat up straighter, listening as if in awe.

At last, Laura said, "You know where our home is?"

"I do. Write a note to your ma but don't write down where you are. I'll tell her, but if it's not in writing, Edgar Beaumont can't find it. I'll deliver the note, and I swear on my life, as a Christian and as any decent man would, that your stepfather will never again lay a hand on your ma, not while I'm alive. I'll stay there until you girls find it safe to return, even if that means I stay for the rest of my life. I'll get news from your ma and mail it to Zane. He'll bring it to you."

His eyes shifted to his boss. "Won't you?"

"I will. And I'd go with you if I could. Do you want me to send more men?"

"No, once I'm there, I'm certain I can find twenty men, fifty men, in that logging camp who will throw in with me to protect Mrs. Stiles. And if I can't, I'll do it myself."

"You can't trust everyone," Jilly said. "Some of them have come in since our stepfather . . ."

"Edgar Beaumont." Nick said the words as if they burned his tongue.

"Yes. Some are his men, and they are dangerous." Jilly reached out for him again. This time she laid her hand gently on his arm. "Be careful. And please, please hurry."

Nick jerked his chin. "Write your note. I'll tell her all I know, but I think it will comfort her to get a note in your own hand."

Laura turned to Michelle. "You have paper and pens?"

"Yes. Hurry." All three girls rushed to the wagon and began digging out paper.

"Nick, thank you for doing this." Caleb felt like a failure.

135

"I should have figured this out. I knew they had secrets, but—"

"It might help to remember those girls—no, those women—are probably smarter than the three of us combined. There was talk of that in the logging camp, too." Nick gave a quick nod. "It will give me great pleasure to go protect their mother. She came out to the lumber camp one evening the summer I worked there. Beaumont had gone somewhere. Now I can see she came out because he wasn't around to stop her. She smiled, thanked us, and had a kind word for the lot of us rugged, sweating oafs. She told us their lumber company wouldn't work without us. That we were honorable men, and she appreciated our hard work."

Nick smiled. "The kindest words I'd heard since I'd left home, and Ma hugged me goodbye and spoke of missing me and loving me. Mrs. Stiles—the men always called her Mrs. Stiles, as if her second marriage hadn't happened— was all that was gentle and beautiful in the world. And the loggers spoke of the daughters, too, with absolute respect, almost reverence. We caught a glimpse of them a few times but from a distance. They stayed mostly to the house. The men said that was different than it had been. Their pa had always brought them out to see how the lumbering worked. He was raising them to take over. They were the most highly educated women I'd ever heard tell of."

Nick went to collect the letters, and Caleb looked over at the three sisters in their badly soiled servants clothing. He remembered Michelle sewing a pair of trousers to her skirt. Laura studying a haunch of venison with absolutely no idea how to turn it into a meal. Jilly with no notion of how to wash clothes. The worst servants possibly in the whole world because they'd been raised as educated ladies. And he hadn't heard a breath of complaint.

"They need clean clothes. They only have the clothes on their backs." Then Caleb thought of the women and children helping build the corral. Feeling helpless, he pointed to that group. "They only have the clothes on their backs, too."

Caleb turned to Zane. "And you already did more for those women than I did. I may not be cut out for mission work."

Zane gave his head a little tilt. "You got me up here. You convinced me to give them two free cows."

Caleb smiled. "I did indeed."

Nick came over, moving fast. "Sorry to desert, Boss."

"Your job'll be waiting for you." Zane stood and pulled coins from his pocket. Caleb saw a few twenty-dollar gold coins. "Let me help to this extent at least."

Nick gave his head a firm shake. "No. Thank you, but I don't see this as a problem that involves money."

"You never know. Sometimes it smooths the way."

Nick hesitated still.

"Take it for the Stiles women, not for yourself."

"Thanks, Boss." He pocketed the coins, then strode to his horse, swung up, and galloped south.

"I'd've never ridden that direction. I hope he knows where he's going," Michelle said as the women came back.

And that pretty much reflected the thoughts going through Caleb's head.

"He'll find his way," Zane said. "He's a man to depend on."

"He's got the most distinct case of heterochromia I've ever seen." Jilly still faced the direction Nick had gone, even though he was out of sight.

"What?" Zane looked at Jilly with one arched brow.

"Eyes that are two different colors. Very rare. Often the result of an eye injury."

With a shrug, Zane went to finish the corral, and Caleb, with little idea how to build a corral but probably as much of an idea as the women and children of Purgatory, followed after and got to work.

His mission field, with only a bit of help from him, now had livestock, a corral, and very soon a church.

God was truly with him.

FIFTEEN

GOD SEEMED TO HAVE ABANDONED these people. Or more likely, they'd abandoned God.

And yet He sent help in the form of three strapping men.

Zane worked until after dark, then he and Shad lay down by the fire and slept.

Michelle watched the two men sleeping from where she was, almost under the wagon. They'd been so much help. Zane, a strong, generous, bossy leader. Shad only paused once to eat, then he went right back to work until full dark.

Nick had ridden off to protect Mama. Michelle had to fight back tears, and she wasn't a crying kind of woman. But to think Mama would have someone to stand between her and Edgar. Michelle could hardly believe it was really possible. She thought men had power over their wives. But Nick acted like he'd do it, and no one would dare tell him he couldn't.

A sniffle escaped as she lay there, and Laura, who always

slept between her and Jilly, rolled to her side and rested an arm on Michelle's middle.

"I want to cry, too."

"To think of Mama being safe?"

"Yes, do you think he can do it?"

From Laura's other side, Jilly said, "I think he can. I *know* he can." Then she added more quietly, "I hope he can."

The three of them lay together, just as they had when they'd moved into the same bedroom to protect themselves from Edgar.

It had been Jilly's idea, and there'd been an edge of desperation to it. Michelle had pressed her about it, but Jilly wouldn't say why it was so important. It had reminded Michelle that, of the three of them, Jilly was the one who had had misgivings about Edgar. She'd been only a faint voice of caution because she'd been taken in, too, but she had wondered if their mother's marriage should wait.

Once Jilly suggested sharing a room, Michelle and Laura had quickly agreed, so there'd been no reason to force whatever secret Jilly held that had given her the idea.

Still, Michelle had to wonder.

THEY AWOKE THE NEXT DAY to long hours of hard labor. The church went up. The corral was finished. The cows got milked, and the food kept coming, so everyone's bellies were full.

They all went to bed exhausted.

And then the men came home.

Drunk. Loud. Any money they'd made digging gold was probably spent on whiskey while their families starved.

Michelle watched as Laura rose up on her elbow to see four men, two of them with their arms slung around each other. Two others staggering along, laughing.

One of them burst into a song with lyrics not fit for women and children. Honestly, not fit for anyone.

Since she didn't have much exposure to drinking men, not even that horrible Edgar was a complete sot, Michelle simply quoted, "'For the drunkard and the glutton shall come to poverty: and drowsiness shall clothe a man with rags.'"

"The men aren't as thin as the women. But they're plenty thin. Not much sign of gluttony here." Jilly sat up. They were on the far side of the wagon, so she bent to look under it.

Laura dropped back to lie flat on the ground. She likely didn't care to see. Hearing was bad enough.

There was a stretch of silence, then Jilly said, "It's Saturday night. They'll be gone again Monday morning." She lay back down, too.

Laura asked, "Do you think they'll all be in church tomorrow?"

Michelle felt a very unaccustomed giggle escape, and she clapped her hand over her mouth. "Good thinking, Laura. We'll make a point of inviting them. Early."

Laura punched her lightly on the arm.

The men went into their cabins.

Eventually, silence settled over Purgatory.

MARGARET WAS READY FOR TROUBLE. And it *would* come.

For days now, she'd stayed mostly locked in her room. Edgar hadn't tried to get in. He'd've found himself thwarted if he had, but it would have been frightening to hear him raging and pounding.

Margaret assumed he was still limping.

Sarah brought her meals. They'd agreed to a certain knock so Margaret wouldn't open the door to anyone else. Sarah stayed quite often to talk about what was going on in the house or just so Margaret didn't spend the day alone.

"I eavesdropped on him in his office, ma'am, talking with one of his awful men about sending people out to search for the girls."

"He can't know where they are. I don't even know where they are." Margaret's heart pounded, and her gut twisted with fear. She could do nothing but hide in her room and pray for God's protection over her girls.

Sarah had very definite opinions about who in the household could be trusted, and Margaret listened carefully.

Margaret knew she wouldn't surprise Edgar with a physical attack next time. But she was an intelligent woman, some might even say shrewd.

There were many ways to surprise a man.

The day finally came. He knocked firmly.

"Margaret, we are going to clear things up right now."

She thought of the mark she'd made on his face. Probably that was what kept him away. He was an extraordinarily vain man. He traveled with a valet like some kind of British aristocrat. As if a man couldn't dress and shave himself.

Maybe it had taken this long for his valet to make his face presentable.

With a solid oak door between them, Margaret walked closer and said, "Say what you want from out there. I've taken my last slap from you, Edgar, and most certainly my last closed fist. My daughters will be back soon, and they will bring with them enough strong men to throw you out, and they'll have all the papers in order to make it legal. Until then, you won't get another chance to put your hands on me."

Not in violence and not in the intimate ways of a husband. Mostly that had ended after a few months of marriage. She was certain he had another woman, or more likely women. She hoped those poor things didn't get treated too roughly.

"Hear me, Margaret. You will come out of that room, or I will return with an ax and chop my way in."

"The door is solid oak. My Liam made them double thick with sturdy locks for reasons of personal safety."

Honestly, he'd used this particular oak because it was beautiful, and they'd both fallen in love with the way it glowed when it was polished. But Edgar didn't need to know that.

"I doubt you've ever worked hard enough in your life to chop through this door. It will be interesting to see you try. And if you do get through, I'll meet you with my trusty poker."

She chilled her voice. "I've daydreamed about coming out of my room late at night to sneak into yours and bash you a few more times. Those daydreams are so entertaining. No matter what you do to me, I can promise you that if you take an ax to this door, even when you fail to get through it, I'll make those dreams a reality. You'd never be able to risk closing your eyes. Not one more time while you're in this house. Maybe I'll do it tonight. Don't sleep deeply, Edgar. Unlike you, I have a key to your room, so you can't lock yourself away from me."

She laughed what she hoped was a wicked laugh.

There was a long silence. "You won't win this fight, Margaret."

"I already have. My daughters are safe, and that is my first and most important victory."

"They won't stay safe for long. I'm ready to teach them some respect. I spared the rod when I shouldn't have."

"If you harm me, I'll retaliate. If you kill me, you will be thrown out without a penny to your name. You've already lost. You're just too stupid to know it."

She pictured his henchmen searching for her girls and couldn't talk anymore.

With a growl of fury, Edgar turned and stomped away. She heard his bedroom door slam.

How could she have been so stupid as to marry him? He'd been a very skilled liar. He'd made himself into everything she'd wanted him to be. But now she remembered moments that should have been warning signs.

But she hadn't heeded them, and it had led her to this.

She'd spend more time on her knees before God than ever.

ZANE DRAGGED A LOG he'd split yesterday to the church, the first board for the roof. They'd finish it today, except for fine work on the door and altar, those things could be set aside while they worked on the cabins for the women.

That's when Caleb woke up.

Throwing back his blanket, he rushed up to Zane. "You can't build a church today. It's the Sabbath."

Zane stopped leading his horse, which was pulling one

end of the split log by a chain. "I only slept here last night so I could work today." He looked at Shad, who was heading for the log pile with an ax to begin the notching needed for the roof.

The only reason Shad hadn't started earlier was because he didn't want to wake anyone, except maybe those half-wit drunks who staggered in late last night. Waking them up would be a pleasure.

There were already quite a few logs notched. The thinnest ones would be used on the top half of the wall. Zane wasn't sure what the plan was, but that seemed right to him. Zane thought there were enough logs to finish the church, though they might need a few more for the roof.

"You don't have to work on the church, Parson Tillman, but I do. I'll break off the building for the church service, then get back to it." He started his horse moving again. "Do you have a preference between shingles or a split-log roof? Shingles would do better at keeping the rain out, but they're more work. Maybe you could skip church on the Sundays when there's rain. Or time the service between downpours."

"Zane, please. No, we mustn't build. A person might make an exception, if their conscience allowed, for their own home. But a church? Would we be so brazen as to ask God to bless a church built on the day He commanded us to rest?"

"I suspect what God wants is for us to worship Him, and He knows our bodies and minds need rest. But whether He'd mind if we built today and rested tomorrow, when we've got the church done, that's a question."

"'Remember the sabbath day, to keep it holy.'"

Zane nodded and unhooked his horse from the log. "I'd

better ride home today then and make sure the men are keeping up with chores."

Michelle wandered over to Zane and Caleb. She'd slept in her housemaid dress. It was filthy, wrinkled, and smelled none-too-fresh. Still, she was about the prettiest thing Zane had ever seen. She and her sisters were an absolute treat for the eyes.

Caleb had said the other day that none of the Stiles women had a single change of clothes. Zane needed to fix that.

A string of furious cursing, a woman's cry of fear, and the sound of something hard hitting a wall came from one of the cabins. A woman, pushing two girls ahead of her, rushed out. The door slammed so hard Zane was surprised the building didn't collapse.

"And keep those kids quiet!"

The cabin was silent.

The woman cuddled two half-grown girls close and shushed them as they cried.

Zane took a step toward the woman. He felt a hand grab the back of his shirt.

"No, let's talk before we go over there." Michelle's urgent voice turned Zane around. "Did you hear them come in last night?"

"Yes, how could I miss that racket?"

Zane noticed the woman had a red mark on her face. The right size for a backhand or a fist.

"A couple of days ago, one of the women left," Michelle said. "Emma Kate's husband, Charlie, came."

"I don't know those names." Zane had taken time to talk with all the women and several of the children.

"They were already gone when you got here. Charlie came

home all excited. He'd had a big gold strike. He came in and said, 'Leave everything. We're getting out of here.' When Emma Kate stopped to grab her baby some diapers, Charlie hit her."

Zane growled.

"Not hard, he just knocked those things she'd grabbed out of her hands and told her to leave it all. She said, 'We need diapers.' Then he said to grab them, and she did and ran after him happy as all daylights."

"And you're telling me this, because . . ."

"Because if you go over to her husband"—Michelle jerked her head at the woman who was walking her daughters toward the corral—"and try to punch some sense into that drunken fool, you're likely to earn his *wife's* fury. Look at that woman, quieting her kids. Trying to get them away from her husband. She's stood by her man all the way down to the bottom of the barrel where they live now. Whether it's wise or not, she's loyal to him. You punching him isn't likely to change that. And there's a good chance it'll make her hate you."

Zane glared at Michelle. Turning it all over in his mind. "So you think we should just stay over here while that woman and her children cry?"

Breathing in and out deeply, Michelle met his eyes.

She was a truly beautiful woman. Dark hair, a match for his. Her eyes were a shining shade of blue. But what blazed out of her was a keen intelligence that he had to pay attention to. If Michelle thought she was right, there was a good chance she was.

"No, we need to go talk to her," Michelle said. "But we don't solve this with violence."

"And when do I get to talk to that sweet man she's married to?"

Michelle's brows beetled as she considered it. She thought with a concentration that spoke to Zane of real power in her thoughts.

Caleb, still standing beside them, said, "Maybe before we do anything, we should pray."

He closed his eyes.

Michelle closed hers, too.

Zane felt ashamed of himself that it hadn't even occurred to him to do the same.

Wisdom, that was all he could think of. "Lord, give me wisdom."

Zane opened his eyes to see Caleb opening his.

Caleb said, "I'll go over to her first, alone."

"If she thinks you're meddling in her happy marriage," Zane said with a voice as dry as the desert, "come on back, and we'll debate some more."

Caleb walked away.

Zane gave Michelle a grim look. "I reckon I'll ride on home today, come back tomorrow to do more building."

He gave the shacks a dark look. "If I do a good job of building, those folks may never leave. Maybe more will come and expect me to build *them* a nice cabin."

"I don't understand a world where a man drinks up his week's pay while his family goes hungry," Michelle said. "But then I don't understand a man who lies like Edgar did, acts like the finest gentleman, charms my mother and me and my sisters, too. Then reveals himself to be a vile pig later."

She turned from watching Caleb approach the woman,

who was well away from her cabin now and had collapsed on the ground, holding her children.

Zane could hear the crying all the way over here. But she was far enough from her cabin her husband couldn't hear.

"So you're the daughter of a lumber baron, huh? The heir to a dynasty, reduced to being a servant by her evil stepfather."

"Yep." Michelle crossed her arms and studied Zane.

"There isn't a fairy godmother or a glass slipper in sight."

That quirked her lips. "Doesn't matter. There's no royal ball being held anytime soon. And in the meantime, I can chop down trees."

"Would you like me to bring some fabric? So you and your sisters can have a change of clothes?"

Michelle's cheeks went pink, and Zane found that fascinating. She seemed like a very calm, smart woman. What was there in what he'd said to bring on a blush?

"We, well, we actually have a change of clothes, and we are going to wash the clothes we're wearing today. If Caleb doesn't think that will break the Sabbath."

"I'm sure you're allowed to change clothes on the Sabbath." Zane didn't know all the rules, but he was clear on that one. Unless they were some strange branch of the Christian religion that forbade such things.

"Even if we change into . . . into . . ." Michelle inhaled and slowly exhaled. "Into trousers?"

"That's your only change of clothes?"

"Yep."

Zane couldn't stop the grin. "I might just stay around."

Michelle gave him a nice firm punch on the arm.

"So there's just the three of you then, no more siblings?"

"Laura carries it deep inside that something about her birth harmed Mama. I know there were other babies. None lived long enough to even be born. I caught Mama crying a few times, and once found her crying in Papa's arms. I saw him crying, too. They stood there, Papa rocking Mama a bit.

"I remember Papa saying, 'We've been blessed with three wonderful children. And I've been blessed with a woman I will love for a lifetime.'

"Mama said, 'But you wanted a son.'

"Papa answered, 'I want what God has given me. A beautiful family. Please don't cry, it's unbearable.'"

Michelle shook her head. Zane thought she was trying to shake away the memory.

"I felt like the ground was shifting under my feet. Mama was bad enough. But my father's tears, that was what made me slip away and spend an afternoon on my knees praying. I didn't even know for what."

"And then your pa started training you to take over the business?"

That got a real smile out of her. "He did."

Zane wanted to hear more, but Caleb approached them with the woman and her children.

"We're going to have a prayer service now," Caleb said, "and I think we should have it in the church."

Laura and Jilly came up beside Zane, and they all turned to look at the small building. Its four walls standing, a frame peaking up in the center that would hold the split logs for the roof.

"I'll stay for the service," Zane said. He turned and gave Michelle a long smile.

The pink on her cheeks had faded, but it bloomed again.

"Then I'll head home and be back tomorrow with enough men to build four cabins in one day." He nodded at the scattered shacks. "They'll be better than those but not much."

Gretel called them to breakfast. The women in the shacks must have heard because they came out fast, children in tow.

Not a single man woke up to eat.

And when none of them came to the prayer service, Zane wasn't shocked.

SIXTEEN

CALEB STOOD AT THE EMPTY DOORWAY of the church and shook hands with each person who'd come to the prayer service.

"We'll have a regular church service in an hour."

There were four women. The one with the red welt on her face, who didn't want to hear a word against her Barney, was Rose. She had two girls named Anna and Susie. Both shy little things, and so skinny it hurt Caleb to see it.

Next was a tiny woman, Janine. Sally Jo was her daughter. She also had an older son who worked with his father every day. He hadn't come home last night. Janine said it would be her third son to run off this way. She seemed hostile to . . . everything. Caleb, the church, life in general.

The third was Clara. She didn't talk, and Caleb couldn't figure out if she was shy or a bit touched in the head. She had four children. They came to church but rushed out the moment the service was over. They had come for breakfast, too, but they ate the food near their cabin, almost as if they were scared it would be taken from them.

The fourth was Barbara. She had two children so young she carried them both. She was pale and painfully thin. She had her limp blond hair knotted at the back of her head, and she was dressed in tattered calico so faded Caleb could only guess it might once have been blue.

She looked to be at the end of her tether. Caleb was surprised she could lift the children.

He made sure she ate her full share because he saw her try to slip food to one of her toddlers. He'd done his best to act calm when he went to her with a second plate of food and took her older child, a boy of two, onto his own knee and fed the tyke.

He noticed the three Stiles sisters talking, a bit away from everyone, then Laura gestured toward the woods, and all three went out of sight into the forest.

Caleb had to force himself to stay by the church and talk to the women.

Gretel came up and said, "I've made a pot of coffee, and there are some biscuits and honey. We could visit and eat together between the prayer service and church. After church there'll be dinner."

The women already had a good breakfast, but they followed Gretel as if they were starving. There was a good chance they were.

Caleb looked toward the woods, where those mysterious sisters had gone, then his eyes were drawn to those awful shanties. Men slept there. Praying fiercely, maybe even desperately, he asked God for wisdom, guidance. *Give me words to speak, Lord. What do I say to these men?*

His only deep assurance was that the men needed God. They needed faith. All their other problems stemmed from their lack of faith.

But how was he to get them to even listen, let alone accept God into their lives?

And what in the world were those sisters up to in the woods?

****

"That's quartz." Jilly dropped to her knees by the rocky outcropping.

Laura stood back so Michelle could take a good look.

Then both sisters whipped their heads around to Laura.

"You found this yesterday," Michelle said, as if it was an accusation.

Laura didn't waste time on that. "What are we going to do?"

Her sisters, smarter than all good sense should allow, fell silent, immediately thinking of a dozen twists and turns. Most of them bad.

"Are we still on the Hart ranch?" Jilly brushed dirt away from a slab of quartz and saw the veins of gold in it.

"I think so. It's called the Two Harts Ranch. The brand is two hearts lying on their sides with the tips touching. But it looks like a sideways number eight."

"An infinity symbol," Michelle said breathlessly.

"That's how it looked to me. Anyway, Zane says he owns a lot of wasteland up here, including a couple of mountain valleys to the south and a steady spring that runs year-round to the north. That would take in this area."

Jilly stood, looking grim. "We can't say how deep this vein of gold goes, but what we're seeing is enough to start a gold rush."

Nodding, Laura said, "And it all belongs to Zane Hart.

But it'll be tough to stop the rush, if this is a rich strike. And those folks in the shanties would end up overrun, driven out."

"They couldn't be much worse elsewhere." Michelle ran a hand over the rough stone. "Can we dig it up ourselves and give it to those women and somehow hope a truly rich packet of gold will be enough to keep their husbands from throwing it all away?"

"Those men will end up crowing about their big strike and draw killers." Jilly plucked a small loose stone from the ground and held it at eye level. "Those families aren't the only ones who'll be overrun."

The three sisters stood silently, each of them mulling it over.

It was Laura who broke the silence. "Should we tell Zane?"

Michelle sounded very skeptical when she said, "We should."

Jilly asked, "Should we dig it ourselves and . . . give it to the women and tell them to run and never look back?"

"I think we need to tell Caleb. It's his mission field." Laura's mind twisted between her love of chemistry and her love of the Lord. Her love of her mama and her desire to round Caleb up like a balky horse, marry him, and go home. Throw in a gold strike, and it was enough to make her head explode. No dynamite necessary.

"Not yet." Jilly clenched her hand around the rock.

"What are we waiting for?"

Jilly went back to silence, but this time Laura didn't interrupt her thinking. As long as Jilly was thinking, Laura decided to do her own share of it. Papa had encouraged all of them to think things through. Think of the consequences of any decision. Think beyond the immediate result and consider long-term changes that might stem from their actions.

Laura saw potential chaos. She saw Zane going mad for gold. She saw Caleb getting gold fever. No, not that. Not Caleb.

Those women wouldn't take the gold and run. They'd take it and share it with their husbands, who would run mad.

At last Michelle spoke. She usually tried to run things. Laura usually let her because she had an orderly mind. But it wasn't just an act of mindless obedience. If Michelle wanted agreement, she had to convince them.

"We wait," Michelle said. "We get to know these folks a bit more. Get to know Caleb's true nature. He seems uncommonly decent, but gold is the breaking point for a lot of people. Zane seems like a good man, too. But will he throw everyone off his land and be overtaken by greed? If we tell the women—" Michelle visibly shuddered. "No, we can't tell them. Probably never, but for certain, not now, not yet. We wait."

"It's probably the right decision." Laura spoke cautiously. "So why does it feel like lying? Like we're the greedy ones. I don't want the gold. We're already wealthy women."

She looked down at the filthy servants dress she wore and longed for a bath and clean, pretty clothes.

Jilly giggled. "I sure feel real wealthy right now."

Shaking her head, Laura said, "It's not our land. It's not our home. It's not our mission group. It's sure as can be not our gold."

"But you did find it, Laura," Jilly said. "In the gold world, you make a strike, you're rich."

Again silence.

Again, Michelle said, "We wait."

Laura looked from her to Jilly. "Since we don't know what to do, doing nothing seems like a good answer."

She glanced at Jilly's closed fist. "Should you take that with you? What if someone sees it?"

Jilly studied that little rough-edged, gray-and-gold stone. "Something so small is going to cause really big problems."

"That is the plain truth," Michelle said. "Keep that, Jilly. Put it in the pouch with the money Mama sent. We'll have evidence of what we've seen when the moment comes to talk about it to whoever we decide gets to know. Now, let's get back before we're missed."

SEVENTEEN

CALEB HAD SOME QUESTIONS he wanted to ask the Stiles sisters just as soon as he had two minutes together.

After church, there was a meal. Gretel was working hard. She might not be building a church, but feeding the mission group and the settlement and caring for her baby were all essential jobs she handled without complaint, despite all the load falling on her shoulders.

Caleb talked quietly with the Hogan sisters and asked them to assist her. It occurred to him that he'd more or less forbidden Zane to work on construction, but he was letting Gretel toil away.

Praying for wisdom nearly nonstop kept Caleb busy as he chipped in to help as much as he could.

Shad had ridden off after the prayer service and only returned as they were dishing up the meal. He had a buck draped over his saddle.

Did hunting count as work?

Caleb just prayed harder. As God whispered of forgiveness

and love and unity, as Caleb was starting to feel more calm and joyful, the first man staggered out of his cabin.

"Where'd you get to, woman?"

Rose, whose reddened cheek had begun darkening to a bruise, scooped up her last two bites of stew. Janine and Sally Jo took the children.

"Rose, where are you?"

Rose hurried to heed her master's voice.

Zane, eating very lightly of a plate of stew, narrowed his eyes and watched Rose and her husband. Zane's eyes went cold as the man stormed around, demanding his wife come home.

Caleb braced himself for who knew what. He was sure Zane wouldn't stand by while Rose got hit again. Caleb wouldn't stand by, either.

And that's when Caleb decided to act before this turned into a fistfight. He set his plate aside and hurried after Rose.

"Here I am, Barney." Rose reached her husband's side fast.

"I work hard all week. I expect a meal come mealtime."

Caleb knew from visiting earlier that there wasn't a bite of food in Rose's cabin. Before she could respond, Caleb said, "We've got a meal right over here, Barney."

Belligerent eyes lifted to Caleb, then slid past to see the crowd behind him. A scowl twisted Barney's face, but he sniffed the air. He wasn't as skinny as the rest of his family. The company housed and fed the men through the week.

"We've made enough stew for everyone. Come join us." Caleb watched Barney and stayed close, in case the man struck out at Rose again.

The scowl faded. Barney's stomach growled, and he said, "Smells good. Appreciate it."

He looked at Caleb, and it was like rusty wheels were turning in his head. "Who're you, mister?"

"I'm Parson Tillman. We're traveling through the area and are camping here for a time, holding church services. We already had church today, but the meal is ready for you."

Barney's expression turned wary, but the food was too much temptation. He started for the fire.

Caleb mulled over the food being a temptation. That didn't seem exactly like a good thing.

Barney slumped down on a log. Janine, Sally Jo, and Barney's two little ones moved away to give him elbow room. Rick put a plate in his hands with a good-sized serving and three biscuits.

"See you brought down a deer. This area is hunted out lately." Barney said it as if he'd looked for food. Caleb wondered if that was true.

After he'd filled his belly, as if he were a truly hungry man, Barney said, "So what's that you're building? A cabin? Are you all going to live up here?"

"It's a church."

Caleb saw the Stiles sisters wander off, heading for the woods again.

Gretel and the Hogan sisters went to work cleaning up after the meal. They left a fair-sized pot of stew warming for the rest of the men when they woke up.

Harriet touched Gretel's arm gently and pointed to the church. Gretel nodded, picked up the tiny blanket she wrapped her baby in, and went inside the building. A chance to get little Willa down for a nap. Maybe Gretel would get one, too.

Rick took the women and their children to where the cows and horses stood grazing in the corral.

Zane and Shad took the deer out of sight, probably to butcher it. Provide them all with food for a few more days.

Everyone had backed away, leaving Caleb alone with Barney. "We've been here a few days. You're working long, hard hours. Do you have your own claim?"

Barney nodded. "But I ain't workin' it right now. Never found any color there. There's a big claim bought up by some rich man from San Francisco who hires on men. All of us here at Purgatory work there. Barely pays enough to keep body and soul together. Hard to feed the family. Your meal was welcome, Parson."

Barney seemed open and sincere. So why did he drink away his paycheck? It didn't fit. Caleb had expected a harder man, cruel.

"We'll have services again tonight. Not another sermon but prayers and some singing, some Bible reading. I hope you can come."

"I was raised a Christian, Parson. I miss meetings. We were faithful attenders back home."

"Where is home?" Caleb was pleased at how easy it was to talk to Barney.

A second man emerged from his cabin. This one had a sad expression. Like life was a burden that weighed his shoulders down. He was Barbara's husband, Herbert. He went to his wife, talked quietly to her, took the older of the two babies she was always toting, then came over, accepted a plate of food, and joined in their quiet visit.

He balanced the toddler on his knee and ate, and did it with surprising skill.

Robbie was Clara's husband. He talked a bit too loud and boasted a lot for a man whose family was starving.

By the time an hour had passed, Caleb had all four men sitting and visiting with him. There was coffee in the pot, and they all drank as if it was life to them.

All but Janine's husband, Lou, agreed to come to the evening service. He was surly and didn't join in much beyond eating and sipping coffee.

Janine came to the fire, plunked her fists on her hips, and said, "You're done with your eatin', Lou. Now we need to talk. It can be here, or it can be in private."

Lou looked sideways at his wife. His eyes narrowed. He stood, coffee cup in hand. Caleb noticed Sally Jo, the cow milker, was a few paces behind her ma.

"You come, too, Sally Jo. This is a family matter."

Lou grabbed Janine's arm roughly, but Caleb didn't intervene. The couple strode toward their cabin, Sally Jo lagging behind.

Caleb looked at the three men still seated. "Is he going to hurt her?"

Zane approached the group. He said with quiet menace, "I won't stand by while a man hits a woman."

"Better to ask if she's gonna hurt him," Barney said. "Janine gives as good as she gets mostly."

Caleb and Zane looked at each other, then turned as voices rose in the cabin. More Janine than Lou, but he had a few things to say.

Soon enough, Sally Jo came hurrying out and put some distance between her and her parents. She sat on the ground outside her cabin, drew her legs up to her chest, and hugged her knees.

The way she buried her head on her knees, Caleb thought she looked like the saddest, loneliest person he'd ever seen in his life.

Laura and her sisters came out of the woods just then. Laura noticed Sally Jo, said something to her sisters, and walked toward the despondent girl. Laura spoke quietly to her, and the two of them left the cabin behind.

LAURA LED SALLY JO FARTHER AWAY from her shouting parents.

Sally Jo walked along beside her in sullen silence. Laura let the silence stretch. She didn't know what would make this better. She led Sally Jo to a downed tree, and the two of them sat side by side.

Sally Jo finally said, "My brother didn't come back with Pa last night."

Laura didn't respond.

"It's the third of my big brothers to take off. They all worked alongside Pa on his claim, then at the job he does. One by one, they've taken off. I reckon I knew it'd happen, but my brother, the one nearest me in age, he'd always buy flour and some side pork. Potatoes. Whatever he could stretch his money to. Last night, Pa came home with empty pockets because he drank his money away. And no food."

Sally Jo turned to look at Laura. "If you hadn't shown up here, we'd have nothing. Not one blasted bite of food to eat for a week. Ma's scared. But she'd rather fight with Pa than talk things through with him. Or even leave this awful place. Leave him and find work for herself."

"A marriage is serious business, Sally Jo. It's hard to get out of it." Laura thought of her own ma and how trapped she was.

"I know. But it's a pa's job to take care of his family. Not work himself half to death six days a week, then drink his money up. He says he's exhausted and needs to relax at the end of the week. Needs a few hours of fun before he comes home to listen to Ma nag at him. But there ain't much fun in hunger. Ma's not the only one who's scared."

"What do you want, Sally Jo? Can I help somehow?"

"Not unless you've got a big old pile of money."

Laura thought of the money in the little sack she wore. It hung across her middle just under her breasts. But she wasn't giving any of it to Sally Jo. Not if it ended up in the hands of her father and went straight toward a whiskey bottle.

"Anything else? Do you—" Laura quit talking. She didn't want to hurt Sally Jo with suggestions that might be impossible to carry out. Impossible, wrong, sinful, stupid. Let the girl find out what she really wanted and ask for it.

And what about that gold? That would ease everything for everyone. But Sally Jo's father seemed so foolish. Why would he handle a great deal of money better than he handled a meager amount? There was a Bible verse about that.

"When is it my turn? When do I get to leave? My brother just took off with a week's wages. But I'll never get to do that. Because there's no week's wages for me. I'm trapped here." Her voice broke. She added through her tears, "Trapped here forever."

Laura was supposed to be very smart. She prided herself on it. She knew just how to separate that gold from the quartz and suspected it was a rich vein. She could give this girl money, and Sally Jo could run off and— What? What would become of her?

Michelle left Zane on the far side of the settlement and came toward them.

Laura watched her big sister, then looked beyond her to Zane, who wandered to the stew pot and the Hogan sisters.

Praying, thinking, listening to Janine and Lou shout at each other, Laura got an idea. A ridiculous idea. But she'd been praying and thinking. No idea, especially an outlandish one, could be ignored.

"Sally Jo, can you wait here for me?"

Sally Jo pulled her knees up to her chest and wrapped her arms around them. "Sure, I ain't never going nowhere."

Laura went to meet Michelle and led her away from the cabin.

Michelle hissed, "I don't want to look at the . . ." Michelle looked all around her and dropped her voice to a whisper, "The *you know*."

"You seem to get on with Zane a little better than the rest of us. I want something from him I doubt he'll like. And I want you to figure out how to get it for me."

Laura knew Zane would probably give them most anything he could. He was proving to be a very generous, if slightly cranky, man.

"What do you want?" Michelle sounded a little nervous.

It was Laura's turn to look around. "I want him to give Sally Jo a job at his ranch and get her away from here."

Michelle jerked her head back, eyes wide. She glanced at Zane, then Sally Jo. Crossed her arms and went to thinking.

Laura waited patiently. If Michelle thought it was a bad idea, it probably was.

"Do you think she'll be safe?" Laura knew better than to interrupt Michelle when she was organizing her thoughts.

"I'm past safety or whether it's a good idea, or whether Zane will do it," Michelle said. "I'm on to deciding which of the Hogan sisters to send along."

Which meant Michelle agreed. Laura rested one hand on Michelle's upper arm. "You'll figure it out. Good luck."

"Better than wish me luck, you should pray for me. A lot of people have to cooperate for this to work."

"I've been praying since I had this hairbrained idea." Oh, that wasn't even close to true. She'd been praying since they snuck out of the house heading for a flume ride.

Michelle went off to talk to Zane just as the door flew open on the cabin full of shouting. Lou stumbled out and fell on his backside, holding one hand over his eye. Janine charged out after him, grabbed him by the shirt front, and started in yelling again.

To Laura it mostly sounded like the same thing over and over.

Janine threatening to leave. Let Lou try to feed himself with the money he drank up. Other things in that vein.

Laura settled into a daydream about her own parents. How kind they were to each other. Of course, they'd had money, and it looked like money, or the lack thereof, caused a lot of problems.

Through the daydream, Laura noticed Zane walk over to Sally Jo and speak quietly to her. Much too far away for Laura to hear.

Sally Jo's eyes lit up. Zane pointed, and Sally Jo took off

walking, then she turned onto the trail Laura had used coming and going, and headed into the woods downhill.

Meanwhile, Shad had saddled three horses and led them toward the same trail. Michelle was busy talking with the Hogan sisters.

It surprised Laura a little that they both nodded and went to fetch their satchels, which contained more things than Laura had, including two changes of clothes and nightgowns they had yet to wear for reasons of propriety. They headed for the trail.

All of this with the backdrop of shouting that went on for so long Laura was beginning to get used to it.

Zane came over to talk to Michelle again. She nodded and gave him a little wave, and he walked away, after Shad, the Hogans, and Sally Jo.

Michelle came over to Laura. "We need to break this to Parson Tillman."

They both looked at Caleb, deep in conversation with two of the settlement women as they watched a third milk the cow. The children played nearby, under the watchful eye of the oldest boy.

"We just cut his mission group by twenty-five percent." Laura thought of counting baby Willa. That made the percentage a little better.

"Yep, we lost him two good mission workers." Michelle seemed satisfied with the outcome. "We couldn't let Sally Jo go off alone with two men."

"I'd thought maybe just *one* of the Hogan sisters could go."

"Apparently they're a team. They'll get Sally Jo settled cooking and milking for Zane and keep an eye out for another woman to come live in his house with Sally Jo. Zane's an honorable man, and he vouched for all his hands. But he did say it'd probably take one crook of her finger and Sally Jo would be married by the end of the month."

Laura looked at the trail where so many of their group had gone. "She's sixteen. That doesn't seem right."

"No, it doesn't." Michelle lapsed into silence. "So was it wrong to get her away from those two?"

They saw Janine kick Lou in the shins. He flung his arms wide in anger. He didn't hit her, and he wasn't intending to, but it wouldn't take much more to make him.

"She'd be better off away from her parents."

The shouting finally broke Caleb's attention from the friendlier members of the settlement.

He looked around, and Laura wondered if he was searching for Zane and Shad. He squared his shoulders and went toward the arguing couple.

Laura gasped. "I don't know if he should step into the middle of that."

Janine slapped Lou hard across the face. Lou grabbed her forearm and jerked her forward. The two stopped yelling, both breathing hard as if they'd run a long distance. Caleb reached them.

"I'd better get over there in case Caleb needs saving." Laura might need saving herself.

"Papa focused his money on educating us." Michelle's brow furrowed with worry. "He maybe should have had us take boxing lessons along with mathematics."

Nodding, Laura headed toward the man she intended to marry. She didn't want him badly hurt before she got the chance to bring him around. She also didn't think she could win a fistfight with Lou. Janine either, come to that.

Maybe she could drag Caleb out from the middle of a war. A family war that looked for all the world like it'd been raging for . . . well, if they had three grown sons, then possibly as much as three decades.

A miracle was going to be needed to calm these two.

EIGHTEEN

CALEB PRAYED as he approached Janine and Lou. He'd been searching for a pastoring job back east. But his disreputable past was too well-known. He attended church faithfully, but he'd never found a job. When that missionary gave his talk at church, God lit a fire in Caleb's heart to help. He had a bit of money, nearly enough to outfit him for the trip and pay for the boat ride and the train ride. He found others who'd heard the same calling to go. All of them turned what they could into cash, a few more donated, and the mission group headed west. He'd found he could work on the ship, and it gave him a bit of money left over. All that. He'd come all this way only to realize he had no idea what he was doing.

Building a church? He'd expected that and counted on Rick to handle that.

Cooking? Hopefully Gretel and the Hogan sisters would take that over.

He intended to preach, pray, lead singing, and share his faith with every person who would listen.

He hadn't considered he might have to break up fights between a husband and wife.

He came up to them just as Janine slapped her husband again. And Lou's cheeks were already red and puffy.

"I want you to stop shouting at each other." Caleb felt like simple statements were called for. He kept his voice low, friendly but firm.

He glanced around, wondering where Sally Jo was. How awful for her to witness this. And yet there was a good chance she'd lived with it all her life.

She was nowhere to be seen, but maybe she'd long ago learned to walk away from the fighting.

Janine and Lou did stop shouting, but they were still furious. Except now they were glaring at him.

He'd . . . what was the word, he'd heard it somewhere in his pastoral studies . . . he'd . . . uh, redirected them from their fight. That was it.

"You're very angry with each other. But the yelling doesn't do a bit of good. Let's talk through your problems and see if we can solve them."

Laura reached his side at that moment. Caleb mentally wished her away, but he didn't take his eyes off the challenge before him.

"Sally Jo left a while ago," Laura said very cautiously.

Janine's furious gaze pivoted to Laura.

"Quite a while ago."

Caleb thought she sounded like she wanted to head off a pursuit.

"She and the Hogan sisters decided they'd take a job with Zane on his ranch."

Janine's flushed face calmed to a slightly less vivid shade of red. "Do you know what this means, Lou?"

"Yep." He rested both hands on her upper arms. "The kids

are finally grown. You can get out of this place and come on back with me."

"I'll get a job, too. Cooking or cleaning somewhere."

She said it as if she'd been busy mothering Sally Jo when the truth was she mostly ignored her.

"Let's get packed." They both headed for the cabin, swung the door open, and slammed it shut behind them.

Caleb turned to Laura. "The Hogan sisters abandoned my mission group to work on a ranch?"

"I take full responsibility for this. I talked with Sally Jo, and she was so bitterly angry that her brothers have left the family because they could work. They'd each picked their own time, taken their week's pay, and headed off somewhere. For her, that was never going to happen. So I asked her if she'd like a job. Then I had Michelle ask Zane if he'd give her a job."

"Why didn't you ask Zane yourself?"

"Because I've got a notion Michelle should marry Zane, so I've been giving her all the chances to talk to him."

Caleb slapped himself in the face, his eyes covered, then he drew his hand down slowly so he could watch what this woman would say next.

Janine and Lou came out of their cabin with two gunnysacks stuffed full and hurried away.

"I've lost half of my missionaries."

"Actually, it's under half."

Caleb stared at her. "You're counting Willa? An infant?"

"She brings a lot of joy. I think she counts. Anyway, your mission team got smaller, but you've lost two families out of the original five, so we're still about even."

"My plan isn't to drive these folks away and empty out Purgatory. My plan is to reach them for the Lord."

Laura winced a bit as she shrugged. "I won't say you had success with Janine and Lou."

Caleb felt his eyes lift to heaven as he prayed for patience. "No. Really? You think you need to warn me that the people who've walked away from here didn't exactly make a commitment to turn their lives over to the Lord?"

Laura grinned.

Caleb needed to stop being sarcastic and start growling more. He was almost sure that would be the way to handle this.

"The thing is, Caleb, the folks who live up here are as low as people can go and still claim to have a roof over their heads. Any help you give them, any lift to their spirits, any wisdom as to how they should live, is bound to result in them leaving." She added hastily, "You'll have a good effect on them." She patted him on his upper arm in a way that wasn't entirely sincere. "On their *souls*, I mean."

Caleb walked over to the circle where they'd eaten. It was away from the fire. He hadn't seen Gretel in a while. He knew she'd gone into the church, probably to feed her little girl, change her diaper, and get her to nap.

The families still here were standing by the corral.

"What I think you have, as far as a mission," Laura said, "is an ever-changing group of people. I suspect they fall on hard times, then get some kind of second chance and leave. So you'll need to . . . to structure a ministry for always being an . . . an outreach. A call to new believers." She grinned again. "Do you ever preach fire and brimstone? That might be the most effective."

"I really don't. I'm not sure I can. I feel God calling me to love these people. Care for them. Feed His sheep. I think their lives are hard enough without me scaring them with talk of hell, especially when they already live in a place called Purgatory." Caleb watched the women and their men. Clara wasn't out here. She'd gone back to her cabin with her four children. They had to be sitting in that little building doing . . . what?

"What am I going to do, Laura?"

She leaned against his shoulder. "Tonight, you'll hold a singing and Bible reading. Tomorrow, we'll finish the church. Jilly's a good builder. Michelle and I aren't as good as her, but we're good. And Rick is excellent help. If you feel God calling you to love and serve these people with kindness, then honor that calling. Now I need to go have a little talk with my sisters."

Caleb watched her go and wondered what in the world God had in mind to put the Stiles sisters in his path.

Do you really want me to marry Laura, God? What about this mission field? She wants to go back home, protect her mother, run a lumber dynasty of all things. Where does my call to this humble mission field fit in?

He listened after he prayed. He really listened. No still small voice goaded him to propose. Neither did it tell him not to. Was God saying not yet?

Which meant yes only not now. And Caleb felt his heart speed up a bit to think of marrying such a beautiful, brilliant, kind, sassy woman. A woman who took charge and found milk cows her second day on a mission field. Found them for free, too, and brought back a work crew. And found Sally Jo a job, and lost him the Hogan sisters, the women who were supposed to teach school.

Shaking his head, Caleb knew she was a good woman. A

man like Caleb might look high and low and not find one better.

But he didn't see how he could be with her. God would have to find a way.

MARGARET SLAMMED TO THE FLOOR. The blow came out of nowhere.

Her head hit the hardwood. Fighting to remain conscious, she rolled, kicked out. Caught Edgar in the knee.

He stumbled and fell. It must've been the knee she'd hit with the fireplace poker.

As she shoved herself backward along the upstairs hallway carpet, Edgar roared, his fist clenched as he lurched to his feet. She came up against the wall and used it to heave herself up just as his fist slammed into her belly.

No air. No way to catch her breath. She collapsed to the floor. He stood over her, a vicious smile on his face.

"No woman is going to threaten me."

"If you kill me, you lose everything."

That wiped the smile off his face, but he didn't unclench his fist. "I'll be careful not to kill you then." He reached down, caught the front of her dress.

She'd watched out the window, seen him ride away. She'd been so careful for so long.

"Tell me where those girls went."

"No."

"You will." He slapped her hard across the face.

Her cheek felt like it exploded. Her ear rang like a church bell. Her head rapped hard into the wall behind her. She brought a hand up to guard her face and knew it was a wasted effort.

Edgar didn't hit again. He waited, watched. Enjoyed her pain. Was ready to add more but in no hurry.

She prayed, digging deep for courage. She was glad she didn't know where the girls had gone in case weakness from pain would drag it out of her.

Then the prayer took hold, and she found her courage, found it was easy to be brave. All she had to do was imagine Edgar doing this to one of her girls.

Imagine her girls married to men who'd do this to them for a lifetime.

Margaret lifted her chin, looked him in the eye, and said, "I will give my life for my children. I will allow any pain or torment you can deliver. To live is Christ, to die is gain. I'll endure anything and do it joyfully knowing my girls are beyond your reach, and I helped get them away."

He shook her until her teeth rattled, but she held his gaze boldly. She saw the minute it touched him, her words gouging into his hard heart.

He knew nothing of sacrifice. Nothing of love. Certainly nothing of God or faith.

"Do your worst, Edgar. I don't know where the girls are, only that they've traveled far and fast and have been gone for weeks. They are beyond your reach."

Something calculating shifted in his eyes. "Maybe not. I have men hunting. But maybe not enough men. I think I'll add to my crew of searchers." He grabbed at her in a way that sickened her until she realized he was frisking her. When he reached down the front of her bodice, triumph shone in his eyes. He produced the key to her room.

"You won't lock your door against me again, my foolish bride."

Foolish was right. She'd married Edgar after all.

He shoved her hard against the wall. Her neck whipped back and her head hit. She saw stars. Edgar let her go, and she sank to the floor, sliding sideways. He prodded her middle with his boot, but she was numb and didn't notice if it was a true kick.

He laughed and turned down the hall. She heard his feet pounding on the stairs and his shout for one of the minions he'd brought with him into this nightmare of a marriage. Violent brutes he paid for with her money.

The door to the library slammed shut.

Sarah rushed to her side and crouched beside her. "Ma'am, Mrs. Stiles, can you get up? Should I get help to carry you to bed?"

Sarah's voice broke, and Margaret decided crying was an idea with merit.

"I'm not badly hurt. He just knocked me down."

"I saw every moment of it, ma'am. I saw what he did to you. I'm sorry. I should have stepped in. I'm a coward, a weak, worthless—"

Margaret pressed trembling fingers over Sarah's mouth. "Hush now, hush. You couldn't have stopped him. You'd just be lying here beside me on the floor. Help me up. I was going for food when I saw him leave."

"He must've known you were leaving your room while he was out riding. I'm guessing spies in the household told him. He rode off, then must've slipped back on foot to catch you out. I didn't see him come back."

Margaret rolled to her hands and knees, then with Sarah's

supporting arm, gained her feet, and leaned against the wall while her head seemed to circle a few inches above her shoulders.

Her stomach ached, and each breath was hard. The back of her head banged like lumberjacks were trying to chop their way out.

Her ear was still ringing. That had happened once before when he'd slapped her.

"Beneath the pain, Sarah, is joy that my girls got away." Margaret's aching stomach swooped. "Do you think he'll find them? What men are so horrid that they'd hunt down innocent young women and drag them home?"

"We can only hope they've done a good job of hiding. Let's get you to your room, ma'am. I have another idea how we can make you safe." Sarah slid an arm behind Margaret's waist and helped her take each step. By the time they got inside, Sarah was nearly carrying her. They made their way to the bed, and Margaret lay down on her back.

Sarah, her eyes wide with worry, adjusted pillows behind Margaret's head. She went to the pitcher of water and poured water into the pretty china basin, dipped a cloth into it, and brought it to bathe Margaret's face.

When she folded the cloth to keep the cool side on Margaret's skin, Margaret saw blood. She hadn't noticed she was bleeding, but now that she saw it, she was sure her lip was split, and she might have a nosebleed.

The sight of her own blood made her head spin, even lying down. When that eased, Margaret was able to ask, "What's your idea to make me safe?"

"Well, it's a simple one, honestly. You've been locked in

your bedroom because you made sure there wasn't a second key to your door, and you kept the one key to hand."

"He has it now."

"But I've been fearing this day would somehow come." Sarah dug her hand into her pocket and produced two keys. "You can lock yourself into your daughters' room."

Margaret closed her eyes and felt tears trickle down her cheeks. "And from now on I'll be a lot more careful about when I leave the room."

"Let's get you moved now, ma'am. I'm afraid he's going to be inclined to do you more harm, and very soon, just to work over his bad mood."

"That sounds like Edgar. Yes, let's move now."

"Just so you know, ma'am. We can keep moving you for weeks, maybe months. I've stolen nearly every key in the house."

Margaret managed a laugh, when she'd've been sure there was no more laughter in the world.

Sarah helped her stand, and Margaret found the strength to bear most of her own weight while they scurried to another place to lock themselves away like a pair of timid mice.

Margaret brought her fireplace poker, but she no longer believed in her own strength. No, she had to rely on her wits, and her head was pounding too hard for her to find any such thing as wits.

NINETEEN

LAURA WANTED TO KNOCK her head against a wall. And she sort of wanted to build a bomb. She had the chemicals on hand.

Mostly she was so confused she didn't know what to do. For a smart woman, she felt just plain stupid.

She'd listened to Caleb's Bible reading, listened with a bowed head to his prayers, and joined in with the singing.

He was wonderful. Reaching people for Jesus Christ was his true calling.

He couldn't be dragged away from here to run a lumber dynasty. And of course, *she* was the one who was going to run a lumber dynasty, whether she truly wanted to or not. But she thought her husband might live with her.

Nope.

And she couldn't ask him to give up his ministry. Not when God had called him here. Not when he had such a gift for lifting spirits, drawing people into faith. It would be a sin. It would be dishonorable.

The church service was over, but she remained in the little

church building, the stars shining down from overhead. They planned to build benches, but for now it was a dirt floor with no seats to be had.

Beneath that unfinished roof, she prayed.

The bad part was, even as she was admitting it would be wrong to wrangle sweet Caleb around to propose, she was starting to really think he'd be a wonderful husband.

And she could be a great help to him as a parson's wife. But running a lumber company wouldn't match with his calling from God, and she had no choice but to help with the company.

Shaking herself out of her deep pondering, she heard Caleb outside the church, talking quietly with at least two of the husbands, maybe all three. He wasn't scolding or even advising. He was offering love and kindness.

Laura could stay here with Caleb. Forget all about the lumber. But what about Mama?

Tears burned in Laura's eyes as she tried to get the turmoil in her thoughts to calm.

Bending low over her knees, she sat on the floor, leaning against the wall in the back southwest corner, to the right of the doorless doorway.

Think. You're supposed to be so smart. All those years of mathematics, all sorts of sciences, and plenty of reading of classic literature. Oh, didn't she just think she knew everything.

But none of that book learning was doing her any good. Maybe Michelle with her orderly mind could help.

Maybe Jilly, who knew how to apply all things to the real world. Well, all things scientific. She wasn't good with romance.

Laura needed her sisters.

The gaping entry to the church was suddenly in shadows, and Laura looked sideways, hoping it was Michelle.

"Are you all right?" Caleb came in and hunkered down in front of her. "No, I see you're not."

He dropped the rest of the way down to sit on the floor in front of her. Hoisting her up, he settled her on his lap. "Tell me what's wrong."

She really couldn't. Could she? She rested her head against his chest. He was strong. The way he'd lifted her, now the solid support as she leaned against him. She thought of him as a gentle man of God, but he was also tough.

"I wanted a husband I could manage." She looked into those hazel eyes. Light enough in the shadowed church she could see the goodness in them—in him. "I don't think I can manage you."

He laughed quietly. "I'd hoped for a wife who was . . ." He paused as if he didn't have a real list. "I would have liked one who was meek and agreeable and always let me be the big strong man—the spiritual leader of the home, as well as the leader in all other ways. Obedience appeals to me." Then he laughed again. "There's nothing wrong with that list, it just doesn't sound like you, Laura. In fact, off the top of my head, I can't think of any woman I've ever heard of that fits that description."

"I'd want a spiritual leader. And I'd want a big strong man. But for the most part, I think I'd prefer to be a fully equal partner in a marriage. And in truth, I would prefer to be in charge."

He laughed again. "You need a husband, little woman?"

"Yes, I do. But you were wonderful tonight, inspiring. The

men and women who were here really listened to you. You're where you're supposed to be."

"You need to drag me away from where God wants me to be?" He asked it gently, but she heard what he didn't say. What she'd already thought.

"It would be a sin." She knew it and admitted it out loud.

"I want to live my life within God's will. Right now, His will calls me to be here."

"So I should hunt up another man. But Caleb, when I think of being married, I can only think of you."

Caleb's strong fingers touched her chin. He eased her back from his chest and lifted her until she looked him in the eye.

Then he lowered his head and kissed her.

It should be sinful, this kiss in the mostly built church. But it was such a kind kiss. So reverent. So . . . so . . . confusing.

Laura pressed both hands flat against Caleb's chest, and he lifted his head and smiled.

"I've decided to accept your proposal, Laura."

Long seconds ticked by. She really shouldn't be sitting on his lap. It took some effort, but she managed to crawl off him and stand. She reached her hand down. He took it and stood to face her.

"I've decided to withdraw it, Caleb."

He should be terribly hurt. Instead, he smiled. "Because marrying me would be a sin?"

"Yes."

"Then let's don't sin. Let's marry. You'll be the owner of a third of a lumber dynasty, but you can let your sisters go off and run it."

"But I'm supposed to dynamite holes in mountains so Jilly can build train tracks through."

"That's the plan?" He slid his right hand up and down her left arm. "You dynamite, Jilly builds? What does Michelle do?"

"She handles the machines. She's doing the calculations to plot a course though the mountains. And she's working on several inventions. Getting a train up a steep slope is complicated. Besides that, she intends to organize the whole thing. She will make sure I have plenty of chemicals to blast my way through a mountain and men to clear rubble. And she will see to shipping in the lumber Jilly needs to build trestles across gorges and bridges across rivers. Michelle will manage the whole company."

Caleb shook his head. "And you all know how to do these things?"

"You should see Jilly do Euclidean geometry. Or Michelle combine topographical maps, apply trigonometry, and plot a course straight through a mountain." Marveling at it all, Laura added, "And what I can do with a careful mix of chemicals would fill you with wonder." She leaned close. "Have you ever heard of dynamite? It's a new invention. A way to stabilize nitroglycerin."

"That kiss filled me with wonder. And you can go do some chemical wonders, then come back to me. Or maybe I'll go with you. Take a break from my ministry to watch you blow mountains up. Then we'll come back together."

Laura stepped closer and leaned in to whisper, "Two of us have to marry and go back to obtain a majority ownership. B-but, Caleb, I have a secret. You said you could keep confidences, right?"

Nodding, Caleb rested both hands on her shoulders and pulled her close enough no one could overhear, especially not her sisters. "You have my word, I'll keep your secret."

Laura's head lowered until it rested on his chest. Then she looked up and over Caleb's shoulder toward the door.

"I don't really want to blow up mountains. Dynamite, well, it's a fascinating thing to study, but . . ." She leaned closer. "But it's loud and dangerous and—" She sniffled, hating to be such a weakling. "But I have to go back and help Mama. I can't abandon her. If I tell her I'm unhappy about the work I've been trained to do, I'll be abandoning her to—to . . ."

Caleb's hands flexed on her shoulder. He studied her, then pulled her into a hug. She realized she was shaking.

Caleb didn't speak until she began to calm down. He slid one hand to the nape of her neck and massaged gently.

"Why is it so upsetting to admit that?"

Looking into Caleb's eyes, she said, "To turn my back on the company is a betrayal."

"The others can take it over."

Shaking her head, Laura said, "There have to be at least two of us married for controlling interest, and I figure it will be hard to really convince Jilly to find a husband. She objects to marrying."

"Why's that?"

Laura realized she was no longer shaking. Caleb's steady strength had calmed her. But she was no less determined to help with the family business. She glanced at the space where a door would be tomorrow and drew Caleb away from it toward the front of the church, where there'd soon be an altar.

"She won't speak of it, but it has to do with Edgar, I'm sure. She was never like this before." Laura kept her voice as silent as a breath. "I-I don't know if it's something awful he did to her, or if just knowing how cruel he was to Mama set her against marriage. But getting her married isn't going to be easy."

"Hm . . ." Caleb watched her so carefully, paid such close attention, it awakened something in Laura's heart she hadn't noticed was sleeping.

"If you and Michelle marry, you'll have the majority ownership of your father's company. Jilly can remain single and still take advantage of your ownership. Then they could go, and you could stay with me."

Laura hesitated, considered. "I just don't know."

"Marry me, Laura. I can't, in good conscience, want to kiss a woman and hold a woman as much as I want to kiss and hold you, and not think of marriage."

She looked as closely back at him as he looked at her. "There is another secret that my sisters and I haven't told you. I-I don't think I can say yes until I've made a clean breast of this. And I can't tell you without my sisters agreeing. We promised each other, and I have to talk to them."

"Secrets? More secrets?"

"This is a rather new one. I believe you know everything we held as secret before we met you."

"You and your sisters went off this morning between the early prayer service and church. I could tell something was going on."

"Let me talk to them."

"Of course, you can talk to them about revealing a secret. But I think, before you do, you need to decide whether you want a real marriage, Laura. You know I can't just be some item you check off a list. I'm a living, breathing man, and you're going to have to include me in your life. After we're engaged, when you and your sisters sneak off to talk privately and conjure up new secrets, you're going to have to take me, too."

She rested one hand on his cheek. "I know that. That's one reason I'm hesitant to say yes."

"I'm not going to hold you and kiss you anymore unless you do."

Nodding silently, she whispered, "Give me time. I'm still afraid saying yes would pull you away from your ministry and be a sin."

He looked long into her eyes, and then, as if he dredged the words from somewhere deep inside, he said, "I-I have some things you should know. You're not the only one with a story to tell."

"You have secrets?" She watched his eyes. Saw them shift so he wasn't meeting her gaze.

She thought of Edgar.

Then he looked at her, directly at her. "We both need to be fully honest with each other. And I think maybe my secrets are . . . well . . . bigger than yours."

Nodding, she said, "Getting married is complicated. For some reason, I thought it would be simple. Find a man, round him up, and marry him."

That took away his somber expression, the slightly shifty expression, and his eyes lit up again.

"But I can see now it's going to take some time. Time I think we both need. If I could honestly believe Nick can keep Mama safe, I'd be willing to take that time."

"I'll give you time, my beautiful, brilliant Laura." He leaned close and kissed her again, exactly what he'd just said he wouldn't do. After far too long, he pulled back and said, "But I think . . . not too much time."

She nodded and left the church and Caleb behind.

As she walked out, she heard him mutter, "Euclidean geometry?"

She smiled as she went to hunt for Michelle and Jilly and reconfigure their plan. They had to find room in their secret for one more.

TWENTY

CALEB WATCHED HERBERT AND BARBARA walk away after church on Sunday, Herbert carrying both toddlers.

It'd been a week since Caleb had met Herbert, since he'd met all the men. This week, all the men came back directly after work, and Herbert had his week's wages, a bag full of supplies, and a bit of gold dust he'd found on his own claim. He'd scraped out enough to rent a decent house in Dorada Rio, and they were leaving right after church. Caleb liked to think he'd been a help, but there was a good chance it was because Janine and Lou had left. Lou was a bad influence on the other men.

Caleb had counseled both Herbert and Barbara and urged them to find a church wherever they settled. He was hopeful this new step they were taking would include a true faith.

Clara had begun to speak a bit. And her four children had lost the worst of the gaunt, hungry look.

The men were hungry, and Gretel kept food coming, now with help from the ladies in the settlement. The women milked the cows, too. Rick, Caleb, and the Stiles sisters had finished the church and begun patching the cabins so the rain wouldn't come in.

Zane had come back with three men, and they'd been ready to work as long as they were needed. Caleb figured if they put their backs into it, they could build a whole town. After some serious talk, they decided building new cabins might be the wrong thing to do.

This place was for those who had nowhere else to go. It was where families went when they hit bottom. If the cabins were a good size and inviting, then people in not such dire straits might come, and there'd be nowhere for these nearly homeless folks to go.

Caleb prayed about it and could find no peace with leaving the cabins so small and rickety, neither did it feel right to build all new ones.

Watching Barbara and Herbert leave with their children reminded Caleb of Laura's words. To succeed at this ministry was to lose his congregation, one by one, and always there would be new folks in terrible need.

His successes would be gone and only his failures would remain. It would be demoralizing, but at the same time, he embraced it as pure service to God.

Laura hadn't come back to him and accepted his proposal. She hadn't shared her secret. She'd been working endlessly, as had he. From before sunrise every morning, until long after dark each night, and the days were getting long.

But maybe, after the midday service and the noon meal, they'd have a chance to revisit their conversation. He turned to find her just as the door to one of the empty cabins creaked open and a young woman holding a baby peeked out.

Caleb didn't know when she'd come. During church services? In the night?

All he knew was she looked terrified and desperate. Her baby cried, and it was a thin, weak cry that sounded all wrong.

Laura was at his side. "You get milk for the baby. I'll go talk to her. She might be frightened if a man approaches her."

"Laura, after we get these newcomers settled with a meal, we need time to talk."

Laura patted him on the arm, then left his side to approach the woman like she would a nervous forest creature. Laura was going to make an excellent parson's wife.

"WHEN ARE YOU GOING TO TELL HIM?" Jilly scowled, looking across the camp at Caleb.

"There hasn't been much opportunity," Laura said. "I'd hoped to get a chance to talk to him today, and I still mean to, but Melinda and her baby have taken the whole afternoon. Now it's time for evening services."

"A widow, so young." Michelle looked at the frail, timid woman.

"Barney and Robbie both said they'd heard about the cave-in at the Dorada Rio mine two months ago. Several men were killed," Laura said. "She held on to her claim as long as she could. She'd been threatened several times, even though it had never paid out much. Her food was gone. She didn't have the time or strength to work the claim with a baby in her arms. She'd heard there were cabins up here, so when she finally ran, she came to Purgatory."

"I imagine there are terrible stories behind every one of the folks that come here." Jilly crossed her arms. "I can't imagine being so helpless. So at the mercy of the world."

Considering they'd ridden down a flume, thrown in with strangers, and now lived deep in the wilderness, it seemed like they *should* be able to imagine it, but Laura really couldn't.

Caleb left Melinda's side, and Gretel took over talking with her. Both of them standing with a baby held to their chest, rocking the way mothers holding babies all rocked. Gretel was able to get the woman talking about motherhood. Melinda even found a smile.

The evening service was starting soon, but Laura could tell by the determined glint in Caleb's eyes that he wanted to have their talk right now. Not put it off yet again.

"We'll let you two talk." Michelle turned away.

"I want to talk to all three of you." Caleb's voice, always kind, held a thread of iron that made Laura want to smile. He really was a strong man in spite of his kind and loving ways. Or maybe because of them.

Jilly narrowed her eyes. Michelle crossed her arms to match Jilly.

Laura scanned the group. The missionaries and settlement people were all accounted for. She spoke quietly so no one could overhear.

"We discussed it and decided we have to tell you what we found. I hope when you hear what we have to say, you'll understand our misgivings about it." Laura glanced at Jilly and Michelle, squared her shoulders, and went on even more quietly. "When I tell you this, don't yelp or jump or react in any way."

Caleb's brow furrowed. Surely his imagination was going wild.

Laura looked left and right, glanced behind her, then said, quiet as a breath, "We found gold."

Caleb reared back, but he quickly controlled himself, managing not to yelp. "Up here?"

Laura nodded. "There's a deposit of quartz back in those woods." She discreetly pointed to the thick stand of trees that framed the north side of the level stretch. "I went in the farthest to chop down trees, and there it was. It's a fine quality of gold." She barely moved her lips on the word. She was sure others could lip read well enough to get that one word, considering. "There's a lot of it. It has to belong to Zane, right?"

"Ummm . . ." was all Caleb managed to say.

Laura went on. "It seems like the kind of thing that could cause a lot of trouble. Bring on a . . . gold rush."

Caleb was nodding. She thought he was a little flushed. Maybe from trying not to yelp. Or did people with gold fever run an actual fever?

"It might upset and excite people, including the ones in our mission group." Good heavens. Laura tried to imagine what they'd do if Gretel went mad for gold.

"And it might draw in outsiders who might be willing to fight to get the"—she glanced around—"*you know*, so we decided to think about it for a while."

"And what did you decide?" Caleb scratched his head, clearly confused.

"We never decided anything. It's not ours. It's not these

folks', it's not anyone's but Zane's. He doesn't need it, but since when is need the basis for the madness that comes when there's a strike?" Laura shrugged. "We just don't know what to do."

"Give me a minute. Let me think. Let me pray."

CALEB LOOKED AT THE THREE WOMEN. Two who might soon be his sisters. One, much more important, might be his wife. He'd really never seen women like them before.

All he could think of was how honorable they were. They'd had secrets they'd felt hesitant to share, but they'd done it. He hadn't.

His secrets were different. But he felt a need to be honest with Laura, for sure, and with all of them, as they'd been honest with him.

He studied them. Beautiful, the three of them. Blond, delicate Laura, who thought marrying him might be a sin because it might pull him away from God's will.

Fiery, redheaded Jilly, who was opposed to marriage for a reason he, as a good pastor, should probably try to find out. Help her face what was bothering her, help her heal.

Dark, stunning Michelle. The strongest of the three, strong enough to be the natural leader of two very strong women.

All so brilliant that, if they'd wanted to, they might have been able to secretly mine for gold and make off with a fortune.

Caleb knew what was right. It bothered him deeply, but this was Zane's land, and any gold found on it was his. But

Zane was an honorable man, too. He didn't want to see these folks suffer. What might he decide?

And just handing out a load of gold to the families up here might be a very good way to get them at the least robbed, at the worst killed.

"I wondered . . ." Laura said hesitantly.

She was not usually a hesitant woman, so Caleb paid strict attention. "Yes?"

"We've seen three families leave here and one come. I fear that Janine and Lou didn't leave for any decent reason. But the others who left seemed to be moving on to a better life." Laura looked about her again. "What if we mined the gold, slowly and with Zane's permission, so each family that leaves could be given a small gift of gold to help them on their way."

"Or maybe we could give them some of the money we have. That would take gold out of the equation," Jilly said. "We could do it for a while until our money ran low. Or maybe replace our coins with the gold here."

Caleb wondered how much they had. He remembered a life where he'd done a good job of separating innocent people from their money. Now he looked at three very smart but very innocent women and wanted to protect them.

"If we did that, Parson." Michelle spoke slowly. No one interrupted her. "You could say it was a gift from our mission group. Do it discreetly. Give it to them after you've talked with the women and hopefully assured yourself they are on a steady path. Ask them not to tell their husbands until later. Maybe even weeks later, because they likely won't be leaving unless the man of the family straightens things out with his work, his drinking, and his gambling or wherever his weekly wages go."

Caleb wasn't a liar, but he certainly knew how to lie. He was good at it. "I won't ask these women to tell a lie. That could cause a rift in their marriage and do damage to their faith."

The sisters looked at him in that way they had of being quiet, not really seeing the world around them as they considered, added, and subtracted details. Probably multiplied and divided them, too. Probably ran their ideas through some Euclidean geometry tangle.

Finally, Michelle shrugged. "You're right about the lie. Keeping secrets could damage a marriage. As women who've been keeping secrets, we know how it holds us apart from others."

Caleb wondered how his secrets held him apart from his mission group and his church flock.

"Let's consider possible ways to handle it," Michelle went on. "My sisters and I have been praying for a week, and we don't feel God telling us a single thing. Maybe somehow we get Zane involved in giving money to the folks up here. Money coming from him might not raise questions. And he stands to make a fortune, so that might encourage him to be generous."

"Time is probably a good idea." Caleb ignored her mentioning a week. How much time might they need? A month? A year?

God, what am I supposed to do about this?

And he felt it. An itch, the tiniest possible itch, easily left unscratched, to find that gold, chisel it all out, and head for the hills.

Satan whispering in his ear.

Get thee behind me.

"From what I know of the folks at Purgatory, none of

196

them are leaving anytime soon." But three families had left already, so he knew nothing.

The sisters nodded and turned to go. Caleb caught Laura's arm. "You can do your thinking later. We need to talk."

MARGARET HEALED AND HID.

She'd quit leaving the room.

Edgar had figured out where she was and pounded on the door, shouting threats. But Sarah must have been thorough with the keys, and he'd yet to get a hatchet.

The oak door was solid and thick. It had aged until it was iron hard. Margaret doubted Edgar had the strength to chop through it, but she suspected his henchmen did. He hadn't resorted to that yet, and she could only think he liked making a prisoner of her, even if she had imposed the sentence on herself.

And while she healed and hid, her girls were being hunted. Margaret felt almost desperate to go to Edgar and demand to know what he had planned. He'd never tell her, but she needed to know.

Sarah came only late at night with a tray of food. Each time she brought enough for a full day and a bit more, in case she couldn't get back.

Margaret had no doubt Edgar would harm Sarah if he caught her going to or coming from the locked room.

So Margaret lived like a mouse in a fine hole with a nasty cat right outside.

She'd been so determined to stop being a coward. But Edgar was big, and she was small. She remembered that

Michelle had told her there was a gun in this room. She'd found it, seen it was loaded, then returned it to its hiding place. She didn't want to shoot Edgar. She couldn't bear the thought of it.

And then one night, very late, she heard the key turn in her door. Sarah came in and behind her was a man with two different colored eyes.

Margaret, heading for the door in case Sarah needed help carrying anything, stumbled to a halt. She looked at Sarah for signs of fear, of being forced at gun point to let one of Edgar's men in.

"Don't be afraid." The man held out several pieces of paper.

Sarah closed the door and quickly locked all three of them in.

"I have letters from your daughters, from Michelle, Jilly, and Laura. They are safe."

Was this a trick arranged by Edgar? Or had the girls been found and coerced?

"They are hiding in a very unexpected place. I hope and pray they can't be found. I know it won't be easy," the man said. "Has Beaumont harmed you?"

Margaret pressed her hand to her stomach. Still tender from Edgar's fists and his boot. There was a mirror in the room. She knew her cheek was bruised and swollen.

The man frowned. His brow furrowed into lines too deep for such a young man. He didn't approach her. Instead, he handed the notes to Sarah and stayed back.

Margaret took them with trembling hands and read each one quickly. Could she believe this? It was a very tall tale to be made up. No mention of where they were, but each girl included a small personal memory that no one else could possibly know.

The man talked quickly. "I'm a cowhand for a man near where your girls are. Your daughter Laura, the blond one, came to Zane's ranch and asked to buy milk cows."

He ran through the story, and Margaret felt herself begin to hope. When he finished with his having worked here before, his disgust for Edgar, and his admiration of her when she'd come out to talk to the men, she began to trust.

"If you're lying, then this is a made-up story, perhaps to get me to tell you the truth, but I don't know where my daughters are. Or if you're in league with Edgar, then he's gotten past the door and will soon be here. I'll trust you because I have very little choice."

"I've been out with the loggers for a half a day. I remember a few of them from when I worked here before. I told them how Edgar was treating you and, ma'am, I give you my word he will never harm you again. The foreman of your lumberjack crew knows who he can trust. And he knows which men are still loyal to your first husband."

"Mr. Dooley?" Margaret asked.

A smile flickered over the man's face. "It's Old Tom Harmon, ma'am. I reckon that was a test."

It had been a test. Margaret trusted even more at the sound of their longtime foreman's name.

"My name is Nick, Nick Ryder. I've talked with your daughters, and they are in a fine, good place. I'll tell you every word that passed between us to ease your mind. And I want you to know, Old Tom said he'll send twenty men in here to stand guard around you. In fact, five men are now stationed under your window, including Tom himself."

"How I would love to see Old Tom. My husband and I used to go out among the men often. Rough men but so hardworking and decent. Always kind to me, and they treated the girls as if seeing them was a better treat than Christmas gifts. But if they stand for me, Edgar will fire them. They'll be cut off from any income and sent away."

"If he fires them, then they'll have all the more time to stand guard around you. None of them will leave. I'll signal them, and we can let them in, then you can get out of this room and move about without fear."

Was it possible?

Margaret found herself trembling. "Where's Edgar now?"

"He's asleep, ma'am," Sarah whispered, looking scared for her mistress, for herself. For this man.

Nick gave Margaret a mean smile. Somehow, though, the mean wasn't aimed at her. It was all aimed at Edgar.

"Signal your men."

He went to the window, pushed it open, and called out, "Tom, are you there?"

"Yep, here and ready to help."

"I left the front door unlocked. Come up the flight of stairs you'll see right before you. We're on the second floor, and I'm looking to tell Mr. Beaumont that things are going to change."

Margaret went to Nick's side. "I'm here, Tom. Yes, please come up."

"Be right there, Miz Stiles, Nick." He stood in the dark, but the moon was bright, and she saw him tug on his cap. A gesture of respect he'd made to her many times. She leaned back inside, turned to Nick, and smiled.

He smiled that mean smile back. "Let's go wake Beaumont up and tell him the new rules of the house."

TWENTY-ONE

LAURA, LET'S STEP INTO THE CHURCH," Caleb said. It was about the only private place available, unless they took a long walk into the woods in some direction no one else happened to go.

Once they were inside the stark little four-walled, one-doored building with eight benches and an aisle between each pair of them, he led her all the way to the front, down the center, not unlike a bride walking down the aisle.

They'd considered a fireplace but decided, for simplicity's sake and to move quickly, they'd forgo warmth. For a few months in the winter, churchgoers would have to bundle up.

Jilly had created an altar out of split logs, rustic but so well made it was beautiful. Laura had used a red-hot iron to burn a cross on the wall behind the altar. He led her so they stood beneath the cross.

He faced her, took both her hands in his, and said, "I've given you time to do plenty of thinking."

For Laura that was no small job.

He held her hands tighter and pulled her so close their hands were the only thing keeping them apart. He leaned across that small space and kissed her. It was a chaste kiss.

"I want you to marry me, Laura. We will work out all that you need to do somehow. If you feel you must work for your family, then you will. If you find it in yourself to tell them you're not going into the lumber business, I'll support you in that decision. And I won't give up my calling from God, either. But that's not the reason I am asking."

"It's not?"

"No, I'm asking because through prayer and time, through getting to know you better, I have decided you are the woman God has prepared for me to share my life with."

She felt her heart melting.

"At first, that seemed outlandish, until I realized how God guided your path, my path. We are both far from where we started out. God set things in motion so we could find each other. Meet and come to know each other and care about each other. I've fallen in love with you, Laura. I want you to please do this humble man the great honor of saying you'll marry me."

Laura pulled one of her hands free and rested an open palm on his cheek. She looked at him for a long time, but not too long for Laura.

She leaned forward and kissed him. "You're the one who's done me a great honor, Caleb. I know my life is complicated, and you're taking on a lot when you ask to join your life with mine. Yes, Caleb. I love you, too. I would be delighted to accept your proposal."

He dropped her other hand and wrapped both of his arms around her waist and kissed her.

CALEB KISSED HER WITH ALL THE LOVE and longing, the hunger and the humility, a man could contain.

He was marrying a woman who fulfilled all the finest callings of a wife. As the woman did from Proverbs 31. *"Who can find a virtuous woman? For her price is far above rubies."*

Sure, that woman in Proverbs didn't blow things up, but the virtuous wife had work and did it with zeal. Just as Laura would.

Then he thought of another verse. *"Her children arise up, and call her blessed."*

Children with Laura.

He couldn't wait.

He broke off the kiss and said, "We should get married right away."

Laura nodded. He guessed she was more concerned with rescuing her ma than creating those children who'd call her blessed. But that would certainly come, too.

He wondered if he should insist she not work with explosives when she was with child.

That could be settled later.

"When do you want to marry?" he asked.

"D-do we need to find a preacher?"

"Absolutely not. I'll perform the ceremony. We'll need witnesses, but me speaking the vows is completely legal."

"Then how about we get married right now?"

He smiled. She smiled right back. She might be thinking of more than just her ma and her lumber dynasty after all. He sure hoped so.

"Let's go invite everyone out there to a wedding," he said.

"Oh, Caleb, wait."

"I don't want to wait." He grabbed her hand and started towing her to the church door.

She laughed and dragged him to a stop. "But you said you had secrets just as I did, and that there shouldn't be secrets between married people."

He froze. Caleb wanted Laura, but he wanted to keep his own secrets.

She thought *she* struggled with the decision? She knew not a fraction of what he hid. And if he told her, she would distrust him. She might tell the mission group, and they would distrust him. All he'd left behind might catch right up to him.

But her secrets were here and now. Her truth had to come out, or he couldn't be what she needed in a husband. His secrets, on the other hand, were best kept dead and buried.

He'd worked it all out and just could not risk telling her of his past. He'd told her he had secrets, so would she accept that he didn't want to talk about them? This woman who'd proposed a week after they'd met? Or had it been sooner? He was losing track. It'd been really fast.

But she wanted to know.

"Um . . . my secrets are . . . are a-about when I wasn't a Christian. I have left that behind me. I will tell you, but it's something that shames me greatly. I wish we didn't have to speak of it except for me to say I'm not that reckless, worthless young man anymore." He faced her fully.

He saw her kindness. Her willingness to listen, understand, and not hold his past against him.

"I saw my mother marry a man who kept his true character from her. Who lied and cheated with no intention of being honorable or keeping his vows. I've been so trusting with you, Caleb, and I find myself still trusting you. But I think I should know all about you."

He nodded. "I spent some time in prison. I committed crimes."

Laura gasped.

"I found God in that jail. I changed my life. You probably shouldn't marry me quite so fast, but I do swear to you that my past doesn't affect who I am today."

"I can't quite see you as a man to distrust."

"We can postpone any wedding plans for as long as it takes for you to know everything. But I don't want to speak of it here. I'd want to be sure of privacy."

"So no one else will hear of your past?"

His shoulders slumped. "It got between me and those I tried to minister to back in Savannah. I'd hoped to leave the past behind out here."

Laura was silent as she looked at him. At last she said, "I trust you, Caleb. I feel God leading us to marry, and I want it to be here and now."

Her kindness remained. He saw only openness and trust. She was a woman who'd made her choice and intended to live with it.

She said, "Let's go invite everyone out there to a wedding."

"DEARLY BELOVED," Caleb began.

Michelle whispered to Jilly, "'Love' on such a short ac-quaintance? I doubt it."

Laura ignored her. She stood facing Caleb, he being the parson as well as the groom.

Caleb grinned in reaction, and then he ignored Michelle and went on, "We are gathered here today in the presence of these witnesses to join . . . uh . . . this woman and I."

"Those aren't the right words." Jilly hissed more than whispered.

"It's this woman and me." Michelle had always been fussy about grammar.

"What's important isn't the exact words," Caleb said patiently. "What's important is two people making sincerely spoken vows before God and man. With a parson and witnesses to declare it to have happened."

"That's important, no doubt about it." Jilly wasn't hissing now. "But it's important that it's legal, too."

"It's legal." Laura saw Caleb's desperate fight for patience.

"I'm making up a marriage certificate. A bunch of us are going to sign it." Michelle stood past Jilly, who was closest to Laura. That probably made Jilly the maid of honor.

"I'm not even sure a marriage certificate has any standing in California. I'm not sure of this state's rules," Caleb said. "But our vows are before God, and that makes them holy, more important than some certificate."

Michelle hadn't been that happy about the sudden marriage. No . . . *unhappy* wasn't exactly fair, more like, she had severe misgivings. So she'd refused to stand closest. That made her a bridesmaid and a poor one. But Jilly was closest, so it was her foot Laura stomped on.

A flicker of impatience replaced the humor in Caleb's hazel eyes. Laura didn't want a grouchy bridegroom. Nor grouchy bridesmaids. She was starting to get grouchy herself.

"Do you Laura Stiles . . ."

Jilly hissed. Caleb flinched. Laura glanced to see if the

congregation was listening. They most certainly were. They seemed fascinated. She suspected Caleb hadn't meant to say Laura's last name out loud in front of everyone. But he was probably required to. No sense drawing everyone's attention to it. The whole settlement sat on the benches, except for the woman who'd come today. She'd skittered back to her cabin with her baby as soon as she was finished eating. A knock on the door had gotten no response.

"Uh, do you take this man—me—to be your lawfully wedded husband, to have and to hold from this day forward?"

He went into some pretty big vows. Sickness and health. Laura sure hoped he didn't get sick. Richer or poorer. And she had no intention of being poor, the present situation where she slept on the ground and had a single change of clothes notwithstanding. So those were easy vows to make since they didn't apply to her. For better or for worse set her to wondering just what secrets he was keeping from her. Why had he gone to prison? Why wouldn't he tell her if the reason wasn't pretty darned worse? She probably should have insisted. . . .

Jilly jabbed her between the shoulder blades. "Say 'I do,' idiot."

"I do." And she didn't like being called an idiot, which was exactly why Jilly had done it.

"And do I, Caleb Tillman . . ."

Michelle muttered to herself as Caleb went on with his vows.

Laura was starting to regret inviting the rest of the mission group and settlement to the wedding. It was nothing she was proud of. She'd been to plenty of big weddings in San Francisco. Fancy. Fine gowns, flowers everywhere. Bridesmaids who were happy to stand witness to the ceremony. Delicious feasts afterward.

And here she stood in a tattered, filthy servants dress. Better than her trousers but only just. She should have at least taken the time to pick a few of the spring flowers blooming. But she hadn't thought of it until now, and she guessed Caleb would object to pausing his vow speaking so she could pick posies.

Caleb finished up his vows, and Laura smiled at him. He noticed her lips and stared a bit too long. By the time he managed to look into her eyes, he'd seemed to cheer up.

He began to speak about commitment and love and spiritual union. She tried to pay attention, but she kept stumbling over that long look at her lips. It made her think of the night to come.

She always slept between Jilly and Michelle. Which side would Caleb sleep on? Between her and Jilly? Or between her and Michelle?

Which of course was nonsense. They'd go off and sleep together. It gave her a chill to think of it. A warm chill, granted.

Where would they go?

The Steinmeyers and little Willa slept in the wagon. The church didn't seem right.

Maybe they could sleep in one of those ramshackle cabins.

And that didn't bear thinking about so she didn't.

"I now pronounce us . . . uh, I and wife."

"*Me*," Michelle said dryly. "And it's wife and me."

"It's man and wife." Jilly jabbed Laura between the shoulder blades again. "Make him say it right, or I'm not signing."

"I'll be glad to sign in your stead," Gretel said from where she sat in the front row. "I remember my own wedding, and this is just as romantic."

Jilly snorted.

"I now pronounce us man and wife and two sisters." Caleb was growling by the end. He was realizing, Laura feared, that in some ways he really had married all three of them. Or at least he'd joined the family. He was in no way married to anyone but her—and that was that.

"You may kiss the bride." Caleb grinned and did just that.

Laura wondered if a ramshackle cabin might be acceptable because she wanted him to kiss her again and for much longer. And she didn't like the idea of a bunch of cranky witnesses to *that*.

"Are we done? I've got a marriage certificate to write up." Michelle headed for the door to the church and the wagon, where she'd stored her paper.

"We are most definitely done." Caleb offered Laura his arm very formally and escorted her to the front bench of the church. She sat beside Gretel and baby Willa. Rick scooted over to make room. There wasn't room for Jilly, so she sat behind Laura. Laura was going to make a fuss if Jilly poked her between the shoulder blades again.

Caleb proceeded with the evening singing. Laura decided the songs were a fit ending to the wedding.

Michelle came in with a marriage certificate she'd written out with an ink pen in very elaborate, swirly handwriting. And every adult in the room signed it . . . except the people who couldn't sign their names, which turned out to be most everyone.

Clara shyly offered to make her mark and, thinking that meant she could sign her name, they watched while she made a rather uneven X on the page.

In California that was most likely legal. Though they'd need a witness to the witness, and that seemed complicated.

Michelle muttered that they needed to teach their congregation to read.

An idea with merit. Laura thought they should probably make a list.

And their teachers had left the group and gone to live on a ranch. If Sally Jo was possibly going to end up married within the month, Laura wondered if the Hogan sisters might find men there, too. The female shortage sounded dire.

TWENTY-TWO

CALEB HAD TO ADMIT he was looking forward to the wedding night. It might have inspired him to sing with a great deal of . . . energy.

When he'd stood at the door to shake everyone's hand and sign Michelle's marriage certificate, he'd had Laura stand with him. The proper place for his wife, by his side.

She seemed to enjoy it, or at least she kept stealing glances at him and smiling.

Maybe she was looking forward to the wedding night, too.

The last person left. Except Michelle and Jilly were standing there watching them.

"Laura, would it be all right for us to have a few moments alone?" Caleb gave the sisters a meaningful look.

It meant "go away," but apparently, they didn't communicate well nonverbally.

"Michelle, Jilly, yes, Caleb and I would like to spend time

alone together now." Laura gave them a meaningful look, too. When they didn't move, she shoved Jilly. "Go on. I mean it."

Caleb's look, well, he'd meant it, too. But he was glad the shoving was left up to Laura. He'd have to be in the family a long time before he could start shoving her sisters around.

Which really hit him hard. "You're my sisters now."

It lifted his spirits. "I'm the only one of my parents' children who lived to adulthood."

Laura slid her arm around Caleb's shoulders. "Our parents lost babies, too. It's a terrible thing to lose family."

"I had two little sisters and a brother. I was the eldest. They died in a house fire the year I turned twelve. I still can't think of it without pain. I like the idea of joining a family, having sisters. And your mama. I hope I can be a good enough husband to Laura that your mama will want to claim me as a son."

Laura hugged him.

Instead of scowls, Jilly and Michelle looked sympathetic, even kind.

It was all true, Caleb hadn't lied. But he knew people well. Knew how to handle them. And he'd manipulated them to gain their acceptance.

Was that a sin? It wasn't like he was going to swindle them out of their money.

"Of course you'd like to be alone. I guess we might as well turn in," Jilly said to Michelle.

They looked at the little pile of blankets they used every night on the hard ground. Michelle went over and brought one to Laura and Caleb.

She gave Laura a hug and, after a long hesitation, kissed Caleb on the cheek. "Welcome to the family, brother. I suppose our papa would have been delighted to finally get a son. Mama, well, you'll have to win her over, but you seem to have a talent for that."

Caleb wondered if he'd lost his knack for manipulation because Michelle's direct look didn't seem all that convinced.

Jilly hugged Laura, then patted Caleb on the shoulder, perhaps just a bit too firmly, and walked away with Michelle. All fifteen steps to the wagon to sleep on the ground. Of late, with the good weather and the dwindling of their supplies, Rick and Gretel had taken to sleeping in the wagon bed.

Caleb said to Laura. "It seems we need a place to stay. It doesn't seem right to use the church as a home. And it doesn't seem right to build a house for the parson that is nicer than the ones his congregation lives in."

He took her hand and raised it to his lips. "There are several empty shanties. It embarrasses me to offer you such a poor place to stay." He looked into her eyes, felt the worry lines across his forehead. Tried to tell if she was offended or sad or . . .

"I think . . . well . . . it would . . . now that you say it . . . we should all move into those shanties. There are several standing empty. We can move in understanding that if someone comes, we have to give them the shelter. We can keep making repairs to the buildings. We haven't yet repaired the ones no one lives in. I think we should let these people know we don't consider ourselves too good to live as they live."

Nodding, Caleb clasped her hand tightly. "That's a fine notion. Let's always make sure one cabin remains empty. There are three of them occupied now, and seven more are empty. Take out the one that has collapsed and the two with no roof. But maybe that's me speaking from a place of wanting too much. There might be people who would welcome a cabin even without a roof over their heads."

"We can move into the farthest one for tonight. We need a place to talk, to get to know each other better. And if Rick and Gretel would welcome the shelter for their baby, then they can have one of the others with a roof. And my sisters can get up off the rocky ground, too. Tomorrow we'll put a roof on two more cabins, and we'll have plenty of room for anyone else who shows up."

No one had gone to bed yet. The sun was setting, but it was a lovely spring night. They'd soon hunt their beds but not yet.

"Will the settlement folks mind?" he asked. "Will they think we are taking cabins that should be left for those seeking shelter?"

Laura studied Caleb, and he studied her. He really was looking forward to knowing her better.

Finally, Laura said, "Let's ask them."

"We'll see if we can repair the one that has collapsed." Caleb studied the tangle of fallen timbers. "We could each have a cabin with a few to spare. Why haven't I thought of this before?"

"I suppose because necessity is the mother of invention."

"I've heard that one. Shakespeare maybe?"

Laura smiled. "Him too. It's an old saying. I think Plato said it first, though not in that exact form."

Shaking his head, Caleb said, "My wife quotes Plato."

"Let's go talk to your congregation. Then we can move into a cabin."

Hand in hand, they went to make their first pastoral visitation as man and wife.

CALEB PICKED THE CABIN at the far end of Purgatory. He really wished they'd change the name of this place.

The two roofless cabins were between them and the Steinmeyers. Next was the collapsed cabin and then the folks from the settlement.

When Laura proposed fixing the roofs on the two cabins, Jilly got all excited. She and Michelle now slept in the wagon bed with plans to take over a real structure tomorrow.

Caleb wanted that bit of privacy, and he led his beautiful blushing bride into a complete hovel.

No furniture. No back door. No windows. Dirt and stone floors. There was certainly no food or clothing. They did have Laura's blanket and satchel. Caleb had a satchel, too, and his own blanket, plus his Bible and a few things more.

All stacked on the floor beside the wall.

"Happy honeymoon, huh?" He smiled at her. She blushed.

"Every time I've kissed you," he said quietly, pulling her close, "I've had to stop long before I was done. Not this time."

He lowered his head and kissed her with all the longing he'd been feeling since the first time he'd looked into her eyes on that station platform. Even then, that first moment, there'd been a strong pull between them. Or maybe it had only been him.

Now he had her to himself, and all the laws of God and man approved of the closeness.

He paused from the kiss and found their blankets. He threw them on the floor, wondering about cutting grass to cushion their primitive bed. Not tonight, but maybe he could do that by tomorrow night.

He drew her down onto the blanket and pulled her into

his arms. Between kisses, he said, "I love you, Laura. I'm so happy to be married to you."

And the kiss lasted until it turned into something far more intimate.

THE GUNSHOT JERKED CALEB AWAKE.

Someone screamed.

Caleb was on his feet, dragging on his trousers under his nightshirt. Laura fumbled to straighten her dress, glad for once that she'd been forced to sleep fully clothed since running away.

They were both outside, barefoot, within seconds of the scream.

Another gunshot fired from inside the cabin that Melinda, the newest woman in the settlement, had chosen. Her baby howled, and a man shouted at Melinda to shut up. They heard the dull thud of fists as they ran. A wild, raging laugh followed the thuds.

Caleb wrenched open the cabin door so hard it ripped off and landed flat on the ground. Laura dodged the flying door.

"Billy, no!" Melinda cried.

Caleb charged in and grabbed Billy just as he raised a fist, ready to slam it into Melinda's already bruised face.

About to run inside, Laura backed away quickly as Caleb yanked the violent man outside and punched him right in the nose.

Then Rick was there, dressed only in a nightshirt. He clawed at Billy's gun arm. The pistol flew out of Billy's grip, and Rick was cast aside like wash water.

Caleb kicked the gun away, and it slid right toward Michelle, just as she and Jilly came running up. Michelle picked up the gun and hid it in the folds of her skirt.

"Stay back," Caleb snapped.

It worked on everyone but Billy. He was huge, not fat but tall and heavily muscled. A wild black beard and shaggy hair nearly covered his face until he looked more beast than man.

Growling in the dark, he swung at Caleb. Ducking, Caleb punched the man in the stomach.

Melinda's screams and the baby's cries added to the chaos.

Billy shoved Caleb hard enough he landed on his backside. He kicked Caleb's belly, but Caleb was rolling and the kick didn't land hard. Caleb leapt to his feet with catlike grace.

Billy swung a massive fist that caught Caleb on the chin.

Rick threw himself against the man, nearly dangling from one heavily muscled arm.

With a savage roar, Billy swung his arm and flung Rick off. Caleb dove at him, sending the big man stumbling backward, then Caleb landed another blow and another. A fast, skillful, painful battering of the man's face while Rick got back ahold of that one arm, helping to keep Billy off balance.

After several minutes of the three grappling, Caleb landing punches with machinelike power, Billy collapsed in a heap on the ground. With one last ugly groan of pain, he passed out cold. Silent at last.

Every person in the settlement was out watching, men, women and children.

Melinda staggered out of her shanty, her baby in one arm, the other clinging to the doorway to hold herself up.

Caleb rushed to her side. "Are you all right? Do you need doctoring?"

Shaking her head, she wept and threw her free arm around Caleb. He saw Jilly produce a kerchief from the pocket of her work-worn servants dress and hand it to Laura, then gesture at Caleb's bleeding lip.

"Who is he? Is he your husband? You said you were a widow?" Caleb asked.

Melinda nodded. Which wasn't really an answer. Then she said, "I am a widow. This isn't my husband. He's been coming around since my baby was born. At first, I thought he cared for me. He gave me hope we wouldn't starve. Then he showed this ugly side. I ran off because I knew one of these times he'd kill me."

Laura came close and dabbed gently at the crimson trickling down his chin. He looked at her over Melinda's shoulder and said, "Melinda, here is Laura, my wife. She'll help you."

He settled his hands gently on Melinda's shoulders and eased her away from him. "Let me go get something cool to put on your bruises." He made a neat shift, and Melinda's arms wrapped around Laura's neck without Melinda seeming to notice the change.

Caleb looked down at Billy. He glanced sideways to look at the welt rising on Rick's forehead. "You going to be okay?"

Rick's dark hair hung in his eyes, and his skin had a sheen of sweat. He was breathing hard, but he waved a shaky hand. "I don't get into fights as a rule. Not used to the pounding. But *ja*, I'll be fine."

Michelle thrust a damp cloth in Caleb's hands. Then a second one. "One for you. One for Melinda. I've got one for Rick, too."

She gave Billy a wide berth and handed the cloth to Rick. Gretel was by his side, holding him, all her English language lessons forgotten. "Heinrich, *bist du verletzt, meine liebe?*"

"Hush, Gretel. Hush. No, I'm not hurt. I'm fine, little mama." Rick patted her hand.

Willa must not have awakened because their cabin door stood open, and no crying came from within.

Gretel, her red hair in wild disarray, supported Rick, though he seemed to be holding up. His pin-straight dark hair, always messy, was as flyaway as Gretel's.

Gretel took the damp cloth from Caleb, paused to study Caleb's face for a moment, then went back to tending her husband.

The man on the ground groaned and shifted a bit. His hand came to his eye, which was swelling rapidly. "Whaa happened?"

Everyone stepped back from Billy. Melinda rushed for her cabin. Laura right behind her. When Melinda was inside, Laura turned in the doorway, with a fierce scowl on her face, standing guard so Billy couldn't get in.

"Rick, keep an eye on him. Everyone watch him." Caleb went down on one knee beside the man, then pressed the cloth he'd been given to the lump rising on Billy's eye.

The cloth must have soothed Billy a little because he relaxed, and the next thing Caleb heard was a snore.

He'd fallen asleep. Caleb leaned close enough to get the foul stench of whiskey on Billy's breath. And just what were they supposed to do when violent Billy woke up and wanted to teach poor Melinda a lesson? Wanted to punish her for running off?

"I think we're going to have to post a guard," Caleb said. "There's nowhere to lock him up, and I don't want him waking up and causing trouble before one of us can stop him." Caleb looked at Laura. His wedding night had been bliss until it ended in a fistfight. He wanted nothing more than to return to his cabin and his wonderful new wife.

With a sigh, he said, "I'll take the first watch."

Rick nodded, and Gretel helped him toward the cabin they'd moved into. He did his best to stand up straight, but he moved carefully, and Caleb wondered if he might have cracked ribs, bruised ribs at the least. Caleb had a few of those himself.

Melinda's baby girl quit sobbing. Melinda, too.

Laura came from the doorway and rested a hand on Caleb's shoulder. He met her gaze. She gave him a rueful smile.

"Not the best wedding night ever." She leaned in and kissed him lightly.

"Yes, it was," he said.

She blushed and smiled. "With a very memorable ending."

Caleb didn't think he'd have trouble remembering his wedding night.

"I think I'll stay up with you while you guard the prisoner."

Caleb slid both arms up and urged her to sit down beside him, where they could rest their backs on a downed log. With his arms round her waist, he pulled her close for a deeper kiss. "I'd love the company."

Jilly and Michelle returned to the wagon. The settlement folks, who still milled around, went into their cabins, though Melinda's no longer had a door.

The folks all settled down. Billy kept snoring. Laura and Caleb sat together on the ground far enough away to talk without bothering anyone but close enough to leap into action should Billy wake up with more mayhem on his mind.

"Try to sleep, Laura." Caleb pulled her around and lifted her onto his lap. He couldn't hold her like this for long. He'd lose all the feeling in his arms and legs. But for now, he wanted her close. "No sense in all of us being exhausted tomorrow."

"I have an idea." She hopped up, dashed into their shanty, and came out with two blankets. She moved to a slightly more distant spot, spread one blanket on the ground next to a boulder, and said, "Sit here, you can lean back against this rock."

"An idea with merit."

She doubled the blanket, and it cushioned the ground a bit, then he settled in, and she climbed right back into his arms and pulled the second blanket around both of them.

"I don't think you can fall asleep. You'd tip over and wake up. But at least you can be a bit more comfortable. Wake me if he comes around. I'm not much help fighting him, but I can stand between him and Melinda . . . all the while hoping you keep him from getting too close."

She ran a hand up and down his left arm, the one under her knees. "You're a strong man, Caleb. I didn't expect a parson to have such good fighting skills."

"Well, as I said earlier, I was something of a . . . trouble-maker before I put my soul into God's keeping."

"You mentioned prison."

"I'm ashamed of who I was back then."

She rubbed his arm again. "You'll have to tell me tales of your misspent youth sometime, Caleb. I won't judge you for it."

She might. The judge certainly had.

He kissed her on the top of her head, then pressed her face against his chest. "Try and sleep."

It wasn't long before she obliged.

The gentle rise and fall of her chest as she breathed evenly charmed him until he could barely leave her alone.

He watched her sleep. Her eyes closed. Her dark blond lashes so long they rested on her cheeks below her eyes.

His wife. It was hard to believe he was married to this beautiful, brilliant, sweet woman.

He had to tell her about his past. But did she have to know every detail? He'd left all his sins far behind. The Steinmeyers had been new to the community. And the Hogan sisters couldn't know; they'd been too good to him to have any doubts. His secret was safe.

But a man should be fully honest with his wife.

God, guide me.

He should tell her, wake her up right now and tell her everything. Was that a message from God in an answer to his prayer? He should tell her he'd led a dishonorable life, one far too much like the stepfather she hated and, worse, feared.

Yes, he'd gone to prison for his crimes, but there were plenty of crimes that had gone unpunished.

Caleb had prayed, and he felt God guiding him to reveal all his secrets. As she slept in his arms, the purity of it, the sweetness . . . it was all too much. He didn't want to ruin it. He'd tell her soon, but maybe he'd wait until after he began to believe she wouldn't turn away from him. Yes, then he'd tell her about his sordid past.

He'd do it as soon as he knew he could count on her to stick with him no matter what.

And in the meantime, no one here knew anything about his past, and they never would.

TWENTY-THREE

WHERE'S MY WIFE? Melinda, you get out here!"
Caleb had stepped into the woods for a moment of necessity and was just returning when
he heard Billy roaring. Caleb ran, hoping to arrive before
someone else stood between Billy and Melinda.

He emerged from the woods to see Billy sitting on the
ground and Laura standing in Melinda's doorway.

Throwing herself into the breach.

Rick dashed out of his cabin.

Jilly and Michelle were already up, just done hanging a
cross over the church's sturdy front door. It was the final
thing. Now they could declare it finished.

They dropped their tools and came running.

Caleb nearly skidded into Laura when he reached her side.
Billy hadn't managed to get to his feet yet.

"Melinda, you're mine. You get out here and bring my
baby."

"We aren't married, Billy Nash, and this isn't your baby."

Melinda sounded strong and fierce. Probably easier with people blocking the violent man.

Billy Nash? Caleb barely heard her after that. His ears went fuzzy, and the world spun just a bit. He gripped the edge of the door to keep from toppling over.

He studied the man on the ground. Caleb had known a Bill Nash. He was as big as this man, but he cut a sharp figure. Tidy, clean, sober, quick with a smile, and, above all, charming.

This man, under the riotous hair and thick beard . . . it couldn't be.

"You made the b-baby cr-cry with your yellin'. I'm done with you."

The man shook his head as a wet dog might. He rolled onto his hands and knees, then stood, staggering a bit. He caught his balance, then looked at Caleb. Except not at Caleb, he was looking beyond to Melinda, who huddled behind Caleb and Laura. The baby let out a cry, much stronger sounding than when Melinda had arrived.

One by one, the others emerged from their shabby homes. The settlement men had gone to work.

"You're not running off from me."

"I'll not let you hit me anymore, Billy. I've tried to get you to stop. I tried to learn to live with it, but last time, you only missed the baby through sheer luck, and I came to my senses. I'll not raise my baby girl in your presence. I'm done with you. I'm going to live up here, and well, I think I'll study on being a Christian and maybe throw in with these folks and just be a missionary. Baby Hannah and I will be fine with these folks. You go on away from here."

Caleb listened to his newest volunteer and wondered

what the rules were about new members. With the Hogan sisters leaving and a new mom and baby, they were back to full numbers—since apparently babies counted. But at this rate, they'd soon have more need of a nursery than a school.

Billy was unsteady, but he lowered his head like an angry bull and advanced toward Melinda. Rick came to stand by the door, Laura between him and Caleb.

"Laura," Caleb said quietly, "please step out of the way. This is men's business."

Laura didn't move.

Caleb hated to draw attention to himself, just in case under that uncivilized fur this was the man Caleb had known, but it had to be done to protect Laura.

He raised his voice for Billy's benefit. "If we were dealing with a decent man, I'd keep you here, Laura, because a *real* man would never hit a woman. But Billy has shown no hesitation about such a thing."

Billy swung his shaggy head in Caleb's direction and truly looked at him for the first time. Caleb's stomach twisted when Billy's eyes lit up.

"Cal Tillman, as I live and breathe. Well, I'll be horn-swoggled. You've managed to stay out of prison this time? Never figured you could resist swindling people. You were too good at charming the ladies."

LAURA'S INDRAWN BREATH was almost an inverted scream.

She turned to look at Caleb. Cal. Cal Tillman. All she could say was "Charming the ladies?"

She saw the expression on good old Cal's face and knew this awful, filthy, dangerous man spoke the truth.

"I-I . . . w-we . . . that is . . . you're a swindler?" Laura shook her head. "B-but you're a parson. We've spoken of our faith."

It was tempting to turn toward the shack and take a few moments to pound her head on the doorframe. It might clear her thoughts.

On second thought, maybe she should pound Caleb's head on the doorframe.

"I was going to tell you, Laura." Caleb spoke quietly, but they were all close together. No one missed a single syllable.

"*Was ist* prison?" Gretel asked her husband.

"*Gefängnis.*"

Gretel gave Caleb a frightened look. "*Komme weg*, Heinrich. Come away."

"*Nein*, Gretel."

Gretel tucked Willa close and hurried into her cabin.

Into the silence, Michelle said with vicious sarcasm, "So what were you in for, Parson Tillman?"

Billy laughed. "Didn't tell 'em, huh? I thought they might be in it with you. Instead, you've got another swindle runnin'. Not much money up here, but Bible thumpin' can be good money. Practicing on these folks till you get the right act going?"

Billy looked at Laura. "He was in prison, same as me, for cheating folks out of their money. We were a team and mighty slick. Finally got caught. He got out and ran off before we could team up again."

She'd married a man who was just as good a liar . . . no, a better liar than Edgar. A man who swindled people for money.

"For the love of money is the root of all evil."

"Bill, there is good in you. I know it." Caleb sounded the same. His voice, his sincerity. His kindness. "I know you were raised in a home of faith. Think of your mother. Think how this hurts her, still."

"My ma is dead. Don't you speak of her." Bill's laughter was gone, replaced by rage. His huge fists clenched, and Laura saw bared teeth in the midst of his wild beard. She backed away so both Caleb and Rick were in front of her.

"I'm sorry to hear that. I really am. I know you always cared for her. She was a good woman. Remember we went to visit her once, in that little house in Atlanta? She didn't put up with much of our oily charm, remember? A wise woman. I'll bet she's looking down from heaven right now, praying for you. Hoping to be with you again someday."

Laura thought Caleb sounded sincere, but then a good swindler was talented at making those around him believe every word. Or maybe he was sincere. How could she ever be sure?

"And I am here, with these people, to give, not receive. I have no ugly motive like you're trying to say I do." Caleb squared his shoulders and stood solidly near the doorway. "And I won't let you touch Melinda again. If you're not willing to talk, to pray with me, then you'll have to leave. Melinda's staying. I could always beat you, Bill, despite your size, and you know it. And you're in worse shape than when we were locked away together. You won't win a fight with me."

Bill fell silent. He glared at Caleb. Laura watched him. Sure he wasn't capable of anything but a vicious reply. Then she saw him . . . She couldn't quite describe it.

Collect himself might be about right.

He was filthy, long unbathed, and unshaven. She could smell him from where she stood. But for all that, he stood straighter. His expression, beneath all that hair, turned calm. As she watched him transform, her only thought was *It's a lie*. He was trying to don his old swindler persona.

If he was dressed well and clean. If he'd shaved and combed his hair. And if he hadn't behaved like a drunken brute up to this moment, she suspected they'd all believe it.

Just like she believed Caleb.

Believed him enough to marry him.

With no idea what to do, all she knew was that she needed space. She had to get away from Caleb and think. She stepped fully into the shack. She turned to Melinda, who stood cowering, her baby in her arms.

"Come out," Laura said loudly. "He won't touch you. Come and eat breakfast. For all the madness going on, it's still breakfast time, and I'll help you make it. Your Billy is trying to pretend like he's a decent man."

Laura glanced outside. Caleb and Rick stood shoulder to shoulder. Beyond them, she saw Billy's eyes narrow. He'd taken her shot right to his pride. He had no friends in this settlement, and if he wanted to pretend he was changing, turning decent, he'd find an audience to his falsehoods that was hard to convince, Laura most of all.

Walking out of here with Melinda would be a fine test. Let him prove he wasn't going to put his hands on her, when he had to be sorely tempted to do just that.

Melinda let Laura draw her forward.

Laura touched Caleb's shoulder. "Let us pass, please. Look at how he's trying to act like he's not evil. Let's see how long the performance lasts."

Melinda, either because she had no backbone at all and obeyed whoever gave her orders, or because she was trying to be brave, Laura couldn't say which, came along. They walked toward the fire. By the time they got there, Gretel had come, probably circling around behind the cabin to stay well away from Billy and maybe Caleb, too. The three of them, Melinda, Gretel, and Laura, built up the fire and got potatoes on to fry. They'd add shaved pieces of venison to make hash.

The voices from the taut exchange between Caleb and Billy, with Rick there as a witness, went on but low enough Laura couldn't make out the words.

Michelle and Jilly passed Laura. Michelle laid one hand on Laura's shoulder and said, "We'll talk later."

Her sisters went back to pick up the tools they'd dropped by the church. They had planned to fix up the newly occupied cabins, too. But there was trouble near the cabins. That work would wait until later.

"Eggs would really make this better." Laura stirred the potatoes in their large cast-iron skillet, an odd pan they called a spider, with three long legs, so it would stand on its own over the campfire.

"Eggs?" Gretel said haltingly.

"Yes, eggs. What is the German word for *eggs*?"

Gretel seemed to be searching inside her head. "*Eier ist* eggs. *Ja*, eggs *wurde be gut. Englisch ist hart.*"

"It just takes practice. I'm sorry we haven't talked more, Gretel. I could work with you to learn English." Rounding up Caleb to marry her had been Laura's main focus. Now avoiding him, she'd have plenty of spare time.

Gretel gave her a confused look, and maybe she didn't understand what Laura said.

Willa yelped and began to cry with some serious anger. Gretel picked her up from where she lay on the blanket and took a clean diaper from a short stack. They washed diapers daily to maintain a supply. Greta took Willa into the church to change her.

Was Gretel confused because she didn't understand? Or was she confused that a brand-new wife who'd just discovered her husband had been in prison wasn't running into the woods screaming?

Laura hadn't had time to tell anyone Caleb had warned her. Not enough, not what his crimes were, but she'd known he had a past.

Laura was all too tempted to start running, so she didn't blame Gretel if she was wondering.

TWENTY-FOUR

H OW'D YOU END UP LIKE THIS, BILL?" Caleb sat on a log, with the settlement cabins between where he sat and the mission church.

He didn't have any hope that drawing Bill away from everyone would keep Caleb's past a secret. That was out now. But he saw the calculating look in Bill's eyes and knew he would set out to lie and cheat and charm his way into acceptance.

Bill was good at it. But the beard, wild hair, and tattered, filthy clothes put him at a deep disadvantage.

He gave Caleb a sheepish grin. "I got out of prison and heard tell of gold. I headed west, threw in with a wagon train, lied my way into being in charge of it, got paid well for it."

"You don't know anything about wagon trains."

Bill tipped his head and smirked. "They didn't know that until we were well on the trail. I figured, How hard could it be? Follow a trail a few thousand people had already followed."

Since Caleb didn't know much about leading a wagon train, he couldn't comment.

"Things went bad soon enough, but we were on our way, and I had their money in hand. I didn't know what I was doing, but none of them knew what I was supposed to be doing, either. People don't make a habit of going on wagon trains. Any troubles that came up we just mucked our way through. I about had a fight on my hands a few times, but we made it to California."

"And did you ever find gold?"

"I never even looked. I found folks to swindle instead. Took a liking to Melinda. A young widow-lady who was in a terrible way."

"So you found a desperate, hungry, beautiful woman and took a liking to yelling, threatening, and giving her a beating."

"Aw, Cal, she's worthless. Fussy, nagging woman."

"If that's so, then why did you come after her? You should've been well rid of her."

Fire flashed in Bill's eyes. This had never been there before, or not much of it. Caleb had hoped he could talk to Bill. Reason with him at least, share his faith at best. There'd always been carefully concealed evil in Bill, but never like this. Now there was a touch of madness.

Caleb decided he had to be clear, keep things simple. "You're not welcome here. You're leaving, and Melinda and the baby are staying. Just because I'm a parson now, doesn't mean I'll stand by wringing my hands and praying for holy intervention when a man is hitting a woman."

"I'm leaving all right, but Melinda goes with me. I keep what's mine."

"If you wanted her to be yours, you should have married her. There's a lot of talk in marriage vows about women obeying, women submitting, but the vows God asks of a husband are harder, more demanding. A husband is to love his wife as Christ loves the Church."

"Don't start talking Bible to me, Caleb." He rose. "I say she's mine, and she goes with me."

Caleb rose too. They faced each other. Caleb knew with a sick twist to his belly that he was going to have to settle this with his fists, and since he'd already knocked Bill cold once, even a fistfight wouldn't solve it. He'd just come around and start in making demands again.

Caleb knew one thing: God expected him to protect Melinda from abuse.

Quick as a rattler, Bill grabbed the front of Caleb's shirt with his massive left hand, lifted him to his toes, and cocked his right fist.

Caleb grabbed Bill's fist before he could throw it. Suddenly, Bill's face contorted. Etched in pain.

Caleb released Bill's fist. "What is it?"

Bill didn't answer, just stood rigid. Slowly, he released Caleb.

Caleb lowered until his feet were flat on the ground.

Bill's fist opened, dropped. The look of pain faded until Bill's face was blank.

Then he fell forward. Caleb tried to catch him, and they both went down hard, Caleb underneath. When Caleb leaned forward to see what was going on, he saw a knife sticking out of Bill's back. Blood running hard and fast.

Beyond him stood a stranger, looking with satisfaction at Bill.

Faint noise invaded the quiet and got louder until a dozen men emerged from the woods, bedraggled, staggering. Someone tripped and fell. Another man fell over him, leapt to his feet, and punched the man beside him.

One man lifted a bottle to his lips. An ugly curse came from somewhere as they shoved and shouted. Caleb dragged himself free of Bill's dead body. The closest man yanked the knife from Bill's back. Caleb was on his feet, hands raised hoping to calm the crowd.

The man with the blood-drenched knife seemed to size Caleb up for his next target.

LAURA WASHED DISHES while Gretel took Willa into the church to feed and change her and hopefully get her a nap. With a solid door and a latch that could be closed from the inside, the church was a sturdy building.

Laura decided Melinda should be in there with her baby, too, well away from Billy. The church was turning into a nursery. Well, better that the nicest structure in the settlement got used rather than sit empty waiting for church services while everyone around went without solid shelter.

Laura was about to toss the dishwater away when a crash and racket from the far side of the camp stopped her.

Men. Stumbling, growling, fighting, cursing men. Five, no six. Then seven, ten, too many to count at a glance, all shouting, came into the settlement.

Caleb stood, backing toward her, or better to say backing away from the encroaching mob.

"Michelle." Laura's voice cracked like a whip. Well-known

for her easy smiles, Laura could find a temper and the skills to take charge if needed. "Jilly, get everyone in the church and lock the door. Where's Rick?"

Rick was rushing toward the women, who had gathered near the corral to visit, the children all about them, while Clara milked. The women were all looking at Caleb and the mob.

"Inside the church." Rick's heavy German accent took on the tone of a military officer. "*Schnell*! Hurry! Fast, get the children and get inside."

Clara climbed through the corral posts and brought the milk pail with her, without spilling a drop. The children, who had probably already faced more trouble than most adults did in a lifetime, didn't have to be carried. They sprinted for the church door. Michelle had rushed to it and held it open. Jilly grabbed all the axes and took them in.

All Laura could imagine was Jilly worried they'd be used against Caleb and all of them.

Sickening thought.

Caleb was backing faster now. Laura saw Bill on the ground. Someone tripped over him. She saw the blood and complete stillness and knew Bill was dead.

The children dashed inside. Jilly's arms dragged them deeper into the building. The women followed close behind.

Michelle charged straight for Laura. "We've got to get inside."

Rick had one of the axes. Laura had the wild thought that the mission group needed guns.

"I want to help Caleb." Her lying, former-prison-inmate husband.

Michelle dragged her toward the church. "A mob of men

like that might do terrible, unspeakable things to any woman they catch. You help Caleb most by getting to safety. Get inside. We'll lock the door, and if possible, pull Caleb and Rick in with us."

Then Laura thought of something else that could be used against them. She tore free of Michelle, dashed for her precious packet of chemicals, grabbed them, and sprinted toward the open church door.

She crossed the threshold one pace behind Michelle, just as the mob reached the campfire. Michelle slammed the door. Jilly was there, and she dropped the stout latch into place.

Whoever heard of locking a church? Jilly had built the latches without consulting anyone.

CALEB GLANCED BEHIND HIM to see Laura rush into the church a step behind Michelle. He heard the dull thuds of the church door slamming shut and the latch dropping into place.

For all that he was terrified of these madmen, he nearly cried out with relief that the women had the sense to get behind the only lockable door in the whole settlement.

"What are you men after?" Caleb asked.

"We need cabins."

One of the men fell over the fire. It was chaos, even by the standards of this crowd, as his pants caught fire. Men whooped. A couple slapped at the flames while the burning man rolled and screamed. Someone grabbed the wash water and dashed it against the flaming cloth. The man staggered to his feet.

He snatched a bottle out of someone's hand and took a long drink.

"Food here." A little man, skinny and shifty like a cornered rat, picked up a burlap bag full of venison jerky. He reached in and grabbed a handful of the meat, and someone else took the bag.

The man who'd killed Bill still brandished his knife. He thrust the bloody knife into a loop on his leather belt and took jerky from the bag.

"Why did you kill that man?" Caleb pointed to Bill's body, trampled, bleeding, left behind. It gave Caleb a terrible jolt to think he'd wanted to share his faith with Bill, and it was too late now.

"Bill Nash stole my horse not two weeks ago. I saw him up here, ready to punch you, preacher man. Had a right to kill a horse thief."

Caleb wondered if the man thought he had the right to kill a parson.

Caleb ran his finger along his parson's collar. He forgot sometimes that he wore it. But he had two shirts, and they both had the Roman collar that marked his profession, so he always had it on. It gave him some protection, at least in the normal course of things. It also gave him something to live up to so he wouldn't shame his profession.

The men muttered and shoved to get hold of the food. They looked at the church. They'd seen the women rush in. The talking and shouting changed to laughter and lechery as they discussed the women.

Hoping to distract them from thoughts of the women up here, Caleb asked, "Are you moving into Purgatory? You said you'd lost your jobs?"

"The mine closed. Price of gold booms and busts. When it's a bust, a man's got to get along best he can for a time. We knew there were abandoned cabins around here. We headed up."

Caleb thought of the gold hidden in the forest so close at hand. And if he told anyone about it, many more of these kinds of men would overrun the place and stay forever—or until the gold was gone.

God, how can I do mission work among men like this? Poverty I can handle. But these men are full of vice and sin. They have every depravity among them.

But maybe that's why God had called him here. Maybe these men could be reached.

"Our mission group is glad to share our food with you. Please sit down. Tell me about—"

"Did you see those women running into that building there?" The knifeman interrupted the beginning of Caleb's sermon.

"Pretty ones, from what I seen."

Another one said, "You running a bawdy house up here, Parson?" The man laughed until he almost fell over.

Raucous laughter grew, and the mood darkened.

"Women, up here? Not just the used up old crones who usually live in these places? Where?" The rabble were all talking again.

One headed for the church, another shoved Caleb aside. Someone knocked him to the ground. A heavy boot landed on his stomach.

The mob was past him. He saw Rick try to stop them and fall to the ground.

Caleb met Rick's horrified gaze. Rick scrambled to his feet and shoved at the crowd.

Caleb was right after him. He went around instead of through and hit the church door, his back to it, facing the men.

"These women and children are part of my church. They are to be treated with respect."

Caleb took a fist to the face. He saw Rick get thrown aside. Two men shoved at the door, then one of them kicked at it.

Children cried from inside the church.

A man at the back of the mob shouted, "Let's burn 'em out."

Horror crawled up Caleb's spine as he jumped up and started swinging.

A piece of firewood slammed against the front of the building.

"We need kindling."

Someone slammed his fist against the church door. "You women come out, or we're burning this building down."

Someone inside screamed, and who could blame her.

LAURA HEARD THE THREAT and looked at her sisters, looked at the women and children, cowering together.

She rushed for the front door and pressed her ear against it.

"Go around the sides to start the fire." Someone was taking command. "Leave the front door alone so they come running out right into our arms."

Laura turned to her sisters. "The sides, they're planning to start a fire on the side walls of the church."

"It's log. Fresh cut timber burns slowly." Jilly glanced at the side walls.

It was true it burned slowly. But it did burn.

Laura's thoughts rabbited around, prayers shooting like

sparks upward to God. Think. Think. Think. They'd been trained in logic, in leadership, in chemistry.

Laura felt the bag she still clutched in her arms.

Chemistry.

She looked at Michelle and Jilly, who as one said, "What?"

Laura had never done such a thing before as what came to her right then, but in theory, it should work. "I think I might know how to blow a mob of men back."

"You're going to kill all those men?" Michelle asked.

Laura frowned. "I don't plan to. If I'm very careful, I can create a mild explosion that will knock them out cold. Without blowing us up here in the church. Slow-burning logs might just be the answer."

She pulled open her leather pouch of chemicals and drew out the one that scared her the most. A small packet of powdered dynamite.

She looked at Gretel, clutching her baby. Easily the best dressed of any of them. "I need your petticoat."

Gretel's eyes widened, and she squeezed her baby until little Willa wailed.

CALEB SLAMMED A FIST into the face of a drunken lout. With every ounce of power he had. The man went down and stayed down.

Caleb counted a dozen. Twelve good hits, and this would settle down.

He saw Rick swing a length of firewood, and a man went down and lay limp. Maybe Caleb only needed six good hits. He slugged another one. The man was so unsteady on his feet that falling down and passing out was probably going to happen within minutes anyway.

The next one saw the punch coming, ducked it, and tossed Caleb aside. Caleb hit the ground hard, stunned. He staggered to his feet to see the man rush to their campfire and grab a log burning at about half its length.

Caleb threw himself in front of the man. Someone hit Caleb with a solid jab to his lower back.

Another man scooped up the fine sticks and shredded bark they used to start fires, another picked up logs split into kindling.

The man with the kindling kicked Caleb in the knee. Caleb went down as the man stormed around the side of the building. He had the burning log pressed against the building. The man with twigs and bark dropped them on the flame. He saw men doing the same thing and heading to the other side of the church.

Caleb struggled to his feet and ran at the nearest man.

He was huge, heavily muscled. Not scrawny and hungry looking like most of them.

"You ain't gettin' all them women for yourself, Parson." A harsh laugh accompanied a fist that hit Caleb's chin like a kick from a shod horse.

Caleb landed on his back. He drifted toward unconsciousness. He fought the coming darkness, felt around, searching for the ground.

The crying and screaming from inside built as the smoke crept between the logs. Men continued to batter the front door and shout threats that they'd burn the women alive.

Caleb shoved himself to his knees as he saw, to his horror, fire creep up the side of the church.

"It caught on this side!" A roar of celebration went up from the far side of the church.

The three men standing near glowered at Caleb. Ready to stop him if he tried to knock the kindling away.

"We don't wanna hurt you, Parson. But you can't have all the women to yourself. Ain't fittin.'"

"You men can't do this," Caleb shouted. It was like the men's ears were deaf. And maybe with enough drink, a man had a kind of deafness and blindness.

"WHY DID YOU BUILD THE CHURCH SO SOLID?" Laura glared at Jilly, then went back to poking at the clay mud Jilly had used to fill in the gaps where the logs didn't line up just right.

The only reason they had a tool at all was because Caleb had been building more benches, and he had had a hammer and some nails in here. She'd use an ax if she had to, but it might knock too big a hole.

Laura was chiseling with the hammer and nails when what she needed was a drill.

"There, I'm through." She picked up a ball of fabric even as a curl of smoke came in through the hole she'd finagled. Smoke would kill them faster than the fire.

They were running out of time.

"Come here, Michelle. Remember what I told you to do?"

"Yes."

"Jilly, listen for Caleb and Rick. We don't want them close when we set the dynamite off."

Jilly pressed her ear to the door. Laura had already told them what she wanted, and she didn't need to repeat it for her sisters, but she hoped the plan might calm the frantic women, who had started screaming, crying, and threatening to run out since the word *fire* had been uttered outside.

Jilly had posted herself at the door and shoved back any woman who made a break for it.

Michelle grabbed Laura's arm and reeled her in close. "You're sure this isn't going to blow these walls right in on us?"

Laura narrowed her eyes. "Since this seems to be our only choice. This or burn to death or run out and be overtaken by a mob, the word *sure* is a waste of time."

She held Michelle's eyes for a second.

"Jilly did make these walls sturdy," Michelle said. "They'll hold."

Laura saw the doubt and knew Michelle was speaking to comfort the panicky women of Purgatory.

"We should set both packs off at the same time."

Michelle nodded. "Get ready."

Laura went to her side of the church.

Laura picked up her own cloth bundle. It had a hole poked in one spot and was shaped as much like a funnel at one end as Laura could manage. They'd line the fabric up to the holes, slap them flat, and dynamite would blow out right into the flames and explode.

Or at least that's what she was hoping for. She turned to Jilly. "Do you hear Caleb and Rick?"

"I hear Caleb, but I haven't heard Rick talk. I wonder if he got knocked out." Her eyes flickered to Gretel.

Laura knew being knocked out wasn't the worst of what Jilly feared.

Something slammed against the door so hard, Jilly jumped back.

Melinda screamed, and her baby shrieked along with all the other children.

CALEB ROUNDED THE CHURCH, looking for a vulnerable spot to . . . what? Get inside? Get the women out?

Three men kicked at the door.

"You women will come out. If you don't, you'll burn to death."

A scream sounded from inside.

It wasn't Laura, but it was an adult woman. Her terror echoed in her scream.

Caleb saw three men stretched out unconscious. Then he saw a fourth. Rick. He was moaning, trying to get to his feet.

"There are children in there," Caleb shouted. "Two are babies. You can't burn this church. You can't harm these women and children."

Another solid kick landed on the door.

Someone screamed again. Children wailed.

Caleb came around the corner of the church building to find three men stoking a small fire that had already begun to crawl up the log walls.

"Please, for the love of God. By all that's decent in any man. Stop this. Don't throw in with this madness. Won't some of you help me stop this?"

A mob. Caleb tried to think through such a thing as this. Men gathered together, whipped up into a frenzy. All sense and order, all law cast aside, both the law of God and man.

It echoed in his ears. *"Crucify him. . . . We have no king but Caesar."*

A mob could do terrible things.

Desperation had Caleb searching for a weapon. A gun. A knife. Was there one that Gretel used for cooking? He thought of the man who had one in his belt. Could Caleb get it? Could he stab all these men to death?

God, that can't be what you'd want from me.

A long line of flames climbed the side of the church, and the roof caught fire. The crying from inside rose.

A woman, he thought it was Laura, shouted, "Smoke rises. Get low to the ground. You can breathe down there."

The women had only minutes now.

To come out and face who knew what nightmarish abuse.

Or stay in and burn to death.

The devil's own choice. And yet it was the choice God set before these poor women.

The side Caleb could see was engulfed. He went to the three men by the door and charged the nearest one. He swung a fist. Took one that knocked him back, and the other two men came at him. Grabbed his arms. The third one swung one fist into his gut and the other under his chin. He used the men holding him to lift his feet and kick the attacker hard in the face.

Now, his lip split and nose bleeding, the man came at him for the last time. They could kill him.

Grimly, Caleb knew they'd have to.

"NOW!" JILLY SHOUTED.

Laura slapped the little ball of fabric that had a small balloon of air in it with a very small measure of dynamite.

She heard Michelle do the same.

A blast knocked Laura on her backside.

The explosion had worsened the fire. Several chunks of roofing collapsed. Smoke was choking them.

"Let's go." Laura could only hope they'd knocked enough men out to handle the rest.

Jilly unlatched the door and swung it wide.

Laura scrambled to her feet. She and Michelle ran to the front of the church, where the women and children huddled by the altar.

The women broke like a frightened herd of elk and rushed for the door.

THE MEN LET GO OF CALEB when the church exploded.

Caleb collapsed to his knees.

A horse crashed out of the trail at the far side of the settlement.

Caleb wrenched his head around. Zane.

With only a second to take in the situation, Zane had his gun out. Spurred his horse. The men giving Caleb the beating ran. Two more cowpokes came out behind Zane, both armed. Then the Hogan sisters. More cowpokes.

The church door swung open, and he yelled, "It's safe. This is Caleb. Get out. Fast. The church is coming down."

The women stumbled, choking and crying, tugging their children.

Laura! Where was Laura?

Gretel emerged with her baby shrieking in her arms.

Still no Laura.

Jilly came out, fighting for breath as the building's roof

dropped a burning log. Michelle had her back to Caleb, screaming, "Laura! Laura, get out."

Michelle started coughing, and Jilly turned back. The fire roared like an enraged beast. The logs crackled, and flames snapped until the noise was deafening.

"Get out of the way." Caleb as good as tossed Jilly behind him. He dragged Michelle out of the doorway. Another part of the roof rained down in fire.

He dashed in and stumbled over something. No, someone. Laura.

With the last of his own breath, the church collapsing around him, Caleb grabbed Laura under her arms and struggled to reach the door while he choked on the wickedly hot air.

He passed the doorframe, but the inferno seemed to chase him.

Too much heat, too little air. His knees wobbled.

Then Zane was there. He swept Laura into his arms. Someone else grabbed Caleb by the arm and pulled him along.

He heard the church roof collapse and glanced back to see the whole building coming down. He sped up as much as he was able. Cinders shot forward into the air and flew past him. Something heavy and blazing hot slammed into his back.

His shirt caught fire, and whoever had him slapped at the flames, shouting for Caleb to move.

Then the pressure of the fire and the church coming down blew with explosive force. It threw him forward along with the man beside him. They landed facedown on the ground.

More hands hit him.

"Fire! He's on fire."

Then Caleb was breathing clean air. Finally dragged far enough away that the fire couldn't get him.

He heard Zane shout, "Watch the fire! Don't let the forest catch."

Caleb managed to lift his head and see, through eyes nearly swollen shut from the beating, that Laura was out. But she lay unconscious on the ground. Her sisters working over her. Everyone coughing.

His burning eyes wouldn't stay open a moment longer.

TWENTY-FIVE

THE COOL CLOTH REVIVED LAURA.
She blinked her eyes open to see Nora Hogan bathing her face.

Nora's expression was all kindness and worry. "Are you going to be all right, Laura? You and your sisters were the last ones out. And Parson Tillman, of course."

"Th-they made it? Everyone made it?"

Nora gave her a gentle, rather awkward hug. That's when Laura realized she was stretched out on the ground. Nora, always serious, looked around, assessing everyone's condition.

"Everyone made it. Two of the children have burns, not serious but painful, and Clara can't seem to stop coughing. Seven of those wretched men were knocked cold by your explosion. Your sisters told me about the dynamite. That last explosion was the rest of your dynamite blowing up. The men you knocked out came around faster than you did.

"The babies have finally stopped crying. Rick and Gretel have gone into a cabin. I heard them arguing in German. I'm afraid they'll quit the mission group. Gretel is terribly upset. Terrified really, and who can blame her?"

Now that Nora mentioned it, Laura heard the unfamiliar language. It wasn't loud, but there was a strident quality to it when Gretel spoke. Yes, they might leave.

Laura thought of what had happened. "Will we all have to leave? Will we have to give up the mission? Or arm ourselves against the next mob?"

Shaking her head, Nora wrung the cloth out, then scrubbed Laura's face with more diligence than seemed necessary. Probably trying to clean her up. Laura didn't mind.

"I'm afraid Parson Tillman has a few serious burns on his back."

"Burns." Laura sat up and was wracked with a cough from deep in her chest. Nora eased her back, and Laura didn't have the strength to resist.

"Tell me how he is." Laura coughed again but waved a hand at Nora to get the woman talking.

"He ran into the building and pulled you out. You'd collapsed. Jilly and Michelle were heading back in after you when he shoved them away from the church and went in. Zane was running in to help just as Parson Tillman reached the door with you in his arms. Zane took you, and Bo caught the parson as he was falling." Nora told Laura all the horrifying details.

"Is Caleb unconscious?"

Nora gave her a strange look, and it took Laura a second, her mind was a little foggy, to realize she'd used Caleb's first name. Nora must not know they were married.

Before Laura could make that announcement, Nora said, "No, he came around. But he took a terrible beating from those miners, and he's got serious burns on his back and arms. He's in rough shape. He'll need rest. But Parson Tillman is a strong man. He's got the Lord fighting on his side. Or perhaps better to say Parson Tillman is fighting on the Lord's side. He'll make it."

Laura reached out and took Nora's hand. "Parson Tillman and I got married yesterday."

Nora's expression broke into a smile. "That's wonderful to hear. He'll need a strong woman at his side when he's working in his mission field."

Laura thought of all the secrets he'd kept from her while pressuring her to be open and honest with him. Had she married a man just like her stepfather?

Nora's remark about needing strength popped back into Laura's head. "Does something like that mob of men happen very often?"

Laura wasn't looking forward to blowing up a church every time there was trouble.

"Zane had one of his hired men in town overnight. When word got out about the mine closing, his cowhand came running for the ranch. Yes, it seems there's always trouble when jobs are lost, and it happens regularly. No money coming in. Men without any cushion of savings to live on. There's rioting and often mobs form. Men apparently often come up to these shantytowns and hunker down until the mines reopen. And sometimes when they come, they can be dangerous. Zane was afraid of what might happen here. He got us moving as soon as word arrived."

And he'd saved them all from a terrible death. If the women had come out of that church, even with Laura's dynamite knocking quite a few of the men out, they might still have been in deadly danger, and they might have faced something monstrous before they died.

"And what of the women up here?" Laura asked. "What if we hadn't been here? Our presence is what drew Zane's attention. What would these women have faced if they were here alone?"

And had they faced those dangerous men before? Laura hated to even think of it. She struggled against Nora's hold as she sat up, and this time she stayed up without the coughing fit.

"You were in an unnatural sleep for a time, Laura. You should rest a bit."

"I think I'll be able to help. I can't lie here while there is a need. What happened to those men?"

"Zane had them taken away. He can't expect much. What law there is in the nearest mining town has to be overwhelmed. But he'll get them away from here, then he'll leave a guard posted up here. He's talking of building a line shack at the bottom of the hill and keeping a few men there so they'll always be close at hand if there's trouble."

Zane couldn't guard them forever. And if this kind of thing happened every time a mine fell on hard times and shut down, facing a mob might be a normal part of their lives. Laura didn't want to live like this.

Michelle came to her side. "Are you all right?"

Jilly was a step behind. "We were scared to death when you wouldn't wake up."

"Help me up. Let's see if my legs are sturdy. How are you two?"

"Fine, both of us," Jilly said. She took Laura's left arm. Michelle took her right. Nora stepped back, watching, ready to rule over all three of them if Laura looked like she should be lying down. Although Nora couldn't be more than fifteen years older than Laura, the woman's behavior was motherly, and Laura found a deep fondness for the stern woman.

They hoisted her to her feet. Michelle slid an arm across her back. Jilly held on to her on the other side.

"Zane almost had to yank you out of Caleb's arms," Jilly said.

Caleb's arms. Mercy, she was a married woman, and her husband was a swindler.

"It was a tug-of-war," Nora smiled. "But Parson Tillman was all in, or you'd've been snapped like a wishbone."

Laura looked around and didn't see Caleb. "Where is he? How is he?"

She twisted in her sisters' arms and was stunned into silence. The church lay in a smoldering heap. The women scattered all around, sitting, lying down, kneeling over their children and bathing sooty faces. Harriet was holding Melinda's baby and talking quietly with her.

Gretel and Rick, in the cabin they'd slept in the night before, continued their conversation in German.

All this pain. So many hurt. The damage a mob could do was a kind of madness, and Laura didn't know how to work with madmen, how to make anything better.

She saw Zane and Caleb talking, a few steps away from what had become a makeshift hospital on the ground in front of the shanties. Caleb was sitting on a stump, shirtless. His chest and belly were wrapped in white bandages. Red blisters stood up on his shoulders. If they'd left those ugly blisters uncovered, what must the burns they'd wrapped look like?

He had one eye swollen shut and turning black. His mouth

was swollen, his nose red and bulbous. He held one arm against his stomach. She couldn't decide if it was because his arm wasn't working right or his belly hurt, but it wasn't a natural pose.

He and Zane were having an intense conversation. Laura hoped, whatever went on in between, it began and ended with thank you.

"Is anyone else hurt badly? Are there any dangerous burns?" Laura looked between Michelle, Jilly, and Nora.

"We all survived. A couple more minutes in that church, and we'd've had to come out." Michelle gave the building a grim look.

"I think I'll build the next one out of stone," Jilly said. "There are plenty of rocks around here."

"I'm a married woman now," Laura said. "I think I'll go home to Mama. I might not have the controlling interest in our company, but I can hire bodyguards and take up residence. Mama will be safe."

"What about Caleb? How will you get rid of him?" Jilly didn't sound like she was opposed to getting rid of him, just considering the details.

Nora gasped in shock. She was very loyal to Caleb, but she hadn't heard of his time in prison and the lies he'd told to cover them up. Or maybe not lies. But he hadn't admitted who he truly had been.

Laura reached out and patted Nora's hand. "I found out Caleb has a past that he didn't tell me about. I'm not sure I'd have married him if I'd known, and I don't quite know how to handle it."

"You mean that he was in prison?"

Laura blinked as she looked at Nora. "You knew that?"

"Yes. We've never told him we were aware. But it wasn't a well-kept secret. And Parson Tillman is a sincere man. I crossed the continent with him, and I trust him."

Laura sure wished she did.

"I'll just go," Laura said. "Maybe Zane will sell me a horse. He already let one of his cowhands leave to help Mama. Maybe he'll let me have a couple more cowhands. Caleb can come if he wants. We can't stay here, not if a mob forms regularly. We need to get these women away from here, too. And their children." Laura shook her head. "And their husbands and every woman in every shantytown, and their husbands and children."

Laura looked at her sisters. "It feels like there's a whole world that needs saving. How can we do it all, and how can we quit without at least trying?"

"I wonder if Zane needs more cowhands." Nora studied the scene around them. "And if these women have husbands who could do that work. Except for a very lucky few, gold mining just seems like a stupid way to make a living."

"To think roping cows pays better. It's a strange world," Laura said. "Jobs working a ranch would solve the troubles for these women. But what about all the other women in danger in these shantytowns?"

"That cowhand who went to protect Mama, Nick, with those heterochromatic eyes? He'd be there to help you." Jilly seemed to remember him overly well.

"Then I'll go. You two find husbands and come when you can."

"I've got a funny feeling about you just taking off," Michelle said.

"Are you worried about being safe?" Laura asked. "Maybe

you'd better come with me. Maybe I should take Melinda. If Rick and Gretel are quitting, maybe they'd like to come. Oh, let's just take the whole settlement. We can leave a note for their husbands."

"It's not us I'm worrying about, it's you." Michelle let loose of Laura, and she stood on her own well enough. Though she missed the support.

"Me? Leaving will be the first step to being really safe."

"I watched Caleb do his tug of war with Zane," Michelle said.

Nora crossed her arms and snorted, but it was a laugh, and there hadn't been much of that around here. "I watched too. Next time I'm afraid he'll hold on to his end of the wishbone and never let go."

"SHE'S UP." Caleb quit jawing with Zane about the insanity that'd gone on around here and groaned as he stood. There wasn't a square inch anywhere on him that didn't hurt, but he needed to reclaim his wife.

Zane grabbed his arm and turned him right back around.

Caleb let Zane stop him because the pain overruled his longing to get to Laura, make sure she was all right, and convince her to trust him again.

"We're not done." Zane just would *not* shut up. "You need to get away from here. I knew it wasn't safe. I've heard of these mobs forming, but I've never really seen it before. It will happen again, Caleb. You can't stay here. Or if you do, you have to make very sure the rest of your mission team is given a choice to leave. Maybe having women here, and outsiders who weren't married to miners, made it worse, but probably that mob would have attacked anyone. But even if the women in your group leave, you'll still have to stand between the next mob and the women who live in these shacks. And that position is dangerous. They'd've killed you if I hadn't come."

"And that would be a risk I'd take, but I have to get Rick and Gretel away from here. The Hogan sisters and Sally Jo can't come back. The Stiles sisters have to go, too."

"And you're married to Laura?" Zane looked over at Caleb's wife. He whistled quietly. "Good job, Caleb."

He gave him a good-natured slap on the shoulder.

Caleb winced.

"Sorry. You probably have cracked ribs along with everything else."

"Probably." But Caleb thought certainly.

"Sore ribs make everything hurt worse." Zane added, "Laura can't stay here."

"Laura really dynamited those men?" Caleb sort of heard the explosion. At the time, he'd been busy being beaten to death.

"Yep. Who carries dynamite around? You're gonna have your hands full with that one."

Caleb sincerely hoped the day came when he could get his hands full of Laura.

"Maybe we can build . . . build . . . some . . . building that won't burn. We need a way to retreat and take the women to safety. A fort with . . . with rock walls."

"Caleb, you . . ."

Laura was standing now, though her sisters stayed near to steady her. Nora stood there, frowning as if her patient was making an escape.

Only just barely hearing Zane, Caleb headed for Laura. He had to talk to her. And she was surrounded by fierce women who probably wouldn't let him get her alone. Plus, she knew how to blow things up.

And still he walked straight for her.

He reached her side and elbowed his way between Laura and Michelle. "Are you feeling better?"

He saw several blisters on her face and wished he'd killed every man jack who'd attacked them.

His next wish was a prayer for forgiveness, followed by complete confusion about how to go on.

"Laura, come and talk to me please. Just the two of us. You know we need to talk, and I honestly don't think I can stand on my feet for much longer."

He saw sympathy, but there was a lot more in her eyes, and most of it didn't bode well. She came along, but he wasn't sure he was going to get to do the talking.

"WHICH BEDROOM IS HIS?" Nick stepped into the hall.

Margaret was behind him and pointed to the door at the far end. Built for Liam and Margaret, the suite had the biggest bedroom, a sitting room, two dressing rooms, and a retiring room, complete with plumbing that carried hot and cold running water, a bathtub, and a water closet.

Liam had worked hard to make this house modern and comfortable.

And Margaret had let the vile Edgar into it. She'd fallen in love with him. Taken him to her bed.

Margaret had to struggle, and not always successfully,

not to hate herself for marrying Edgar. He'd tricked her. She knew he'd deceived her as to his true nature, but she'd fallen so hard for him and married too quickly. She should have waited, spent more time in prayer, trusted more in her mind and less in her feelings.

But it was done. All she had left was to deal with the life she'd brought on herself. And right now, she was dealing with it by hiding behind a stranger. A man younger and no doubt stronger than Edgar but without a fraction of his ruthlessness.

"Mr. Ryder, be careful." She caught his arm, and he turned back to her. As respectful as any son. "My husband is an evil man. You may want to be direct and fair with him, even when you intend to defeat him. But he won't hesitate to use every mean trick in his very large book. And he's got henchmen in this house."

Nick smiled. It was alight with mischief and strength, goodwill and courage. "I've got henchmen, too. And I've got right on my side. The urge was so strong to come here when I realized who your daughters were. I was on the trail, riding hard, as fast as your daughters could get those notes written. I think God put me on this earth to protect you."

He patted her hand and didn't try to escape her grip. Instead, he waited until she felt safe enough, trusted him enough, to let him go.

He gave her a firm nod. And she nodded back. "His room is at the far end of the hall. The biggest and best room. I live as far away from him as I can and stay behind a locked door day and night."

"He needs to learn a lesson, I'd say."

"Let's go teach it to him." And she fell in behind him again.

A strong, intelligent woman, all too happy to hide behind a tough man.

A chill went up her spine when Nick pounded on the door. "Edgar Beaumont, you get out here."

She turned to see five men coming up the stairs with Old Tom in the lead. He'd worked for them for years. Why hadn't she gone to him when she'd realized what a horrible mistake she'd made?

Shame. That's all she could think. And her shame had been strong enough she'd sent her daughters fleeing alone into the night. And Edgar would have fired Tom and any man who defended her. How could they stay if they were fired? But they could. She just hadn't trusted them to help her.

And that only made her feel more shame.

TWENTY-SIX

LAURA SAW HOW NEAR to collapsing Caleb was. The black eye and swollen jaw were the most noticeable, but his face was drawn with pain, and he moved as if every inch of him hurt. She was unconscious when Caleb brought her out of the fire, and she didn't know what he'd gone through outside the church. But she could guess.

She cared for him. But only the man he'd presented to the world. She remembered Edgar and what a skilled liar he was all too well. What if she'd married such a man?

She didn't think so, but then Mama hadn't thought so, either.

Laura and Caleb headed for a boulder set back near the tree line not far from where they were.

Most of the women and children had gone back to their cabins. The Steinmeyers continued their discussion in German. Half of Zane's men were gone, ridding the settlement of that awful mob of men. Enough were left to protect them if another mob came.

Everyone else was either being treated for burns or doing the treating.

Laura sat on the boulder and urged Caleb down beside her. The fact that he was so easy to urge told her how battered he was feeling.

"I married a man I didn't know." Laura fell silent. Caleb needed to talk to her, be honest with her, if she was to remain a wife to him.

A marriage got her a third of a dynasty. Michelle had drawn up a tidy certificate. Laura didn't necessarily have to produce the husband himself. But she also knew that what had passed between them in the night could result in a child. She so longed to give any child she bore a father like the one she'd had. Until Caleb's secrets had come out, she'd thought she'd managed that.

Caleb looked around the clearing. "It's in ashes. My mission field. I felt the calling, the leading of the Lord so strongly."

His topic of choice annoyed Laura. He needed to explain himself, beg her forgiveness, say something perfect so she could trust him.

His shoulders slumped. "Back east, near Savannah where I grew up, I was a known man. A man you could never trust. But I changed, Laura. I found God in that terrible prison. After I got out, I was treated well by the folks I worshiped with, fully forgiven, fully loved. But when I felt led to be a preacher, that seemed to be a line no one could quite cross. They didn't see in me a man to lead their church. I did the study necessary and got the proper certificates to be a licensed minister, but I couldn't find a job. A job I felt God calling me to do. I was a preacher without a church. One day a missionary came to our church and talked of this place and the need out here. I felt God speaking straight to my heart, calling me to come out here and serve in this field. It seemed to be working."

He looked at her as if begging her to agree with him. "I was building a rapport with these settlement folks. I wanted them to know love, know that God loved them, and I loved them. And now . . ." Caleb lifted his hands high as if in total surrender. "It's in ashes. Not just the building but the ministry. I can't ask the Hogan sisters to come back. I can't ask the Steinmeyers to stay. I should get the Purgatory women and children away, but how? I can stay by myself. But I have to get you and your sisters away. And I can see in your eyes you're going to leave. Leave this ministry and leave me, your husband."

Laura looked away, and very deliberately, he added, "Aren't you?"

Laura felt him turn to her. She stared out at the smoldering mound of ash where the church used to be.

"Jilly can build another church," Laura said. "She mentioned making it of stone."

"But what of those men who came raging in here? You know one of them killed Bill Nash. Just stabbed him to death and claimed it was over a stolen horse. The men would have killed all of us. And next time we might not be gathered here, close to the church door, and able to make it inside."

Caleb sighed. "You're supposed to be so intelligent, right?"

Nodding, Laura finally met his gaze. "Right. I am *very* intelligent."

"Then tell me what to do. What does a man do when he wants to walk away from his calling from God?"

And smart as she was, Laura just wasn't sure.

"These shacks up here draw people. We could find a better place to live for every one of these women and their children, then burn down these shacks." And tell Zane about the gold. That'd get a guard posted up here permanently. But she didn't say that. Time later to worry about the stupid gold.

"It's the theme of Parson Tillman's ministry," Caleb said. "Burn everything down."

"It would free you from this calling. You'd have helped every person here. You could encourage them in their faith as we get them closer to their husbands, to a place where there is more safety from a mob like this. In a way, you'd have fulfilled your ministry because no one else would come. Surely that answers God's call."

Caleb was silent, which Laura hoped meant he was thinking about what she'd said.

At last he said, "What of our marriage, Laura? Can you trust me? I didn't tell you about my past for exactly this reason. I knew you'd be suspicious and have doubts, just like those people back in Savannah. But that was selfish of me. I didn't want to lose you. And to me, that man, the one I used to be, the man who got sent to prison, died when I accepted Christ. I came out here to live as a new man and didn't want to have to admit my old life had ever existed. Can you trust me again?"

"Here's the trouble, Caleb. I do trust you. My heart trusts you. But my head is telling me we got married too fast. I don't really know you well enough to have married you, and yet I did. I'm having trouble getting my head and my heart to match. I need to pray about our marriage, and you need to pray about your ministry. Until we've figured out what the future holds, I don't intend to be a wife to you."

"You mean in the sense of the . . . intimacy of marriage we shared last night?"

"That's exactly what I mean."

"I regret that because being with you, as we were, was such a wonderful thing. I understand it. But I want you to stay with me. We can't work out our future if we stay apart from each other. Share that old cabin with me while we pray together and talk things through. I hope we get to a place where you can forgive my dishonesty and know me well enough to trust me."

She wanted to. And she still didn't know what was right and wrong.

"I'm not sure I should agree to that. If we—"

Suddenly, Caleb wasn't quite focused on her. Instead, his eyes took on a glazed look.

"Caleb?"

He turned his head a bit as if he was trying to respond to her. And that little turn toppled him. He fell straight backward off the boulder.

She grabbed for him, but he slipped through her fingers and landed with a thud on rocky ground.

Jumping up set off her coughing again. Through her wheezing and hacking she yelled weakly, "Help!"

Digging for more strength as she knelt beside Caleb, she managed more volume. "Help! Help me."

Michelle was there before she quit shouting. Jilly next, then Zane.

"What happened?" Zane pushed all three sisters aside. "Did he fall and hit his head?"

"No, he just passed out, sitting here talking to me."

"Shad! Bo! Get over here."

Zane was gentle as he sat Caleb up. Then his two hired men were there.

"Help me get him into a cabin." He looked at Laura. "Which one?"

"I'll show you."

Zane took Caleb's shoulders. His men each took a leg. "Be careful of the burns on his back, and watch his ribs. They're at least cracked. He's probably just collapsed from exhaustion and is in need of a good long rest."

They carried him to the ramshackle hut Laura led them to and laid him on the blanket on the floor, because that's all there was.

Jilly followed with water. Michelle rushed to get Gretel. She was the only one up to making some broth. The argument in German ended, and Gretel went back to work. Michelle even dug the milk pail out of the remnants of the church, using a long limb to poke around in the hot ashes until she found it, and ordered Clara to wash it up and finish her milking.

If it hadn't been for the massive pile of ashes, and the unconscious preacher, and the grim-faced, heavily armed cowpokes, and the fresh mound of dirt that marked the burial site of Bill Nash, life would have almost returned to normal.

LAURA HADN'T AGREED to live as man and wife with Caleb, but nursing him turned out to be the same. With a few very big exceptions. For one, her husband was mostly unconscious. For another, she was forced to step out regularly as

Zane or one of his cowhands helped her very groggy husband to deal with private needs.

When she was ousted, which she was perfectly happy to be, she helped Jilly build the new church. Jilly wasn't sure Caleb wanted a new church, but she enjoyed construction, so they weren't asking permission.

It'd be a surprise.

Jilly had set the foundation. Rick's new job was to use the horses to drag in rocks. They'd cut a few trees down to frame the building. "I'm planning to coat the framing logs with the same adobe-like mud I used to chink holes in the log church." Jilly scooped up a handful of the concoction she'd made to act as a filler between the stones and to help them stick together. It was heavily mixed with clay soil and worked similarly to plaster. "It will prevent the logs from catching fire."

"What about the roof? You can't make that out of stone," Michelle asked.

"I'm playing with the idea of a variation of a thatched roof. It would be flammable, but it wouldn't be heavy. If it caught fire and someone was inside, we might be able to knock aside anything that fell and stay in while it burned away."

"I've heard of a thatched roof, but I have no idea how to make one or even really what it is," Laura said.

Jilly shrugged. "I'll have to invent something, but I think it'll work. If not, we might have an open-air church. It'll be cold in the winter and wet in the rain, but we can work around that. The other one didn't even have a fireplace. It's not like church services go on long enough for anyone to freeze."

"It has to be solid enough to be a fortress, remember," Laura said.

Jilly gave her and Michelle a grim look. "Trust me, I remember. I'll make it secure."

Laura did trust Jilly and figured she could make it work. Right now, her redheaded sister was situating a stone on the third layer up. She worked hard at making them fit tightly, and her plaster stuck the stones together and filled in the gaps.

Laura noticed that Jilly was no longer careful to keep her red hair covered, and here the three of them stood, talking, working together. The Stiles sisters.

Their only real protection from being found by Edgar was the odd place they'd chosen to hide.

She decided to worry about something else.

"So I think . . ." Laura looked all around her. Everyone was out of ear shot. Still, she lowered her voice and pulled her sisters close. "We should tell Zane about the *you know*."

She arched her brows and waited.

Her sisters were silent. Thinking. Analyzing.

Finally, Michelle said, "I can't trust myself. It's such a great secret. I'm burning to tell someone."

"We promised to wait. To think about it," Laura said. "I've been praying about it, salted in between prayers for Caleb to get well, me to decide whether to trust him, and Mama to be safe. Oh, and you two, to find husbands."

"Long prayer list and all of it's important," Jilly said. "I'm surprised the *you know* even rates."

"What do you think?"

"What will he do?" Michelle looked at the cabin Laura was staying in with Caleb. Zane was emerging.

"I have no idea. I keep imagining him either going mad with you-know fever or saying, 'I think we should wait.'"

Jilly laughed. "Which is all any of us have been able to think of doing. Tell him."

"Laura, Caleb wants you." Zane was walking toward where the three sisters worked around the new church. They'd moved it a bit so the ground wouldn't be so ashy.

"I have to see what Caleb needs." Laura looked at Jilly.

"I can't quit. My plaster dries too fast."

"Fine," Michelle shrugged. "I've been dying to tell someone."

"Be quiet about it. If he starts ranting and screaming, 'I've struck it rich,' we'll know it was a mistake."

Michelle nodded and walked alongside Laura to meet Zane.

Michelle smiled at him and said, "I've got something to show you." She jerked her head toward the woods and walked away.

Zane looked at Laura. "What does she want?"

"Just go. I need to see to Caleb."

"I changed the bandage on the burns on his back. It's starting to look much better. Gonna be scars, I'm sure. But he'll survive."

He looked after Michelle for a second, then hurried to catch up to her as she walked into the forest. Heading for gold.

Wondering how it would come out, Laura walked toward Caleb. Her healing husband.

They probably should have consulted him before telling Zane. Now that she thought of it, she might've promised to include him in their sister-secrets.

Instead, if his thoughts had finally cleared, she'd just inform him. That'd probably be how their whole lives went on, so she might as well start now.

TWENTY-SEVEN

IT'S WHAT?" Zane yelped.

"Shhhh!" Michelle slashed a hand at him. "It's a secret. You don't want everybody to know, right?"

Zane clamped his mouth shut. He stared at the rock.

Dropping his voice, he whispered, "I know nothing about gold."

Michelle clapped her hand over his mouth. "We don't use the G-word."

Zane nodded. His cheeks were bristly, though he seemed to have no beard. Michelle pulled her hand away, shocked at her brazen behavior. She closed her hand and felt the warmth of his skin, the bristles on his face, and the angles of his high cheekbones and square jaw.

Nope, she couldn't feel that. She just imagined how it would feel. She realized she'd been staring him right in the eye. And for too long. Much too long.

Tearing her gaze away from his, she said, "Well, Laura knows the most geology. She knows what it is. And Jilly and I recognize it. There is no doubt that it's a very rich vein. I assume this is your land. So it's yours. But if you start digging it out, people are going to come flooding in here."

"Not on my land." The cold in his voice sent a shiver up her spine.

"I was sure you'd feel that way. So we haven't told anyone else besides Caleb. I suppose it's your problem now. But it's our problem, too, because you've got to get it mined out of here. You'll never be safe until it's gone. And to do that, you'll have to destroy the Purgatory settlement. We think that might be for the best anyway, but where will all these people go? And what happens to Caleb's ministry?"

Michelle held out both hands in a gesture she thought was very graceful and final, and waited.

"You'll figure it out," Zane said after a moment.

It was a weight off her shoulders. She should have told him right away.

"Someone less honorable and less wealthy than you and your sisters is going to find it sooner or later. We'll find homes for the folks that are here. I send riders into town regularly. They should be able to find decent houses and buy them. Then I will . . . will . . ."

As he fell silent, Michelle knew just how he felt.

"You trust your men, but you worry that you might not be able to trust anyone to this extent. You need to hire more men because you're already stretched thin being up here so much and away from your own ranch. You could hire the men who live here, but they seem to be a disreputable lot, and they would probably just steal you blind—and gamble and drink it away, and their families would be right back where they are now."

"You've given this a lot of thought, haven't you?" Zane asked dryly.

"It's what I do. Give a lot of things a lot of thought."

Zane's head fell back, and he stared up into the treetops. The trees were so thick they canopied until they formed a near dome around them. He seemed to be thinking or praying or both. She supported that.

Finally, he looked back at her. His eyes glinting with decision and something else. She couldn't quite understand what she was seeing. Excitement maybe or a sense of incredible power, or maybe she was seeing gold fever. She sure hoped not.

"I've got three things I'm sure need doing," he said. "I'll do them and make more decisions later."

"I love a well laid out plan." She couldn't hold back a smile. "What are your steps?

"First, I send Shad into town today to find and buy homes for the families still up here. That solves the problem of what to do for these folks to minimize their getting hurt. Considering I'm going to dig—" he glanced left and right and behind—"a fortune out of these rocks, I can easily afford to do this."

"Good idea. Good first step."

"Then I'm going to burn down those shacks, and you might as well tell Jilly to quit building that new church."

"Um . . . not as good. Caleb, for example, is badly injured and living in one of them."

"It will take a few days to find and buy the houses, then get these folks moved. He can use that time to heal up. At least heal up enough to ride, then I'll send him to my ranch to recuperate. You can all come with him. I've enjoyed having the Hogan sisters at my place. Sally Jo too. A few more, Melinda and Hannah, the Steinmeyers. You can all live with me until you decide what to do."

"Is that your third step? It's a very generous offer, of course," Michelle said carefully. "I don't think Caleb will want to leave his mission field."

"No, that's part of the second step. Better that he's outside when I burn down the cabin he's living in." There was a flash of teasing in Zane's eyes, which kept her from punching him. "Anyway, if I provide homes and move everyone out, there's not much of a mission left is there?"

Michelle saw that Zane believed he was right. She liked decisive people, but she liked them best if they decided to do things exactly as she'd have them done.

But since she wasn't sure what to do, she didn't argue the point. She suspected it would be a waste of time. "Then what is your third step?"

"This one's a little on the crazy side, but I'm absolutely sure it's the right thing to do."

Michelle thought burning down Purgatory was on the crazy side, so she braced herself, but not for long. Zane slid his arms around her waist, pulled her close, and kissed the living daylights out of her.

Then he smiled and said, "I need to go buy a couple of houses."

He turned and strode out of the woods.

It took her a while for her misty thoughts to clear enough to follow him.

"WHAT DO YOU MEAN I've got to go outside so Zane can burn my cabin down?"

"I don't believe you can possibly mean, 'what do you

273

mean?'" Laura said. "The meaning is clear as the sky, clear as glass, clear as, as, as . . . carbon monoxide."

"What is carbon monoxide?" Caleb asked.

"You don't really want to talk about that now do you?" Laura knelt beside him. He was sitting up, dressed, his wounds still bandaged but much better. Clearly well enough to ride a horse to Zane's house.

"I'd prefer to stop Zane from burning down this cabin."

"Zane bought houses in Dorada Rio, where the Purgatory residents' husbands work. We spent yesterday getting everyone moved. They're gone."

"But . . . but . . ."

Laura paused, but Caleb didn't go on. So she did. "He found their husbands and informed them of the move, so they won't come back here, but can, instead, go home every night after work."

"But . . . but . . ."

Again she paused, but Caleb didn't seem to actually have anything to say—not counting *but*. "He also bought them a bit of furniture and stocked their new houses with a decent amount of food and gave them a bit of cash and told them if it runs out and they have to hightail it to some slum like this, pick another one because Purgatory is going up in flames."

Caleb slumped over backward, which couldn't be good for his burns, but at least he was sitting on the floor. He probably didn't do any serious damage.

"I should have known this would happen when you told him about the gold," he said.

"He is taking us all to his ranch, where you will recuperate, and he's got some half-formed plan to form a mining company. He said you can take time to decide where you'll set up your new mission field."

Laura didn't say so out loud, but she thought her lumberjacks could use a pastor.

"Oh, and Jilly started a new church, this one fireproof. But Zane convinced her to stop. It's now just a big rectangular rock wall about three feet tall with a gap for a door. Zane might finish building it and turn it into some kind of bunkhouse. Jilly offered to help. That's not settled, but she was enjoying working with rocks and mud."

"I have no idea what God wants of me, where I'm supposed to go."

"God gave you one calling. Surely, He'll give you another."

Laura prodded him in the side until he sat up again. "Let's go. Zane's got the horses saddled, and most everyone has already set out. You and I, my sisters, and Zane are the last, along with a few of his cowhands."

With a helpless look around him, Caleb said, "I smell smoke."

"This is the last cabin not on fire."

Caleb's head drooped forward until his chin rested on his chest.

Laura gave him a little encouraging pat on the shoulder, the one farthest from his burns.

Finally, she reached down, took his hand, and gave it a little tug. "I'm afraid Zane is going to come in here and sling you over a saddle if you don't come along willingly."

"He probably will. Forceful man, Zane Hart." Caleb stood. He looked around the ramshackle cabin, then grabbed up his satchel, conveniently packed. Shoulders slumped, he went outside.

Zane had two saddled horses waiting for them. "I've made more plans. Caleb, how would you like to run my mining operation?"

"No." Caleb swung up on his horse.

Laura could see the movement hurt him, but he didn't squawk.

"Figured you'd say no. But I thought a parson would be an honest man."

Laura didn't disabuse Zane of that belief.

"And you could be the mission pastor for whatever men I end up employing out here. I'd throw in a few guards, well-armed, which would prevent a repeat of that crazy mob that showed up. I'd pay the miners I hired good wages. But honestly, it's tricky to find honest men to dig up gold. There aren't that many who can resist keeping it for themselves."

"Zane?" Caleb asked.

"Yeah?"

"Shut up."

Zane tossed a flaming torch on the cabin Caleb and Laura had been staying in. Their first home. Laura watched it catch fire and turn into a crackling inferno in minutes.

"You men stay and watch. The fire won't likely spread, but best to keep an eye on it until the flames die down."

"Glad to, Boss."

Laura didn't recognize the two here now, but she was getting to know Zane's men. They'd been coming and going all week. Zane too. All of them taking shifts at sentry duty.

Laura wasn't sure how a mission was usually run. She didn't know if armed guards were normal.

"Laura, you lead." Zane waved her toward the trail down

the mountainside. "The rest of the group isn't that far ahead, and I'd like to bring up the rear."

As she took the trail and headed down to that pretty valley full of cows, she decided that taking orders was the easiest way to live. It took almost no thinking. She'd have to start taking control of her life here soon, but for now, she just obeyed. Watching her horse pick its way down a mountain took all her attention, and that suited her. Thinking was putting a crick in her brain.

They reached the level ground, and Caleb caught up to ride beside her.

"We haven't really spent time getting to know each other better. Even though we've been living together, sleeping together. Even though we're married."

"You've been addled or outright unconscious most of the time. You must have a concussion from that beating you took."

"I don't know what a concussion is, but it sounds terrible. I don't think I have that."

Laura shrugged. "So tell me what prison was like. What specifically were you in for?"

Caleb gave her a dark look.

"It's part of getting to know each other."

"I . . . well, I lied my way into the confidence of a wealthy old man. He left me everything in his will. When I came to pick up my inheritance, it turned out he had an estranged son who'd been keeping away from his old coot of a father. The man really was a dreadful old crank, but the son was almost as bad. He'd been circling at a distance, and when his father died, he swooped in with lawyers and accused me of conning his father. Which I absolutely had done. I'd done worse things to people who could afford it less than this man, but that was the one I got arrested for. I got ten years in prison."

Laura gasped.

"But the judge ended up hating that greedy son as much as his father did. The will was clearly written out to me. After the dust settled and the son got the father's money, which is as it should be, the judge commuted my sentence to a year and a day in the state penitentiary in Milledgeville doing hard labor. The prison was a wreck because it had been used as a prisoner-of-war camp during the Civil War, and it had been partly burned and never properly rebuilt. So the prison leased us out like horses in a livery stable to work on the railroad. Hard, brutal work in the Georgia heat.

"There were two men who worked among the prisoners, preaching the Holy Word. For some reason, I'd never felt much guilt over my foolish life until I was in that courtroom listening to that judge declare me guilty. I think that's why I got off. The shame of it was brutal. Then I got to prison and heard those men. Add to it that prison life was awful, blazing hot, the food terrible. I never wanted to go to prison again. Bill was in there with me. He'd had a hand in that swindle, but instead of being ashamed of what we'd done, he lost his temper during the trial. He took a swing at that greedy son, and worse, when the bailiffs restrained him, he punched them, and then he attacked the judge and managed to blacken both his eyes before they got him under control. Bill had to do five years of hard labor."

"I'd say he didn't learn his lesson."

Caleb had no response to that. Melinda was riding well ahead of them, with the Hogan sisters and Sally Jo, who'd apparently come over to witness the burning of Caleb's mission field.

Michelle and Jilly rode a bit closer with Shad but still about a half mile ahead.

"I need to talk to Melinda. Make sure she's handling Bill's death without it tearing her up," Caleb said.

He was a true parson to the bone. It warmed Laura's heart to realize it. And realize she trusted him. Just the way he'd said no to Zane over that gold-mine job helped her believe it. She studied her husband. Pain was etched on his face. His eye was completely black, and his jaw swollen and red. But he looked so much better after several days of rest.

"I think, Caleb, until you feel the Lord call you to a new ministry, you'll find plenty of lost people you can reach out to. That missionary who came to talk to you in Savannah inspired you to come out here. But now that you're here, and the Purgatory settlement is gone, you just have to seek God's will. Figure out what He wants you to do next."

Caleb looked sideways at her. He seemed glum.

Laura wanted to cheer him up. "I still have plenty of money." She patted the purse hung over her neck. "So do Jilly and Michelle. We'll wait for you to find a new calling, and in the meantime, Michelle can marry Zane, and Jilly can do I don't know what. Then we'll all go and take over our lumber dynasty as planned."

"You're going to do it?" Caleb asked. "Go through with taking on your part in running the lumber company, even when you don't want to?"

Laura fell silent for a moment. "I don't see any way out of it. Mama needs us. Taking over my share is part of saving her, isn't it?"

"So you'll do a job you don't like. Choose for yourself a job you don't want, and in the end, you won't have your sisters at your side."

"Yes, I will. They really like the idea of managing Stiles Lumber."

"Do you honestly think if Zane marries Michelle, he'll be willing to leave his ranch, and his brand-spankin'-new gold mine? You should pick someone else out for her."

Laura flung one arm up in the air. "My sisters are taking too much time. Someone has to pick out a man for Michelle, and it's either Zane or one of his cowhands because those are the only men around. And Michelle is so . . . so . . ." She grappled to find a word. "So take-charge that only a really strong man will ever be able to manage her or live with her or even keep from running away from her. Zane seems like he could keep up. But you're right. He seems really fond of his ranch."

Zane came galloping up beside them then, so their conversation planning out his life ended.

"Let's pick up the pace. I've been away from the ranch for too long." He rode on past them.

Laura looked at Caleb. "We have no idea where God will call us beyond where we're headed today, but at least we'll get there fast."

That wrung a smile out of him. She kicked her horse into a gallop, and Caleb came up beside her, and they rode without talking.

Getting to know a man was almost more work than it was worth.

TWENTY-EIGHT

T HERE'S A LETTER HERE FROM YOUR MA." Zane had found a small stack of mail. They were much closer to Dorada Rio here at his ranch, but it was still a long hour's ride to the little town. Men rode to town for supplies and to spend their days off away from the ranch. When they came back, they'd bring mail if there was any.

Laura grabbed the letter with an excited squeal.

Caleb grinned to see her so excited. His face hurt, but it was worth it.

Laura opened the fat letter. Inside was a second letter for Zane from Nick. She handed it over with a suspicious look. "If there's anything in there about Mama and what Nick found, I want to know."

Michelle and Jilly both glared at him with eyes that might light his hair on fire.

"I'll tell you. Better yet, I'll let you read it first." He extended the single sheet of paper to Laura.

She waved it away. "I want to read Mama's first." She

unfolded several sheets of paper. "Nick is there, and she's safe from Edgar."

Michelle and Jilly rushed to stand behind her shoulders and read for themselves.

There was writing on the front and back of every sheet. Caleb counted three. The sisters were a study. Their expressions matched as they read through the lines at apparently the same speed. Frowns, scowls, sighs of relief, squared shoulders, firm jaws, determination flashing in their eyes. And finally huge smiles.

"Nick found plenty of men among the lumberjacks who will stand with Mama. They haven't managed to oust Edgar from the house, and Nick says Mama isn't ready to abandon her home. But Edgar is never allowed to be alone with her. She never walks the halls without at least two escorts. Nick had her write to us that Tom, the foreman of the lumberjacks, stood guard over Mama personally, with a few others, while Nick took the letter to mail. He didn't write the address on the letter until he was well away, and he hasn't told Mama or anyone else exactly where we are, though he's told her of our circumstances and that we're safely hidden."

Caleb saw Laura look around. She seemed suddenly a bit nervous. Not all that well hidden. But she was safe. They'd probably need a lawyer to write up legal documents to wrest Laura's third of the company, but she'd get those documents now. Being married was as good as a cavalry unit riding alongside her. She owned one third of a dynasty.

But Michelle and Jilly weren't yet safe.

"Mama told us not to rush into marriage on her account. We need to pick good men, men we can love and respect. Our notion to just round up any husband we could and get back there fast was foolishness born of fear. If we're not careful, we could end up as bad off as she is from marrying Edgar."

Laura gave Caleb a chagrined look, then shrugged. "Advice that comes a bit late for me, but my sisters can take their time."

"Being married to me isn't foolishness, Mrs. Tillman."

Laura handed the pages of her letter to Michelle, then held out her hand for Zane's letter.

He didn't hand it right over. Kindly, he said, "My cowhand found your ma in a bit of a bad situation. But she's safe now. You're going to read about that in Nick's letter. He's clearly angry, and it comes through. He describes her injuries."

He extended the single page to her. Her hand trembled a bit as she reached for it, then stopped. "You're advising me not to read it."

"Nick has been with me for a short time, but he's a steady hand. Calm in times of trouble. Tough, smart. He's uhh . . . well, he's . . . the letter is, let's say, he chose his words with me in mind. You might find it more than a bit upsetting."

Zane's eyes slid to Caleb.

Laura found her backbone and took the letter. "Good, I'm glad he's angry. On my mama's behalf. I appreciate that. And am thankful he's there."

Caleb came close to Laura's side. Michelle and Jilly had listened to Zane's warning, and they came up to read it.

The bruises. Locked in her room. Edgar sending out men to search for his runaway stepdaughters. Mama served only from a tray once a day, food sneaked into the room by a maid.

"Sarah, I'll bet," Laura said quietly. Nick was angry all right.

After she'd read it, front and back, twice, Caleb tugged the paper from Laura's hand. He had a chore to get it loose.

"We're blessed to have Nick there," he said. "To have your whereabouts still unknown and to know that, after a bad time, your ma is safe."

Laura nodded, then she turned to her sisters. The three of them wrapped their arms around each other, and one of them, Caleb thought it was Laura, cried.

He saw that circle, that band of three.

"A threefold cord is not quickly broken."

It was a Bible verse about two people including God in their friendship, or perhaps a husband and wife including God in their marriage to create a bond stronger than one without God being part of it.

But he saw those three sisters. He knew how they'd clung to each other since their stepfather had invaded their lives. But more, they'd always been different. They'd been raised to be different. A vibrant education, lessons in science, mathematics, physics, engineering, but also in leadership. Three women raised to manage a dynasty in a man's world.

Where did a husband fit in that tight bond? How could Caleb ever find a bond with Laura to equal the one she had with her sisters?

And if she truly didn't want a role in the company, how could he pull her away from it? Bonds could unite, but they could also bind. And Laura was bound tightly to her sisters.

Maybe he was destined to always be the outsider, his marriage taking a lower level of importance in Laura's life.

Grimly, he realized he didn't much like that idea.

Finally, the tears spent, the sister hug over, Caleb said in a voice no one could miss, "Where are we to sleep, Zane?

This house looks huge, but even so, with this many people, you're going to be bursting at the seams."

Laura turned to look at him, blushing. She twisted her fingers together. She'd been staying with him faithfully, but he was conscious now.

"I've got seven bedrooms. Two good-sized ones downstairs in what we call the housekeeper's apartment. When Ma was alive we had a housekeeper and cook, a married woman whose husband worked for us as a cowhand. It was an apartment for them and their children. I'm the oldest of four. Pa built onto Grandpa's house to make it big enough for all of us. My brother, Josh, born next after me, went to sea and comes by once in a while. I've got a sister Annie, married to a rancher. They live a couple of hours' ride south of here. She's got a two-year-old. My youngest sister, Beth Ellen, graduated from boarding school this spring and is being courted by a banker in San Francisco. Since my parents died, I'm left here in this big house alone.

"Harriet, Nora, and Sally Jo sleep in the downstairs rooms. Upstairs, I'll sleep in my regular bedroom. The Steinmeyers can have Ma and Pa's, it's good-sized, and they'll have room for Willa. Melinda and Hannah can have one. That leaves one for Michelle and Jilly, and one for Caleb and Laura." Zane smiled.

That suited Caleb right down to the ground. "Why don't you show us the way. We can all stand to wash up, and we need to figure out some clean clothes for everyone."

Harriet said, "All three of us spent time sewing while we were living here without you. We made dresses, thinking of the women at Purgatory. Loose fitting and we haven't hemmed them yet. They'll work to get everyone here into a clean dress."

"I've got a wash room in the back with a tub and a hand pump," Zane went on.

"I know how to hook up a boiler and attach pipes," Jilly said. "You could have hot water running right into a tub."

Zane arched one brow. "For now, we'll just heat water on the stove. There are hot-water wells, and we'll keep refilling them. Everyone can take turns getting a bath. I'll get out of your way. Caleb you can go first, then get some rest. You look about all in. Then Rick, you clean up, and come on outside, I'll show you around the place. If you're interested, I can always use another cowhand."

A glint in Zane's eyes made Caleb wonder if Rick would get a job offer to run the mining company.

"After Caleb's passed out and Rick is outside, the women can take over the house," Zane said. "Maybe do laundry to get the smoke smell off their old clothes and get washed up and dressed in their new ones before they move into the bedrooms and the whole house smells like a dead fire."

Caleb's life was being arranged for him. He had a feeling, if he wasn't very careful, it'd be that way from now on.

God, where am I supposed to go? What am I supposed to do?

Laura tugged on his arms, leading him toward the back of the house. For the moment, it looked like he was supposed to go to Zane's back room and take a bath.

If he wasn't so tired and didn't hurt so much, he'd've kicked up a fuss. Instead, he let Laura drag him along like a child.

LAURA SLIPPED INTO CALEB'S BEDROOM. Well, her bedroom too. Caleb had fallen asleep so hard after he'd cleaned up that she'd checked him twice to make sure he was breathing. Now, the afternoon gone, it was time for supper.

He needed rest, but he needed food, too.

She sat down on the bedside and rocked his shoulder gently. "Caleb, wake up."

His eyes lifted briefly, then fell shut. Smiling at him, Laura kept up with the gentle rocking. It was nice to be awakened gently. She knew that mainly because she was often awakened very briskly by bossy Michelle, who always had plans for the day.

Once in a long while, Laura would be allowed to awaken gently, and she'd always loved it.

"Caleb, come on now. Wake up. It's time for supper, and you haven't eaten since a very meager breakfast."

This time his eyes opened and stayed. They locked on hers. Laura felt like, in this vulnerable moment, Caleb was completely open to her. And she only saw goodness.

"Laura, I want to tell you every detail about my life. Every sin I've committed. Allow you to know me. And I'll tell you how I found my way to God and salvation in that prison. I don't expect you to trust me right away. But I believe I am worthy of your trust. Will you give me time? Will you stay with me?"

"I do trust you, Caleb. I just don't know if that's wise or not. It's simply the truth. Yes, I'll stay with you, and in time, I'll find out if my trust is misplaced."

She leaned forward and kissed him. A handsome prince being awakened by the princess. Or more accurately, by the chemist.

The kiss was merely the pressing of lips together for a moment, then Caleb seemed to wake up even more. He participated fully and enthusiastically in the kiss.

He took her shoulders and held her just far enough away from him she could see him. "You've decided to stay, or if you go, to take me with you?"

"Or if you go, I'll go with you." She rested both hands on his cheeks and said, "I've decided a God who can love me expects me to love my husband. And I do, Caleb. I love you."

He drew her back in for another kiss. It would have been wonderfully romantic if Caleb's stomach hadn't growled.

Laura giggled. "Come downstairs. Join us for a meal. We can discuss your calling and where our lives will take us next."

"I thought of it before I slept, prayed on it. I have perfect peace with following you home. God helped me see that in loving you, I need to help you through the difficulties you face at home."

"Loving me?"

Caleb smiled, kissed her, then smiled again. "Oh yes. Very much, Laura. I consider myself greatly blessed to have you for my wife."

"Would it be all right if we go home right away?"

She saw him hesitate, wondered at it.

"You won't mind leaving your sisters behind? Or will we all go together?"

Then she knew what made him hesitate. She knew he wanted her to go with him, but he also knew how tightly bound she was to her sisters.

"They can't go. They still aren't safe."

"And what about you running the company? Will you tell your ma of your true wishes? She'd want you to be happy, Laura."

Nodding, Laura said, "I know she would. But there are such plans for the three of us. I can't—"

Caleb pressed his fingers to her lips. "You can. You are an adult woman, married. You can choose your own path. Just as I am searching for God's calling, you can search for yours. We'll go to your home, but you've got time to hear the voice of God. Take that time."

Caleb continued, "Let's go then, as soon as I'm strong enough to travel that far, and that will be soon. I'll see if there is a place for a parson among the lumberjacks."

"I'll leave my sisters behind, and we can go stand in the breach with Nick between Mama and Edgar. Maybe you can even preach to Edgar a bit. Heaven knows the man is a heathen. Maybe he can be reformed. I can make sure the lumberjacks are being treated well and fairly. I can make a difference to them all. My papa taught me how."

She leaned close and, eyes sparkling, said, "Wait'll I show you our flume."

Caleb sat slowly. Still in pain, she could see that. But mending . . . and a strong man to stand at her side. Lead their family in faith. And be the perfect husband for a chemist bride, who was learning all the elements of love.

TWENTY-NINE

ARE YOU SURE YOU'LL BE SAFE?" Jilly as good as wrung her hands.

"I've never seen you this worried before." Laura was tempted to rest a hand on Jilly's forehead, test her for a fever.

"She will be safe," Caleb said with such stern resolve that a few of the furrows in Jilly's forehead eased. "Your stepfather will not lay a hand on her, neither will he touch your ma."

"Let me finish that sentence for you," Michelle said. "'Neither will he touch your ma, not while I'm alive.' Staying alive might be harder than you think."

"He has henchmen." Jilly was just plain fretting, and she would *not* let up. "You have to be wary of—"

Caleb brought a hand up, aimed right at Jilly. "Laura and I have talked this all over. Trust me when I say I've been fully warned. Henchmen, sneaks and liars, greedy backstabbers. Your stepfather is one, and he's hired others. Including men who are searching for you. So we'll pray for your safety, and

we'd appreciate if you prayed for ours. I will protect Laura."
He turned and smiled at his beautiful bride.

She smiled back. "And I will protect you."

Caleb nodded. "And God will protect us both."

"Keep Nick there with you if you can," Zane said. "He
can probably take care of you. He mentioned an Old Tom
in his letter?"

The sisters all had the same fond smile.

"Well, Tom and fifty lumberjacks will also help." Zane
pulled out a pocket watch and glanced at it, then looked
longingly out the kitchen window. A man who had a lot to
do and not enough hours in the day to do it. "Nick said there
are five men protecting your ma around the clock. They take
shifts, and they are all handpicked by Old Tom."

Jilly finally relaxed and gave Laura a hug. "Be careful and
do your best to wrest control of Stiles Lumber away from
that vile man. At least run a third of it well."

"You and Michelle hunt up husbands and get home. But
with fifty lumberjacks on hand, I think you can take your
time and make sure to marry wisely." Laura turned to Michelle and hugged her tightly.

She whispered Zane's name in her ear, and Michelle ended
the hug by slapping her on the back of the head.

But probably not as hard as Laura deserved, so she took
that as a good sign.

Caleb took her hand. "We're burning daylight."

Zane said to Michelle, "Can you really make hot water
run into the house?"

"It's easy. Have you got any . . ."

Caleb dragged Laura out of the house. They had one of
the two horses Michelle had bought and Caleb's. Neither

of them had enough possessions to bother with a wagon or a packhorse. Though Laura had a new dress on with a split riding skirt. And one to spare.

Laura mounted up, then reined her horse around to see her sisters had come outside to watch her leave. She waved.

"Hurry up and come home." She turned and rode beside Caleb.

Away from her sisters. The women who'd anchored her life through bad times and good. She would miss them terribly, but she was surprised at the joy of riding along with Caleb.

They left Zane's Two Harts Ranch behind with all the elements of love riding with them. They'd search out what lay ahead to follow God's call and find their way home.

ABOUT THE AUTHOR

Mary Connealy writes romantic comedies about cowboys. She's the author of the BRIDES OF HOPE MOUNTAIN, HIGH SIERRA SWEETHEARTS, KINCAID BRIDES, TROUBLE IN TEXAS, WILD AT HEART, and CIMARRON LEGACY series, as well as several other acclaimed series. Mary has been nominated for a Christy Award, was a finalist for a RITA Award, and is a two-time winner of the Carol Award. She lives on a ranch in eastern Nebraska with her very own romantic cowboy hero. They have four grown daughters—Joslyn, married to Matt; Wendy; Shelly, married to Aaron; and Katy, married to Max—and six precious grandchildren. Learn more about Mary and her books at

maryconnealy.com
facebook.com/maryconnealy
seekerville.blogspot.com
petticoatsandpistols.com

Sign Up for Mary's Newsletter

Keep up to date with Mary's latest news on book releases and events by signing up for her email list at maryconnealy.com.

More from Mary Connealy

After his father's death, Kevin Hunt inherits a ranch in Wyoming—the only catch is it also belongs to a half brother he never knew existed. But danger follows Kevin, and he suspects his half brother is behind it. The only one willing to stand between them is Winona Hawkins—putting her in the cross hairs of a perilous plot and a risk at love.

Braced for Love • BROTHERS IN ARMS #1

You May Also Like . . .

Falcon Hunt awakens without a past—or at least he doesn't recall one. When he makes a new start by claiming an inheritance, it cuts out frontierswoman Cheyenne from her ranch. Soon it's clear someone is gunning for him and his brothers, and as his affection for Cheyenne grows, he must piece together his past if they're to have any chance at a future.

A Man with a Past by Mary Connealy
BROTHERS IN ARMS #2
maryconnealy.com

Assigned by the Pinkertons to spy on a suspicious ranch owner, Molly Garner hires on as his housekeeper, closely followed by Wyatt Hunt, who refuses to let her risk it alone. But when danger arises, Wyatt must band together with his problematic brothers to face all the troubles of life and love that suddenly surround them.

Love on the Range by Mary Connealy
BROTHERS IN ARMS #3
maryconnealy.com

After living in isolation for many years atop Hope Mountain, three sisters take a risk to face the forbidden outside world—one they've been raised to believe holds nothing but grave danger. Instead, they encounter unforgettable adventure, romance, and friendship.

BRIDES OF HOPE MOUNTAIN: *Aiming for Love, Woman of Sunlight, Her Secret Song* by Mary Connealy
maryconnealy.com

BETHANYHOUSE

More from Bethany House

On the surface, Whitney Powell is happy working with her sled dogs, but her life is full of complications that push her to the edge. When sickness spreads in outlying villages, Dr. Peter Cameron turns to Whitney and her dogs for help navigating the deep snow, and together they discover that sometimes it's only in weakness you can find strength.

Ever Constant by Tracie Peterson
THE TREASURES OF NOME #3
traciepeterson.com

A birthday excursion turns deadly when the SS *Eastland* capsizes with insurance agent Olive Pierce and her best friend on board. After her escape, Olive discovers her friend is among the missing victims. When she begins investigating the accident, more setbacks arise. Finding the truth will take all she's got to beat those who want to sabotage her progress.

Drawn by the Current by Jocelyn Green
THE WINDY CITY SAGA #3
jocelyngreen.com

A very public jilting has Theodore Day fleeing the ballrooms of New York to focus on building his family's luxury steamboat business in New Orleans and beating out his brother to be next in charge. But he can't escape the Southern belles' notice, nor Flora Wingfield, who is determined to win his attention.

Her Darling Mr. Day by Grace Hitchcock
AMERICAN ROYALTY #2
gracehitchcock.com

◈ BETHANYHOUSE